I0784180

"Murder without a Duck was a laugh a minute and a wonderful weekend "away." I know the "real" town and I think author Long has her finger on the pulse of Simpato. Buy a copy of the book and take it to read at the spa after you visit the geyser next time you need R & R. You won't be sorry."

—Ana Manwaring, author of *Kickback*

Truck a Duck

A Simpato Mystery

CLAUDIA H. LONG

Sibylline
DIGITAL FIRST

Sibylline Press

Copyright © 2025 by Claudia H. Long
All Rights Reserved.

Published in the United States by Sibylline Press,
an imprint of All Things Book LLC, California.

Sibylline Press is dedicated to publishing the
brilliant work of women authors ages 50 and older.
www.sibyllinepress.com

Sibylline Digital First Edition
eBook ISBN: 9798897409945
Print ISBN: 9798897409952
Library of Congress Control Number: 2025938505

Cover Design: Alicia Feltman
Book Production: Aaron Laughlin

This is a work of fiction. Names, characters, places, brands, media, and incidents are either the product of the author's imagination or are used fictitiously. Any resemblance to similarly named places or to persons living or deceased is unintentional.

HUMAN AUTHORED: Any use of this publication to train generative artificial intelligence (AI) technologies to generate text is expressly prohibited.

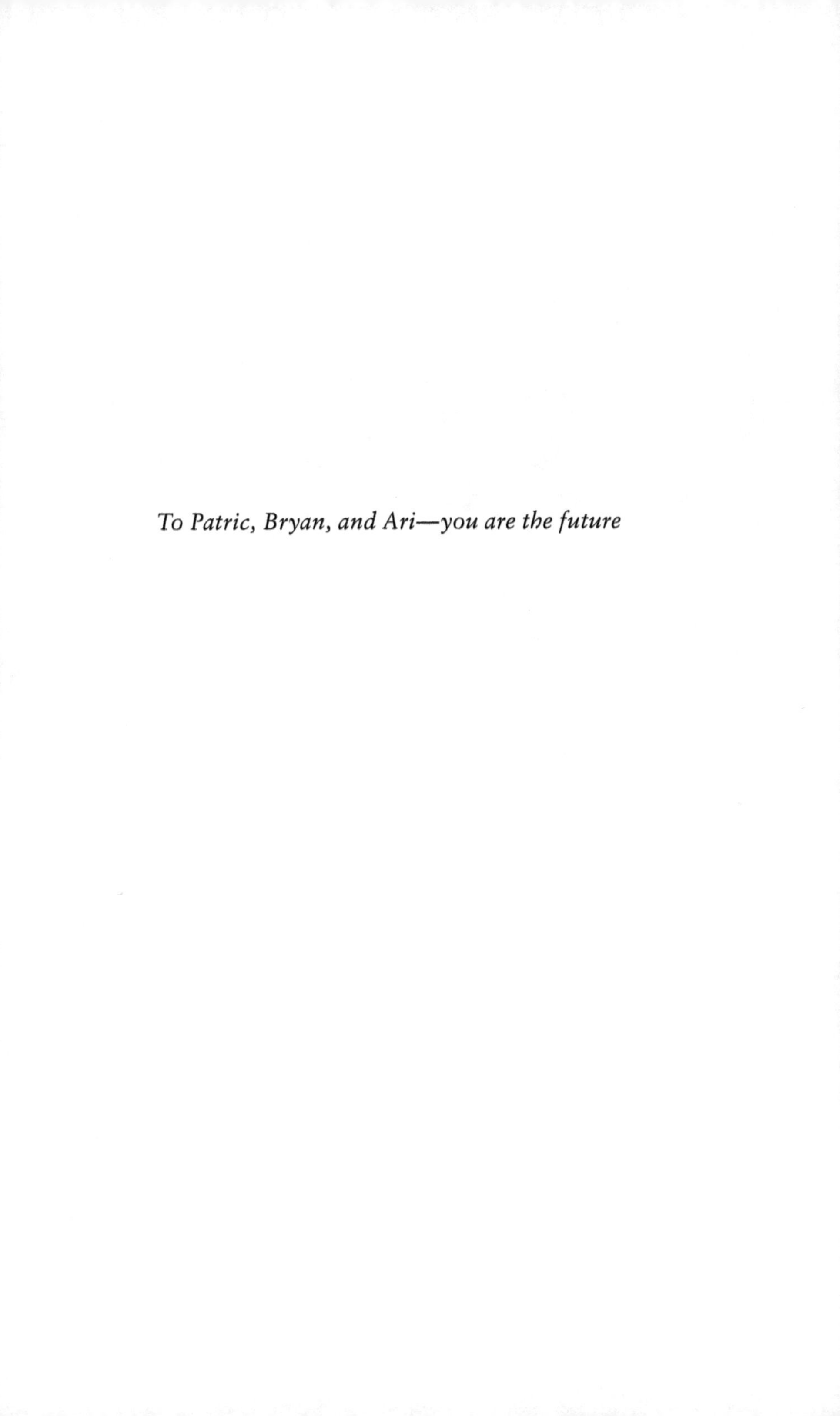

To Patric, Bryan, and Ari—you are the future

CHAPTER ONE

S ometimes you'd kill for a taco.

#

Four food trucks were parked in the Simpato High School parking lot, forming a square, their order windows facing out. *Tacos Buen Día*, *La Sabrosa*, the festively-painted *Happy Tacky*, the deep-blue *La Santa Fé*.

In the center of the square, grills sent smoke up to the nearly cloudless blue sky. A discerning gourmet would be able to distinguish among pork, beef, lamb, and chicken wafting their unique aromas heavenward, but to me it was all just delicious meat. Men tended the grills, flipping the pieces with nearly yard-long tongs, sending flames dancing as melting fat splashed the burning coals. Their voices rose above the crackling and chopping, English and Spanish merging and sliding into one another, a salsa of sounds and scents.

Looking through the order windows I could see piles of herbs, red tomatoes, yellow squashes, chiles of all colors arrayed on the counters within the trucks, and from there the aromas were fresher, more piquant. Women slapped tortillas, both corn and flour, onto the hot griddles inside each truck, then pulled them off charred. As I watched, they filled the steaming tortillas with everything on offer, piled them high with green herbs, rolled and wrapped them in foil. Teens and grannies handed them to the crowds waiting at the windows.

No money changed hands tonight.

On the bed of a pickup truck at the other end of the parking lot, a man played a tuba, its incongruous oompah-blatt softened by the strumming of his friend's guitar. I bit into my *al carbon*; juice ran down my chin.

Just before six, a huge black pickup rolled into the lot, blasting the first four bars of "Never on Sunday." Windows slammed shut. Taco wrappers were quickly stashed in the nearest cans, and we all turned towards the doors of the school.

It was time.

#

I wasn't on my redwood deck on this second Tuesday evening in May. I wasn't receiving the town of Simpato's secrets as I normally did on Tuesdays at six, fulfilling the role of Keeper of Secrets, a post my mother had created, may her memory be for a blessing.

Quite the opposite.

Instead I was now sitting at the back of the Simpato High School auditorium where the Council met every second Tuesday of the month unless they felt like meeting more often. The Brown Act in California prevented them from meeting privately at, say, the Mallard Wing Golf Course or the Duck Bill coffeeshop.

The town of Simpato—named by a drunken founder too lazy to write out *Simpatico*— was known as Sin-Pato, Spanish for *Without a Duck*; Simpato Lake was the Duckless Pond; and Simpato High School was known as No-Duck High (except by the students, who frequently replaced the D with another consonant altogether.)

The auditorium was loud with young energy. Simpato High Juniors were encouraged to attend the Council hearings and be briefed on all the issues before the Council. Many did, especially since attending meant an automatic A in US History that quarter. One student per session got to sit up front with the members. It was a much-vied-for honor.

I was not there as a student, obviously. I was still a temporarily suspended lawyer—only two weeks left on that nightmare—and newly divorced, but I had been tapped by Ed Sharp to cover this particular meeting. The awesomely named editor-in-chief of the local paper, called, yes, the *Quack*, Edwina Sharp was down one reporter from her previous staff of herself and two others. Her absent writer, gossip columnist, Council member in her own right, and local terror Georgiana Noyes, had been murdered last month, and Ed and I had gotten to know each other when I had been instrumental in finding the murderer.

Georgiana used to cover her own meetings. In a small town we wear many hats.

Ed's email had been succinct and properly punctuated. "Sal, could you please cover the Council meeting tomorrow night? Just take notes and write up a summary for me. I'll put it into journalistic style. I have a can't-miss birthday party for my eldest grandson, who's turning 1. If you want a byline, you can have it. Ed."

Request, instructions, reassurance, excuse, and reward. Nicely done.

Not having any work to do, I said yes. I could see myself, *Salvia DeVine, girl reporter*. With a hat with a press card, a note book, a fast car, chasing down the big story, the scoop. At forty-five perhaps "girl reporter" was a stretch, but wasn't forty the new thirty? And if Simpato could be called a city with only ten thousand souls, I could be a girl reporter.

I drove a Prius, though, so no fast cars for me.

#

The auditorium could hold two hundred people, the equivalent of the entire high school. Over one hundred of the seats were filled tonight. Simpato was about fifty percent Latino, so it was not surprising that the composition of the audience was nearly that as well. Besides, there was strong interest in tonight's agenda.

The Council had come to order. There were only four of them, including the pro-tem mayor. There were supposed to be five, but alas, poor Georgiana was neither writing for the paper nor attending Council meetings anymore.

I watched with interest as the pro-tem mayor, Garth Mendez, plowed through the housekeeping items. This was Garth's first foray into mayordom. Our previous mayor, Sebastian Solis, had resigned between the last ill-fated meeting in April and this May meeting. Solis was now living up in Cragstown, meth capital of California. Until a new mayor could be elected, the second-in-command had to take over.

Garth was not a natural. He fidgeted and sweated as he leafed through the papers on the table in front of him. I could almost smell his discomfort. And yet, he was probably the lead candidate for Solis's replacement. He was also the only Council member who was using paper. The three other members, Cindy Scott, who was also running for mayor, Jessica Alvarez, and Matty Buono, used laptops.

I looked at the agenda. After considering what a lawyer would call the "default calendar," i.e. consent matters that were unopposed and were either going to be approved or disapproved automatically, depending on what was sought, the first, and really the only order of business was the Taco Truck Ordinance. Known, of course, as the Duck Truck Law.

Garth was thorough, though, calling each and every item, receiving the vote, and recording it, before he moved on. He shifted his considerable bulk in the chair, adjusted his glasses on his nose, and read the first and only order of new business. "Next item, we will consider the Taco Truck Ordinance allowing up to three taco trucks to park downtown, seven days a week, from ten in the morning to eight at night."

A murmur rose up in the audience. This was what we'd been waiting for. Folks shifted in their seats. Some made their way to the end of the rows, holding sheafs of paper for their five minutes of permitted speech. Others carried tablet computers with their talking points.

Garth looked at his fellow members. Cindy Scott nodded and he seemed to relax. She pulled the microphone closer to herself. "Before we vote, we are ready to hear from the members of the public who have signed up to speak. There are several people signed up." A groan washed over the audience. "You each have five minutes, and we will have to cut you off if you go over. The Council will then recess for ten minutes, and return to discuss the Ordinance publicly. When we have finished discussing, if one of us calls for a vote, we will vote on the matter. Garth?"

Garth took the mic back, and repeated what Cindy had said in Spanish. Having grown up in Sacramento, and having inherited my dad's facility with language, I was very nearly fluent in Spanish myself, with just an annoying California accent I couldn't ditch. Garth was fairly faithful in his translation, adding only that if someone planned to speak in Spanish, he needed to have his own translator with him. And that any speaker who went beyond his cut-off would be, in his words, thrown out. Not exactly what Cindy had said, but it proved that he knew his audience.

In English, Garth called the first speaker. "Ernesto Carreras. Come on up, Nate."

The speaker approached the mic, accompanied by a girl who could not be more than fourteen, her long hair glossy in the overhead light. The speaker's hands shook as he put his papers on the podium and looked up at the Council. "Good night," he said in English. His daughter put her hand on his arm. He turned to the girl, she nodded, and slid into his place. In her high, not yet adult voice, she began. "Honorary Council—"

"Honorable!" someone said from the audience.

"Shut up, Tony!" she said. "Honorable Council," she continued, "I am talking on the part of my dad, Ernesto Carreras, who you know as Nate Carreras, who's got the *La Sabrosa* taco truck that parks out near the closed gas station. Where they're going to build the new hotel. We think that the taco trucks should be allowed to park downtown, because there isn't always building going on, and the—" She looked at her father, mouthed a word. He nodded.

"The Simpato workers can't come out to the restaurants in town because they're priced for visitors, so we want to be able to go out on a Saturday just like anyone else, and enjoy some dinner and play some music," she was no longer looking at her father's notes, "and be able to have fun in the town and right now it's too expensive. So, please pass the law so we can have our truck downtown."

"Thank you, Ernestina," Garth said. "And Mr. Carreras."

They stood at the podium.

"You may sit down."

Ernesto Carreras leaned into the mic. *"Pero solo dos o tres. No como veinte. Porque si no, nos va matar la competencia."*

Just two or three, not twenty. Because otherwise the competition will kill us.

Some of the crowd clapped. Someone shouted, "Two or three, as long it's you, right?"

"Silence!" Cindy said into the mic. "No talking out of turn. The next speaker, Mark Segismundo."

The crowd settled down. The speaker came up, thin and dressed in pressed chinos and a black button-down silk shirt, his sharp voice needing no translator or interpreter. "My name is Mark Segismundo but you can call me Siggy, everyone does. I love this town," he said. "I was born here, I went to No-Duck High, and I have wanted to have a food truck for eight years. I learned cooking not just at the restaurants in town, but at the community college program. We've been closed out of the food business here, as owners, for decades. A food truck permit, with licenses and inspections, would let us have our own businesses, instead of everything being owned by the big hotels. It's about time. Thank you."

He walked back to his seat amid calls of "Way to go, Siggy," and "You tell 'em," as some reached to smack his hand, and others whispered translations to their neighbors.

The next speaker was a tall, thickly muscled man, in a red and blue striped shirt. His hair was pulled into a man-bun, from which wisps of brown hair curled onto his broad shoulders. He looked like he could eat the mic. I made a note of his name for my summary: Michael Charolais.

"I'm Mikey Charolais, hospitality manager for Perdiz Winery. I'm here on behalf of Jack and Victoria Partridge, the owners. Jack and Victoria object to the taco truck program. While we are out several blocks away from the downtown, Jack and Victoria feel strongly that putting food trucks downtown will detract from the food and wine programs that make Simpato special. They'll compete with our fantastic restaurants, and attract crowds, which, as you heard, want to hang out on Saturday nights in town, which is not going to go over well with the visitors. Now, before you get us wrong, we have nothing against the trucks themselves, or folks having fun, but put them where the people who want them live. Not where we get our livelihood. Not downtown, and not in front of the wineries where people come to taste our wonderful wines and enjoy our great pairings. There's something for everyone in Simpato," he smiled, showing excellent teeth, "but everything needs to work together. Without our visitors, we have nothing."

He turned to face a silent crowd. Then one man stood, and started to clap. Then two women stood. And then more.

"Quiet!" Garth said.

The chosen high school student sitting with the Council members giggled. Cindy shot her a look and she clapped her hand over her mouth. I took notes like mad. I also briefly wondered how Georgiana Noyes had managed to participate as a Councilmember and report on the meetings all at once. I was scribbling feverishly on my yellow pad.

A couple had approached the mic for their turn to speak, but the audience was muttering, and those clapping had started to clap rhythmically, joined by others. The pro-downtown-trucks groups were shouting in Spanish and English, calling the clappers racists and elites, and the clappers clapped louder, joined by others, of both races, saying, "The economy benefits all of us!" and *"Sin trabajo no hay comida."*

Without work there's no food.

Cindy and Garth desperately tried to restore order, and one of the other Council members, whose name-plate said, *Matty Buono*, took out his phone. In a minute, the local gendarmerie, in the person of Officer Luke Aureliano, strode up to the front. "Okay, everyone," he said into the mic, *"callense."* The crowd hushed. *"Y sientense, y dejen de aplaudir.* Sit down, and knock it off."

The clappers stopped and sat back down. Everyone looked abashed. I turned and caught sight of an old-fashioned nun's wimple. Sure enough, there was "Sister" Marigold, née Margo Schwartz, who masqueraded as a member of the Holy Order of the Little Sisters of the Earth, who in turn masqueraded as nuns and called themselves monks, and all had plant names, and it was too long a story.

Sister Marigold was a reporter for a very large national magazine, and she had done a blockbusting story about a drug ring with one of the pseudo-nuns at its center. For reasons of her own, Marigold remained at the monastery with the other nuns. She was tall, slender, and had liquid brown eyes behind stylish glasses. She was also one of the only other Jewish people I knew in town, besides, of course, myself. She winked at me. She too was covering the great food truck debate of Simpato.

"We will take the matter to a vote after the recess," Garth said into the mic.

"What about the rest of us?" someone shouted.

"Yeah, I signed up to talk!" another voice called out.

"I think we've heard enough," Garth said in Spanish.

"It's our turn," the woman of the couple at the podium said loudly, and added in Spanish, *"Nos toca a nostros."* She had the most outlandish eye makeup I'd ever seen.

"Enough!" Garth said. "Be back in ten minutes."

The crowd grumbled as they filed out to the parking lot.

As she exited her row, Marigold bent down to whisper in my ear, "Stay tuned to find out if we'll be With or Without a Truck."

#

Like most schools near the coast, the No-Duck High's class-rooms and facilities opened to a quad, with outdoor covered walkways rather than hallways. We spilled out on the flagstone patio that ended at the parking turn-around, as the evening darkened into night. The taco trucks stood in silent vigil.

The couple who had missed their turn to speak were holding forth in front of the auditorium doors, as people milled about in the sweet spring air. While they were speaking Spanish, what they were saying was clear to everyone, bilingual or not.

"It's another shit-show," the man said. "The hotels run everything. That Garth is bought and paid for. No way will he let the trucks in."

"Calm down. We just need to say our piece, and if you're going to go off on them, I'll do the talking," the woman with him said. She had more gray than black in her hair, pulled back into a tight bun. She squinted her heavily made-up eyes, giving the man a glare that would melt an iceberg.

"You say anything, you're not gonna want to come home," he answered, unfazed.

"Knock it off, Arturo," another man said. "Amparo, if he doesn't know how to treat a woman, come on over to my house and I'll show you what love is."

The man called Arturo answered with a foul expletive, and both men laughed. Amparo didn't look amused. Nate, owner of the *La Sabrosa* truck, and whose daughter had spoken for him at the Council, walked up to the squabbling trio. "Look, if we start acting like fools, we aren't going to get our trucks. And the hotels win again. So sober up, Arturo. Amparo, if he weren't such a good cook, I'd tell you to stick a knife in him."

"If he weren't, I would," she said.

"There are better ways," a voice said in English. I turned to see Mikey Charolais lounging by the bug light. "Easier ways to kill someone than stabbing, and a lot less messy."

Amparo turned her back on Mikey. He shrugged and glanced at me. "You here as a lawyer, as the Keeper, or you thinking of starting a food truck, too?"

I tried to look coy.

"Come on, I saw you taking notes."

"Well, I'm here, not on my deck on a lawn chair, with a box of tissues at hand. So I'm not here as the Keeper. And I'm the worst cook on earth, so no, not starting a food truck. Just taking some notes."

He smiled his galactic smile. "You for 'em or against 'em?"

"I'm neutral," I said. "I haven't lived here long enough to know. But I'm surprised at how divided the town is. I thought folks got along, across all levels."

"I guess you should ask those who aren't getting along, then. I'm getting along just fine."

"Why don't you want the trucks? I mean, do you really think that they'll lower the chi-chi factor of Simpato to have places downtown where those who live here, work in the hotels and the wineries, and pick the grapes, can afford to eat?"

Mikey put a heavy hand on my shoulder. I stood still, not shrugging it off. I wanted an answer—one that would go right into my notes.

"I actually have nothing against the trucks. It's my boss. Jack Partridge. He and Vicky, well, I'm not sure Vicky cares much, but Jack, he's adamant. I'm just the manager of his facilities, especially the tasting room and the pairing salon."

I raised an eyebrow. "Pairing salon? Like a dating venue?"

Mikey laughed. "You know, when you serve the perfect food with our perfect wines. Jack had me come because he couldn't. I work for him, so I did. Personally, I love tacos. But I'm not sure parking them downtown is such a hot idea. Out in the neighborhoods, or where Nate has his truck near the abandoned gas station, that's where they should be."

"*Pendejo*," Arturo said to him, as he walked by.

"Duck your mother," Mikey answered, not raising his voice.

Standing apart, behind her dad, Ernestina giggled. Nate clapped Mikey on the shoulder. "Don't listen to Arturo," he said in English. "He forgot to be sober tonight."

"He forgets to be sober every night, Nate," Mikey said.

A bell rang and we started to file back in. "If we get the trucks, you're not going to be one of them," said a voice. A slender man with chestnut hair close-cut on the sides and longer on top, sidled by.

"Justin, my man," Mikey said, holding out his hand. Justin hesitated, then briefly shook Mikey's hand.

Nate didn't answer, but took his daughter's arm and pulled her away from where we were standing, into the auditorium. As he walked by Arturo, he muttered something that made him turn back to us. Amparo moved to stand in front of Arturo, blocking his view.

"Sal DeVine," I said to Justin, putting out my own hand.

"Justin March, county health inspector, meet our Keeper and town lawyer," Mikey said.

Justin ignored my hand, in fact he ignored me entirely, as well as Mikey's introduction. He was staring at the auditorium door.

In front of the open door, Amparo was standing with her arms crossed, looking straight at Justin the health inspector. Their eyes were locked on one another, while people moved around Amparo like water around a rock in a stream. I looked at Mikey. He moved his large, meaty hands as if to say, "Don't ask me."

At last, a group of high school kids, unconscious of the fiery messaging going back and forth, plowed between the two glaring adults, breaking the link, and Amparo turned away. She reentered the auditorium, and I looked back to see if Justin would follow. He had his hand in his pocket, and had stepped back towards the curb where the patio met the turn-around. I watched as he took out his phone, stared at it a moment, then made a call. He strode off into the night, and I went back into the auditorium for the vote.

#

Ultimately the vote was anticlimactic. With four sitting Council members, they had enough for a quorum, but without a leader, they couldn't reach consensus. It was apparently their practice, under Mayor Solis, to work until they could agree unanimously on a plan, and then vote it in. Here, they were left with good old democracy, and its predictable outcome.

The two Council members who had been silent throughout the presentation were undecided. They raised the questions that any good Councilmember should. They asked how many applications would be granted. Shouts from the crowd, "Three!" "More!" "None!" were followed by threats to call Officer Luke Aureliano back in if they weren't quiet. They explored the exact locations where the trucks could park. No one could think of a place that didn't raise a chorus of outrage from the crowd, whether because it was not really downtown, where all the foot traffic was, or the opposite, it was right in front of someplace that didn't want folks lining up for a taco and Jarritos soda.

Garth, surprisingly, was for the trucks, despite the "bought and paid for by the hotels" remark by Arturo outside; Cindy was against. Both were running for mayor, and they were drawing their battle lines with the public. Jessica Alvarez and Matty Buono were undecided, and unwilling to commit.

Suddenly, through a rustle of cloth, a small green tent approached the mic. "May I speak?" said a voice coming from within the tent.

The room was quiet. Turning around, the little figure proved to be Mother Sassafras, the Mother Superior of the Holy Order of the Little Sisters of the Earth, the pseudo-monastery—not a convent—dedicated to stopping climate change, and supporting themselves with cannabis cookies, requesting the floor.

I knew from my earlier interactions with the town that about ninety percent were at least nominally Catholics, and although these weren't "real" nuns, they were treated with the respect that was innate in the townsfolk, regardless of race or ethnicity. So I was not surprised when, despite the fact that public contribution time was closed and some folks had been denied their speaking turns, Mother Sassafras was granted the floor without having signed up. No one objected.

"Perhaps," she started, then pulled the mic from its stand, so she could hold it down where her face was. She stood about four foot ten, at best. "Perhaps, we can compromise. How about if we try it out for two months. We have several trucks operating on the outskirts already. If three of those would be permitted downtown, we could park one in front of our monastery, our Mother-house, one at the fountain by City Hall, and one near the bridge over the Valley River.

"We could see how they did. If they were successful, and not disruptive, then the Council could consider making it permanent. If they were not, the Council would have its answer."

She placed the mic on the table, rather than try to return it to its stand. The room stayed silent as she rustled back to her seat. The Council looked at one another. "We have five owners seeking permits pending the resolution as of now. We could draw lots from those five applications," Jessica said. I made a note. A sensible thought.

I could see that the Council members longed to violate the Brown Act and discuss this option in private, but they were hamstrung by the suggestion's having been made publicly. "Um, that could work," Garth said. "Provisionally."

Cindy sighed. "Shall we put a provisional ordinance to a vote?"

Matty Buono moved, Garth seconded, and they voted. Three to one, with Cindy against, the provisional ordinance was passed.

Garth stood up. In Spanish, he explained the terms. "We have five applications for permits. The drawing will take place at the flagpole on Friday at noon."

There being no further business, the Council adjourned.

The audience sat still. No one spoke. No one got up to leave. I caught Marigold's eye. She smiled a secret, knowing smile. She'd known Mother Sassafras was going to do this.

"Okay, *pendejos,*" Arturo said, finally weaving to his feet. "Who's going to go suck up to the Council to make sure their trucks get picked, huh? Cuz if mine isn't picked, somebody's gonna pay."

He grabbed Amparo's arm, and was the first out the door.

One by one the rest of us followed.

Mikey caught up to me. "Walk you home?"

"No need, thanks. We all know there's no crime in Simpato."

CHAPTER TWO

Luna greeted me at the door, meowing and weaving her fluffy white tail between my legs, covering my black pants with cat hair and nearly tripping me headlong into my kitchen. I fumbled for the kitchen light.

In the six weeks I'd lived in my parents' old summer house in Simpato I had gotten used to the layout—back door from the deck into the kitchen, living-dining room, bathroom, and two tiny bedrooms with miniature closets, the whole house totaled less than 950 square feet. The front of the house faced west to Second Street, but was set back over a third of the way into the radically large, half-acre lot. The rear of the property, with its long driveway leading to multiple deck levels, looked out on the craggy foothills leading up to Mount Santabella.

I'd also gotten used to the fact that my parents, who had died in a boating accident ten years before, had been important people in the community. My mother, Alta, had held an especially dear spot in the people of Simpato's heart: she had developed and established a bizarre practice knowns as the Keeper of Secrets, or "Keeper" for short. Every Tuesday evening she turned her two lawn chairs to face away from the driveway on the deck off the kitchen, put out a box of tissues and a pitcher of lemonade, and for two hours the good citizens of Simpato lined up to tell her their secrets.

Now I'd been pressured into taking on that role, and I had learned by experience that neither forgiveness nor advice was sought. Just a safe place to tell someone.

I was bound to secrecy. Except when it came to murder.

But this Tuesday night I had been play-acting as journalist, so I fed Luna a few "seafood delights" treats, which had the undesired effect of making her even more demanding rather than less, and opened my computer to type up my notes from the Council meeting.

Luna jumped up onto my lap. "So affectionate," I said, faking annoyance. "Did Saul not give you enough attention? Was he too busy with his intern? Did Melissa ..." I nearly choked on the name of Saul's newest mistress, the intern who had signed my name to the documents that Saul had falsified, and had gotten me suspended from the practice of law for two months. Saul had taken Luna as a bargaining chip in our divorce, only to realize he didn't actually want the cat. He also didn't want Melissa. Or, really, a divorce.

I got the cat back, but I made him keep the divorce.

I poured myself a glass of the local specialty, a crystalline Malvasia, crisp and slightly floral. If I was going to live out my suspension in wine country, I was going to drink wine.

I considered something to eat. The Council meeting had run past seven-thirty and I knew that wine for dinner was sub-optimal if I was going to write anything up for Ed Sharp and the *Quack*. Once more I wondered who Margo Schwartz, a.k.a. Sister Marigold, was writing for. She'd published the breaking story of the meth ring being run out of the Little Sisters of the Earth monastery in a large national magazine, but surely covering the city Council meeting of a town of fewer than 10,000 people wasn't going to be national news.

I made myself a grilled cheese sandwich, and with greasy fingers reopened my computer. A quick look at Facebook showed the WAD, or *Without a Duck* page, going absolutely nuts about the meeting. The WAD had been started by one of the women who was tired of the backbiting and nastiness and the trolls that inhabited the rest of the Internet, and so the group was both private and moderated.

I debated whether to read all the comments first or to write my impressions without their influence. I went with purity.

"The Council meeting took up the Taco Truck Ordinance tonight, and ended up voting 3-1 for a provisional compromise, tabling the ultimate passage until after the election to fill the two empty spots. Opposing the provisional ordinance was Cindy Scott, who first appeared to favor a complete passage of the original bill, but ultimately opposed the compromise.

"The compromise bill was suggested by Mother Sassafras of the Little Sisters of the Earth, who spoke out of turn, but was permitted by the Council out of respect for her position as Mother Superior of the Holy Order."

Put that way, it was pretty obnoxious. Especially since it wasn't a real Order, certainly wasn't Holy, and its principal source of income was selling cannabis cookies.

"Mother Sassafras suggested, and the Council adopted, the provisional ordinance, which allowed three trucks, to be chosen at a random drawing at the flagpole on Friday at noon, to park at specific locations downtown for two months. That will bring us past the election, and a newly seated Council can determine the success or failure of the operation.

"It was stipulated," after all, a lawyer was writing this, suspended or not, "that the county health inspector, who was present in the audience but did not speak, would inspect all of the approved trucks—" Didn't he always inspect all the trucks? "—before they would be permitted to park in the designated locations: one in front of the Little Sisters of the Earth monastery, one by the Valley bridge, and one in front of the fountain by City Hall."

The fountain was actually a natural spring, enclosed and surrounded by ceramic ducks, that sat in the paved parking area between the police station and city offices. I saw the wisdom of Sassafras's choices: she got a taco truck for her Order, the police and the city workers got one, and the truck near the Valley bridge was just far enough from the large cross-road that defined the downtown that traffic and congregating wouldn't impose on the aura of perfection that Simpato tried to establish for its visitors. Sort of downtown, but not *Downtown*.

Now I would check the WAD.

#

The WAD, of course, was quacking like mad. I didn't envy the moderators, who were committed to keeping the page civil.

"The cops had to be called! Luke had to baton several people—"

"Not true. No one was batonned. Don't exaggerate."

"Okay maybe not but some of those guys went apeshit and the cops had to come in, right? You're not denying reality, are you?"

"It's a sham. We know the truck owners whore in good with the city are gonna get the spots, and everyone else can suck it."

"Who you calling a whore?"

"Takes one to know one"

"Moderator? You on?"

\#

It was a reminder that I had left out the fact that Officer Luke Aureliano had to come in to restore order. I added it to my summary, and sent it to Ed, with the note that I would follow up after the drawing Friday at the flagpole so the story could be complete. After all, the *Quack* didn't come out until Monday, so a story filed on Friday would get in.

Wow, I sounded like a real journalist. Or at least the way they talked in movies. Salvia DeVine, middle-aged girl reporter, was on the beat.

\#

Wednesday morning came too soon for me, having stayed up late with my Malvasia bottle and very little food. I showered and pulled my hair back into a ponytail. I needed to find a colorist in Simpato, because I wasn't going to go all the way back to San Francisco just to cover the strands of gray that were making themselves known amidst the warm honey-brown of my natural color.

I also needed a good breakfast, preferably with Carinna, known as the White Lady because one, she dressed all in white, and two, she played a shepherd in the town Christmas pageant. Yes, the town Christmas pageant was a real thing. Carinna and I had become acquainted in my first week in Simpato, when her pickup truck and my Prius seemed to have a conversation in the Duck Shop parking lot. Then we'd bonded over finding a body on Mount Santabella. If that wasn't a friend-for-life experience, I didn't know what was.

I texted Carinna and asked her to meet me at the Duck Bill. I had gotten so used to the insane Duck references in Sin-Pato that it no longer struck me as odd that the local coffee shop would have such an absurd name. If only the drunken town founder had managed to spell out the full name on the city charter, we would have been Simpatico, and we would have been spared. But no such duck. I mean luck.

I pushed open the door to the Duck Bill and glanced around for a table. If I weren't meeting Carinna I could just take a seat at the counter, but she'd answered right away, "Be there in 10," so I snagged the small two-top next to the defunct juke box.

I positioned myself so I could see the door.

"Coffee or wine?" the retro-clad waitress asked. This was, after all, Simpato, deep in wine -country. Her black nylon dress was stretched tight over a massive bosom, and her bottom half was encircled by a duck-hunting-print apron, from which she drew out a menu and an order pad.

"Coffee," I said, waiving away the menu. "And a waffle. And there will be two of us."

She nodded, and grabbed a set of flatware wrapped in a paper napkin from her pocket and set it down across from me. I would swear she produced the coffee pot from the pocket of her apron as well, and two little cream thimbles and a pile of sugar packets. I pushed those aside. Perhaps Carinna took cream and sugar. I didn't.

I took a sip of the hot, dark brew, blowing over the top as I did. "It's hot," a man said. I looked up to see Mikey Charolais looming above me. "Can I join you?"

"Actually, I'm meeting a friend," I said. But in the interests of journalism, I added, "But if you want to pull a chair from that other table and sit a bit until she comes, you're welcome to do so."

He'd already gotten hold of the chair, and swung it over to my table before I'd finished my sentence. He sat straddling it from the back. "Thanks. I wanted to follow up on our chat from last night," he said. He turned toward the counter and the waitress nodded. She picked up his coffee and a plate of cut up fruit and brought them over from the counter.

"Thanks, Maeve," he said. He lifted his cup to me in a mock toast, and as he sipped I took a good look at him. He had very dark brown hair, mostly pulled into a bun, with a few escaping curls. His hands and arms were large, and I could see calluses on his fingers as he put the coffee cup down.

"So you're the new Keeper," he said, turning to me.

This seemed to be inescapable. "I guess I am. And you? You said you were the facilities and hospitality manager for Perdiz wines? Where's that?"

"Just past the start of the bike trail. Big black stone building, big black wrought-iron gate."

"Oh, that one," I said. I had walked past it several time on walks with Carinna. We didn't walk up the trail from Simpato Lake, yes, predictably known as Duckless Pond, anymore, after finding Georgiana Noyes dead that time on the lower elevations of Mount Santabella. "Big place."

"Not for a winery, it isn't. We only produce about 5,000 cases a year, most of which is sold through our wine club and tastings, though every now and then some of our older vintages are available at an auction. I've got two tasting rooms, one that's open to the public, and one by reservation for tastings with pairings. Pretty amazing stuff. Arturo, you saw him yesterday at the Council meeting—the one married to the woman with the intense eye makeup, he's probably the best cook in the Valley. When he's sober."

"He's your cook?" I echoed, taking it in. "But he wants to have a food truck. In fact, it seemed like he already did, and if he didn't get lucky in the drawing he was going to be mighty pissed."

Mikey smiled, his high-watt teeth gleaming. I'd never seen teeth like that. More than his massive biceps, now on display in a tight T-shirt, it was his smile that defined him.

"He's a hothead. Especially when he's been hitting the bottle, which unfortunately is more and more often. Of course, Jack keeps him on a string. It's his wife, Amparo, that runs the truck. She usually stations it out by the construction site for the big hotel, and does pretty good business. Arturo cooks up the food for the truck, but he's too nasty for customer service."

"I don't know why women put up with men like that," I said.

"Other guys tease him. They flirt with Amparo to get him riled up. He's all bark and no bite, except with Amparo. Plenty of bite there, from what I hear."

I looked out the window for Carinna. This was pretty interesting, and I knew that I'd not hear any more once she came. I took advantage of the moment. "So why are your bosses, I can't remember—Partridge?" He nodded. "Why are they against the trucks?"

Mikey swallowed the big piece of cantaloupe he was chewing. "A little bit of racism, of course. Don't want all the Latinos hanging around downtown having a good time when the tourists are here. But he really doesn't want to lose Arturo. He's afraid if they get a spot downtown, Arturo will leave Perdiz for his own truck. Right now, Amparo does fine alone, but if they could run two trucks, they'd double their income."

"Then give him a raise."

Mikey almost choked on his coffee. "Right. As if. No, Jack Partridge is as tight as a—"

Carinna appeared at our table.

"Tight as a what, Mikey?"

Her voice was not friendly.

"I'll be going," Mikey said. "See you around town."

\#

Carinna, dressed in a long white T-shirt with a silver parrot emblazoned the full length of her torso, and a mid-calf white skirt, was full-on White Lady today. Although she had changed her name from Karen to Carinna, the term remained apt, and she maintained it by re-purposing her many white tunics as shepherd's gowns. Her coloration didn't help matters, with grey-streaked brown hair that needed a trim, pale skin, and light hazel eyes. She was older than I was, probably mid-fifties, and had had quite a past. In fact, she had quite a present as well.

She pulled back the chair Mikey had been sitting in and turned it to face the neighboring table. Taking her intended seat, she pushed back her bangs from her face and sighed. The aroma of the product she supplied to the Little Sisters of the Earth emanated from her. Her daughter grew cannabis in the foothills near Placerville, and Carinna supplied both leaf and butter to the good Sisters.

"What did that jackass want?" she said by way of *hello*.

I wondered what her animus towards him was based on, but for the moment I brought her up to date on the Taco Truck drawing that was taking place on Friday.

"You writing it up for the *Quack*?" she asked.

"Just sending in the notes from last night's meeting," I answered. "Ed Sharp had to go to her grandson's first birthday, and there's no one else."

Carinna knew that the *Quack* was now short-handed, since the body we'd found had been, among many other jobs, the main writer for the paper, but she raised a point that had troubling me as well. "If you're going to be reporting for the *Quack*, and you're also the Keeper, no one's going to tell you anything if they think it's going to end up in the paper."

"True," I said. "Either it's a great way for me to get out of this Keeper business—after all, I didn't exactly ask for it—or I can tell Ed I can't write for her. But either way I can still cover a City Council meeting, you know. Because of the Brown Act they can't discuss city business in private—"

"You know they do anyway," she cut in.

"Probably, but whatever I cover is just the summary of what happened."

"I tried to watch the meeting on Zoom last night," Carinna said, stirring the coffee that had miraculously appeared before her, along with my waffle and a mountain of scrambled eggs and a pile of toast for her. She had to be a regular, of course. Everyone in Simpato was a regular somewhere. Eventually I would be, too, I supposed, if I stayed after I was back on my feet emotionally and legally. "I couldn't stand watching Garth tiptoeing through the agenda like that, and shut it off. So they're going to draw lots for the three spots?"

I nodded, my mouth full of waffle.

"And this is all going to be a blind draw?"

I swallowed. "Of course it is. Suspicious, aren't you?"

"I've lived here off and on all my life, Sal. I know that Sin-Pato isn't without its cronyism. So who's in the running? Nate, obviously, and Siggy."

"Ernesto Carreras—"

"That's Nate," she said.

"Right. And Siggy is Marc Segismundo. So, them, plus Arturo and Amparo—"

"The A's are going to try to have a truck downtown? Well that answers at least what Mikey-Mike Charolais was doing at the meeting."

"How's that?"

"Obviously, since he works for Perdiz, and Sangiacomo Partridge owns Perdiz and thinks he owns Arturo, he'd be absolutely livid if Arturo left Perdiz to go do a food truck with his wife. When he isn't beating her."

"Sangiacomo?"

"Jack Partridge. Married or not-married to Victoria the Iron Maiden."

I shook my head. "Does everyone here have a nickname?"

Carinna smiled around her mouthful of toast and nodded. "Sangiacomo uses Jack, and who wouldn't? I mean, you use Sal instead of Salvia, and who wouldn't?"

"Thanks. Why is Victoria called the Iron Maiden?"

"Well, not to her face, it's not that kind of nickname. I know that Iron Maiden sounds like a real ice queen, but it really means that torture device like a coffin with spikes, where they used to put people in and slam it shut."

Carinna knew the strangest things.

"Yeah, so why is she, okay, referred to that way?"

"Because when Jack tried to divorce her, she put his balls in one."

#

After breakfast, and now nearly noon, Carinna and I walked up towards the monastery. She had business to conduct, thanks to a recent harvest at her daughter's grow farm, and she spent a lot of time sampling her own wares.

"What's the deal with Sister Marigold?" I asked her. Perhaps Carinna would have an inside track. "She still reporting for that big national news outlet?"

"I wouldn't know," Carinna said, "but she's still part of the Little Sisters of the Earth. Maybe she's discovered her vocation."

I snorted. "We don't do nunneries," I said. Sister Marigold, neé Margo Schwartz, was no more likely to become a nun than I was. Of course, these weren't real nuns. "I wonder what story she's chasing this time. It can't be a small town City Council brouhaha over food trucks."

"Nah," Carinna said, her long strides making me nearly trot to keep up. "She doesn't eat the cookies, you know." I'd gotten used to Carinna's pot-fueled non-sequiturs. "I wonder what keeps her there."

"Free room and board? Slow down a bit."

Carinna shortened her stride, and we walked in silence another block. We were at Second Street, and I could turn off here to go one block to my house, or I could keep going to the monastery with Carinna. I stopped. "Who do you like for mayor?" I asked. "I can't vote in the special election, I'm still registered in San Francisco, but do you think Garth Mendez or Cindy Scott's got the advantage?"

"Cindy. Definitely Cindy. Garth is like a giant slug or something, he moves so slowly it makes me want to scream. I mean, no one actually likes Cindy, but she's sharp and ambitious. On the other hand, she lives just on the border of Valley County and Simpato, so it's possible she's not even qualified."

"Well, everyone would know that already, right? She's been on the Council for what, ten years?"

"True that," Carinna said. "Either way, Miss Ashley Sage is going to be on the Council, because, you know, math."

"Who?"

"Oh, you don't know? Ashley Sage, masseuse, divorcee, look-at-me, is running for Georgiana's spot, and if you have five people on the Council, and one becomes mayor and the other is dead ..."

"Right. You're still one short. Math. I'm headed home," I said. "Glad you could come to breakfast with me."

"Food? Any time. And look out for Mikey. He may be a charmer, but I don't trust anyone associated with Perdiz. Not him, not Jack—certainly not that snake Jack—not Victoria, and not Arturo. They're all their own special brand of slime-ball."

#

I spent the day doing little things around the house. Living in an agricultural area had a negative I'd never expected: dust. As soon as the rains stopped, the fields dried out, and dust blew into the house through every open window and door.

I wasn't much of a housekeeper, but this dirt drove me nuts. After several rounds of vacuuming and dusting, I was sneezing and my eyes were watering.

Luna wove herself between my legs, her fine white hair raising its own cloud. "This never bothered me in San Francisco," I said to her. "It's definitely not you."

I wasn't ever going to tell Saul that the cat made me sneeze.

All the while my mind kept snagging on my conversations with Mikey and Carinna. Nothing stuck, but I'd just met about seven new people in twenty-four hours, and they all hated one another. Odd.

Once the place was decent again and I'd taken a shower, I steeled my courage and went to the State Bar site. It made me nauseated to look at it, with my name flagged and *suspended from the practice of law* next to it, but I had to make myself confront the future.

My lawyer had sent me a reminder that given the short amount of time I was suspended—two months had to be a record in the State Bar tradition of overreach—I was only required to re-take the Professional Responsibility test to be reinstated. I was scheduled for the test in June, which meant that in reality I had a three-month suspension, not a two-month one. Since I had to wait to take the test. And oh yeah, get the results.

I sighed out loud. I scrolled to the practice exams, took yet another one, and scored a 98%. I did every time, missing the few questions that allowed a lawyer to make even more money off of a client. It seemed I was more responsible than the test wanted me to be.

After that self-flagellation I fed Luna a few treats and contemplated the empty afternoon. I wasn't much for retail therapy, but a walk through town would definitely perk me up. Besides, I could pick up a nice bottle of wine on the way back. And maybe I'd swing by the police station.

Our Chief of Police, Devon Plata, had become a good friend of mine, and we often spent the evening, after he left the station, with a glass of wine and some nice cheeses.

I put on my shoes and got my canvas grocery bag. I was nothing if not ecologically minded. If I swung the other way, I could have joined the Little Sisters of the Earth. But I didn't, so instead of a nunnery I was looking forward to wine and cheese with a man.

Tourists tended to surge on Thursdays and stay until Monday brunch, after which the tide of humanity in shorts jaywalking across Central Street withdrew until the following Wednesday. I walked the three blocks to Main, and crossed the little bridge over the Valley River to Central. Across Central, the library was having its Little Ducklings Readathon, and a banner with books and ducks wavered in the light breeze that always kicked up in the afternoons. At the bridge, a knot of men was clustered, and while they were not loud, their body-language told me they were not happy.

As I passed, stepping off the curb to avoid crowding them, I could hear the words bandied about in that combination of English and Spanish typical of Simpato, including "food truck" and "unfair." I took a quick look, recognizing Siggy from the night before, and Nate, and two other men. One I knew, one

I didn't. One was quite tall, slender and wiry, with sleek black hair, longer than was currently fashionable. From the back, he looked like a young man, but as I moved past I could see that he was more likely in his fifties.

The other man was Justin March, the health inspector. He had his hands in his pockets, and he stood with confidence despite the clear indications that the other three men were not happy with him. He lifted his Marlboro-man square jaw and shrugged. As I continued down the sidewalk I felt his eyes on me, and I ducked into the first shop I came to.

Feathers was nearly empty, not surprisingly on this midweek afternoon. It would be bustling by tomorrow. A man stood at the counter, blond and built. When he looked away briefly from the woman behind the counter, I saw that he had blue eyes with pinpoint black pupils that made him look like an AI drawing. And he buzzed like an electric wire.

I gave him a wide berth and went to the back of the store where gorgeous silk jackets, hand-dyed and drapey, were hanging. I picked up one, green the color of the leafing vines, swirled with the yellow of mustard grass and the brilliant blue of the Valley sky. I looked at the price, swallowed, and put it back on the rack.

On the sale rack there were some shorter tops, and some magnificent scarves in deeper winter shades that would work well in San Francisco. I didn't know if I'd be going back, but either way I would love that scarf. I could manage the price. Saul's buyout of our marriage had been very generous, ill-gotten though his gains may have been.

I took the scarf to the counter. The woman behind the glass table was wearing a feathered vest, and dangling red earrings. The twitchy blond man moved aside, she shrugged, and turned to me.

"I'll see you at the dinner next month," the man said, heading towards the door.

"You betcha," she answered, and winked at me. She took my card, ran it, and as I was taking the scarf she put a little bangle bracelet with a duck charm in my bag. "On the house, Mrs. Keeper."

There was no escaping it.

#

Chief of Police Devon Plata wasn't at the station, so I chatted a bit with Tilly, the young woman at the desk. She bubbled with excitement over her upcoming promotion from cadet to officer, having scored spectacularly well on the police academy tests and passed her cadet training.

Luke Aureliano, Devon's second in command, came out through the locked doors that led to the inner workings of the Simpato police department. It had a large duck decal on the bulletproof window.

"Mrs. Keeper," he nodded.

I nodded back. I was tired of saying, "My name is Sal DeVine, not Keeper." It was hopeless. "Off to solve the crimes of Simpato?" I said.

He hitched his pants up. He was a graduate of No-Duck High, as was Tilly, and even young officer Sergio Gallego was an alumnus. "There's no crime in Simpato," he said, and headed out the door.

In less than a minute I saw the police pickup truck race by, sirens and lights going, Luke at the wheel.

"Donut run," Tilly said. "It's almost five.

CHAPTER THREE

Friday, the big day for the drawing, dawned cool and foggy. There was a scent of smoke, which set me on edge. Simpato had had the misfortune of major fires a few years earlier, and any whiff made everyone nervous.

I checked the WAD and there was nothing about a fire. After I got dressed, with my new, beautiful scarf fitting in with the slight overcast, I went out on my back deck. The scent of smoke had sharpened into the aroma of grilling meat. Yes, the food trucks. They would likely be running in force for the event.

Carinna knocked on my door. This time she was dressed in a long-sleeved white sheath dress more suitable to a teenaged body, and wrapped in a white and grey woolen shawl. A pair of brown cowboy boots broke up the color scheme.

Carinna and I walked over to the flagpole a little before noon. A crowd had formed, with nearly concentric circles based on their roles in the event. The Council members were on the inside, right next to the pole. Joining them was a small, neatly-dressed woman who looked to be in her twenties, with long, highlighted hair. She held a small terrier by a leash. The terrier was barking shrilly but without intent, just making noise.

"Who's that?" I asked Carinna.

"Ashley Sage," she said. I raised a brow. "Yeah. The one I told you about. Works at one of the spas as a masseuse. She's running for a spot on the City Council. We could use some young blood."

"I wonder if she's for or against the Taco Truck Ordinance," I said. "Let's go ask her."

"Okay, Lois Lane," Carinna replied.

We had to move through the next few circles of concerned citizens and hangers on. The truck owners from the night before were standing huddled yet apart from one another. I saw Amparo, Nate, Siggy, and the man who had been teasing Arturo, though Arturo himself wasn't present. There were supposed to be five applicants, but to date I'd only seen four sets.

"Do you know who else is supposed to be in the drawing?" I asked Carinna. She shook her head.

Between the truck owners and the Council, other groups had formed. "That guy over there, he owns the pizza shop at the corner, just past the Valley bridge. And those two women, the ones with the bangles and bracelets, they've got the insanely-priced clothing store right before the bridge itself."

I thought I recognized one of them from my venture into the store. "Do you mean Feathers? Yeah, those prices are out of this world but the clothes are gorgeous," I said. "That's where I got this scarf." I pointed proudly to the only stylish part of my wardrobe, conscious that I was appearing in a semi-public role. My jeans were clean, I wasn't wearing my usual yoga pants, and I had on a copper-colored long-sleeved blouse that I thought brought out my eyes and the red highlights in my otherwise wren-drab hair, and maybe went with the scarf. Not Feathers-level, but it would do. "I wonder why they felt the need to come out."

"Not a lot happens here," Carinna said. "Anything for the excitement."

We reached the inner circle and I approached the barking terrier and its owner. "What's its name?" I asked.

The woman looked up at me, a rare event in my five-foot-three life. "Singe," she said, giving it a French pronunciation.

"Oh!" I said. "Monkey. He's very cute!"

"She. But yeah, she is. I'm Ashley, by the way." She held out her left hand, her right one being occupied by the leash. "I'm running for Council member, to take Georgiana Noyes's seat. Are you a voter in this town?"

She certainly didn't wait for small-talk. "Not yet," I started. She turned away, as I was clearly not worth her time. "I write for the *Quack*," I added, watching as she predictably turned back to me. Now I was worthy. "Sal DeVine."

"Nice to meet you, Sal," she said, giving me a closer look. "You writing about the Taco Truck Duck-up?" I had to laugh. She smiled, small even teeth encased in lightly lipsticked lips. "I've got to say, this is a pretty unorthodox way to go about making laws." She added with air quotes, *"Let's just draw names out of a hat! The heck with parliamentary procedure and due process."*

I gave her another look. Carinna had said she was a masseuse, but she talked like a lawyer. I supposed one could be both. "So I take it that you aren't in favor of this temporary measure? Or its implementation?"

"You got that right. While Simpato is for the Simaptans, we can't sacrifice the moneymaking downtown for the whims of those who can't indulge in the fancy restaurants. They forget: without tourists, there are no jobs. Without jobs, they can't live here. So therefore, to live here they need to accommodate the tourists. And tourists won't like it if they come to spend two hundred dollars on a dinner and there's a taco truck outside the restaurant and thirty grape-pickers hanging around drinking *cerveza.*"

Wow. "Can I quote you?"

"Sure. Just get it right, you know?"

I took out my notebook. With the terrible curse of being able to repeat conversations nearly verbatim, I wrote down exactly what she just said. "I will," I said.

"Real reporters just record stuff on their phones, you know. That tall one, the one that pretends to be a nun, she doesn't run around with a yellow pad and a pen. You should observe the pros, that's how you get ahead."

She craned her neck, trying to see what I'd written.

"Don't worry, I won't misquote you," I said, starting to walk away.

"They always do, though," Ashley said.

"Even when they record things on their phones? I guess it would be deliberate, then. I'll get it right." I was getting on my high horse, and I needed to dial it back. "Besides, I'm the Keeper. I've got ethics."

#

I edged towards the truck folks. I wanted to see how they felt about the drawing process. Ashley did have a point, it was a lack of due process. On the other hand, it was fair, unless it wasn't. I thought back to the hubbub on Tuesday night. Someone, I think it was Arturo, had been implying that the drawing would be rigged.

Arturo still wasn't here. I approached Amparo, the men moving apart to let me through, keeping an eye on me as well.

"Excuse me," I said in Spanish. "Could I ask you some questions?"

"I speak English," she said, making that as obvious as possible.

"Of course," I said. "Sorry. Habit," I lied. She gave me the cold look she seemed to have on tap for ready use. "I guess Arturo had to work?"

Amparo gave me an even colder look, one I could never have imagined existing before that moment. "No."

"No?" Did I have the right to ask where he was, then?

Amparo pursed her lips. "He's sick. He don't need to be here. I'm here, that's enough." She turned her back on me, leaving me looking at her graying bun.

"She's not your new best friend, huh?" The man who'd been teasing Amparo last night said to me.

"I'm Sal," I said to him. "What do you think of the idea of drawing names for the temporary trucks?"

"I know who you are. You're the Keeper. You helped figure out what happened to that nosy gossip columnist."

I nodded. "What's your name?"

"Angelo DeVincenzi. But I'm no angel," he said, giving me a wet wink. "I'm a quarter Italian. You can tell by my hands. They're roamin'." He fluttered his hands, grinning.

"Last time I heard that I fell off my dinosaur. But you've got a truck, too?"

"The *Happy Tacky*," he said. "I park out by the vineyards. It's good business."

"So why do you want to move downtown?" I asked.

"Oh, I don't really want to. I just don't want that *pendejo* Arturo to get the good spot. He gets everything. Just because he's a ducking good cook. I gotta hand that much to him. He can make shoes taste like steak. I don't know how he does it. But he treats Amparo like shit."

"She looks like she can take care of herself," I said.

He gave me a side-eye. "Yeah, but I can take care of her better. I got a way with women, just like Arturo's got a way with food. Wanna taste?"

I shook my head and started to walk away.

"Hey, duck-ass," I heard behind me.

Where did Mikey come from? "I didn't see you here," I said.

"I was hiding," he said, with a laugh. "I was mostly trying to see who was here and why. And I wasn't calling you a duck-ass, just so you know. That was meant for Angelo." He turned back to the truck folks. "Amparo, where's your better half? He didn't show up to work again today, and that's not like him."

"Maybe she finally put a knife in his gut," Angelo said.

Amparo narrowed her elaborately made-up eyes. "Maybe I did. Too bad I didn't. He's just sick. Probably from eating at your truck, *Happy Tacky*."

Angelo didn't laugh.

On the other side of the flag pole, the health inspector raised his phone to his mouth to dictate something.

And behind him, also raising her phone, was Sister Marigold, pro-reporter.

#

A hush came over the crowd as Garth Mendez walked to the pole. He looked around, smiled sheepishly, and picked up a stone from the rocks that surrounded the fountain. He banged on the pole as if it were a gavel, to start the process.

"Ladies and gentlemen, *señores y señoras*, we are gathered here—"

"Get on with it," Carinna said behind me, and in the silence her voice carried.

"As the lady said," Justin said.

"Give him a break," another voice came. "This is Simpato, not the rest of the world."

A murmur of approval went through the crowd. This was Simpato, and in this town, folks generally got along. The Taco Truck Ordinance had created an unusually ugly division, but we didn't have to like it.

I saw Mother Sassafras make her way to the front. "Sister," Garth said, "I'm about to start ..."

"I will help you. It was my suggestion, after all. I think it's the only way we can see if the trucks work out. If they do, maybe everyone will get a chance to have a truck. Maybe we'll set up a rotation."

Garth shrugged, helpless against the power of Mother Sassafras.

"Who elected her?" Carinna said in my ear, quietly this time.

Garth banged on the pole again and this time folks got quiet. Cindy Scott brought forth a Simpato High baseball cap, complete with duck on the front, and handed it to Garth. She held up five pieces of paper, and read each one aloud as she folded it precisely in half and dropped it in the hat.

"Ernesto Carreras. Truck name, *La Sabrosa*. You here, Nate?"

"Yeah, I'm here," he answered. She dropped the paper in the hat.

"Mark Segismundo. Siggy?"

"Present, ma'am," he said with a laugh.

"Ha ha," Cindy deadpanned. "No truck name yet?"

"No ma'am," Siggy grinned. "If I get a spot, want me to call it *Tacos la Cindy*?"

She ignored him. "Arturo and Amparo Buendía? Truck name, *Tacos Buen Día*."

"I'm here," Amparo said. "Arturo is home sick."

"That's okay," Cindy said. "You run the truck anyway."

"Damn right I do," she answered.

"Angelo Devincenzi. *Happy Tacky* want a shot at downtown?"

"Happy to try," he answered with a grin.

"Silvestre Sanchez." Cindy paused. "Silvestre, you here?" There was no answer.

"Maybe he's home sick, too!" someone said. "Whose truck did he eat at last night?" There was nervous laughter, but no one answered.

"No one said we must be present to win," Siggy said.

"True," Cindy said. "But, well, his application wasn't really complete, so I'm not sure we can count him in."

I looked around for reactions, and caught sight of a large young man bobbing up and down with energy. "August!" I said.

August bounded over like a Labrador retriever let off a leash. "Hey, Sally!" He was the only person I let call me Sally, and only because I just couldn't break him of the habit. At twenty-eight, he was, in many ways, only eight. In other ways, he was a scarred, responsible man. It depended on the task.

He embraced me with one arm, which could have wrapped the whole way around me. "Is that okay?"

I nodded. "It's okay, but only a little bit." August always asked, but often it was after he'd overstepped. Social cues weren't his forte.

"You know where this missing truck guy lives? Silvestre Sanchez?" I asked him. Born and bred in Simpato, August had never been farther that the city of Valley, twenty miles south, and only as far east as Cragstown.

"Sure. He's a mile past where they're building the big hotel. He has a taco truck but he parks it all different places, not a one-stop guy. He's got a daughter, two years back of me at school, she went on to college. Real smart girl. Alicia. One time, at a football game, she brought cookies to sell so she could do the applications ..."

I stopped him before I could hear the entire family history. "Why don't you take your pickup truck and go see where he is. He's going to miss the drawing and not have a chance at the first downtown spots."

"Good idea, Mrs. Keeper!" he said. Moments later I heard the first four bars off of "Never on Sunday" as August blasted down the road in his black pickup truck.

I moved up to the center of the ring, near the pole. "Cindy, I'm Sal DeVine."

"Of course, the new Keeper."

"Uh, yeah. But could you wait a minute before drawing the lots? August Sanjusto—"

"I know August."

Of course she did. "Right, well he just went to check on the missing truck owner, Silvestre ..." I glanced at my notes, "... "Sanchez. Can you give him a minute? In case he wants to complete anything that's missing before you draw names?"

"They were supposed to be complete by April 30," Siggy said. "Why should he get an extra chance?"

"Why not," I said, "seeing as it's a drawing instead of an award, and no one knew there'd be a drawing today instead of a decision last Tuesday ..."

He shrugged. "Just doesn't seem fair. I play by the rules, he doesn't."

I hadn't seen anyone referred to as Silvestre Sanchez on Tuesday night, I'm not sure he was even there. Siggy had a point. I looked at Cindy. She shrugged.

"Okay, everyone, we're going to give Silvestre another five minutes to get here and finish filling out his application. If he's not here, we go ahead. Meanwhile, are we clear on the spots? Three of you will get to try out downtown. You'll be responsible for keeping order around your truck, keeping folks from getting rowdy, no litter. One spot on the other side of the Valley River bridge, one spot over here by the fountain, one spot in front of the monastery."

"That's not downtown. It shouldn't count." Siggy was adamant.

"I think it should," Mother Sassafras said quietly. "And since right now you can't park there, and if this gets passed you can, someone will be lucky to take that spot."

"It's a loser spot," Siggy said. "It's really two good spots: the bridge and the fountain. And with four of us trying to get in, that's fifty-fifty odds."

"Okay, college boy," Amaparo said. "Let's see who gets what."

"That's because it's rigged," Nate said.

"Don't worry, even if you get the spot, Carreras, I'm shutting you down." Justin March appeared by my side.

"Yeah? You and what army?" Nate said.

"Papi." Ernestina laid a hand on his shoulder.

"Okay, here's August," I said, trying to stave off a fight. I'd have to send Ed an update for the *Quack*.

August jumped down from his big black truck, the engine still running. "Get Chief Plata! Get Luke!"

"What's the matter, August?" Mother Sassafras said calmly.

"He's dead! Silvestre's dead! Dead all over his living room floor! Get the Chief!"

#

I edged away from the crowd, watching the door of the police station. Luke Aureliano came out first, followed by the young officer Sergio Gallego. Sergio looked pale, and he nodded to Luke as Luke gave him instructions. Then Luke got into a squad car, and, putting on both lights and sirens, peeled out of the parking lot in the direction of Mount Santabella and Simpato Lake. This time, instead of donuts, he had a dead man.

"Okay, can everyone just sit down somewhere while we wait for Chief Plata?" Sergio said, his voice shaking. "And can you not talk?"

Mother Sassafras took over. "Sal, take a group over to the benches by the fountain. Anyone who is not on the Council, and not a truck owner, go with Sal. Counsel, gather around Garth and Cindy." I saw Ashley make her way to them. Sassafras raised an eyebrow, but Ashley ignored her.

"Truck owners, have a seat in front of City Hall." City Hall was a two-story stucco building next to the police station. It was the place to get a building permit or pay your water bill. Mother Sassafras herded the truck owners to the benches there, and this being Simpato, and she looking like a nun, even if she wasn't a real one, they obeyed.

I watched as Devon Plata came out the swinging doors of the police station. He was talking on his phone as he walked towards the group of politicians at the flagpole. His powerful shoulders were hunched up as he held the phone to his ear with one, and used both hands to pull out a notebook and a pen from various pockets.

In the distance I heard the wail of an ambulance, and then, as was local practice, a fire engine. Devon took his phone from his ear, and shoved it in his pocket. Garth approached him, and I could just about make out what he was saying, but Plata waived him away. "Let's keep it quiet until I hear back from Luke what's going on. Augustín!" I knew it was serious when he used August's full name.

August, who'd come with my group and was hovering over my shoulder, made a little mewling sound. I put my hand on his arm. August had been wrongfully arrested for murder by the former police chief a decade ago, when he was barely eighteen, and he never really got over it. On the other hand, he went drinking sometimes with Sergio, and told me that Sergio had become a cop because he'd been bullied in high school, and he knew that cops were just people like everyone else.

"Go ahead," I said.

"Come with me?"

I walked over to the flagpole where Devon was standing. "Sergio, go stand with the truck owners for now. And please ask

Mother Sassafras to join us. How you doing, Sal?" he said to me, and I could see a little color come up.

I smiled at him. "Good, Chief." I'd keep it formal in front of the whole town, though in private we seemed to be off-and-on inching towards something a little friendlier than wine-and-cheese.

"August, what happened?"

"I went over to Silvestre Sanchez's house because Sal wanted to know where he was." Devon raised an eyebrow at me. I shrugged. "Because he'd not completed his application right and the Council was going to draw for the spots."

Devon turned to me. I clarified. "You know about the drawing?" He nodded. "Well, there were five applicants, and before Cindy Scott could put the five names in the hat, she called roll, sort of. Arturo's not here either. Amparo says he's sick. But apparently Silvestre Sanchez not only isn't here, he didn't do his application completely, so Cindy wasn't going to include him in the drawing. It was my idea," I felt a little queasy owning up to it, "to send August over to find him. Just to see if he wanted to be in it or not."

"I won't ask why you got involved," Devon said. "And August, I'll take your statement inside—" August mewed again, almost sounding like Luna. "Don't worry, I just need to know what you saw. But for now, you saw Silvestre in his house?"

August nodded.

"The door was open or you opened it?"

August shot me a terrified glance. "I, um, I … I smelled it. I mean, the windows were open, and I could smell something bad, and I opened the door, I mean, I knocked first and then opened the door, when he didn't answer, but he was lying on the floor." Tears started down August's face. This big, ridiculously strong young man, with his round face and soulful eyes, was crying in the street in front of the flagpole and all the City Council.

"There were flies," he said. "And throw-up. Everywhere. I had to get back here. I knew Sal would know what to do."

Sobbing, he collapsed onto the ground, holding his knees.

Devon caught my eye. "Take him inside," he said to me softly. "I need to talk to everyone else. I'll be in soon."

"Find out if Arturo's okay," I said quickly.

"Inside," he answered, and turned away.

#

Tilly, former parking patrol, current cadet, and now in her expanded role of desk officer, took August's hand and led him like a lamb through the locked door with the duck decal, separating the rest of the station from the front desk and lobby. She opened it with her ID card, and led him into the interrogation room. It was also the lounge, recreation room, and place where someone could get a little privacy for a phone call.

I followed, slipping in behind her, and Tilly didn't object. She had August sit down at the large, scratched table, and brought him a cup of the renowned station coffee. She looked over at me. I nodded. She came back with two more paper cups of dark liquid and put one in front of me. She sat down next to August, with the last cup.

The coffee at the Simpato Police Station was possibly the best coffee in the entire county of Valley, and surely better than anything you could get in neighboring Crags County. The coffee was supplied by Sergio Gallego's father, and it was the same good stuff that fueled the finer restaurants in Simpato. Much like the goods supplied by Carinna to the Little Sisters of the Earth, I thought, as I watched August cautiously eyeing Tilly.

I took out my recently-mocked mini yellow pad from my messenger bag and added the best description I could give of the events in front of the flagpole to my notes. I would have a lot more to report to Ed Sharp than which trucks got the spots.

"August, you feeling better?" I asked. He didn't touch his coffee. He nodded. "Can you tell me something? I don't want to upset you more, but can you tell me again how you went up to the door? And then what happened?" I said it all very gently, but I was concerned.

"Maybe we should wait for the Chief," Tilly said. She still called Chief Plata "the Chief," and probably would for her first full year as a cop. Even Sergio had started to slip into "Devon" now and then. "Or I could go and ask him if it's okay for me to ask some questions. Or listen while you do ..." She seemed unsure.

"It's hard," I said. "When you were just doing parking you would have had no question about what to do. Once you're a full officer, you'll know, too. But right now, being neither fish nor fowl—"

August chuckled, followed by a sob. "We say *neither carp nor duck* here." Tilly giggled.

"Okay, neither carp nor duck," I conceded.

Devon appeared in the doorway. "Tilly, we need someone to stay on the desk right now. We can't leave it open when we have an incident." She jumped up, and as we watched Devon take in the three coffee cups, my notebook, and my pen, Tilly edged closer to the door. As soon as he stood aside she dashed out.

I glared at Devon. He shrugged.

"It's okay, thanks for getting everyone settled here," he called out, but she had rushed back to the desk. Devon shook his head. "I need to work on my tone," he said, and sat down at the table. He looked at Tilly's abandoned coffee cup. He cut eyes to me quickly, then picked up her cup and left the room.

"I can't believe she's going to be a cop now, I mean a full one, not a parking cop," August said. "I remember when I was a senior, she was in seventh grade. And she ran track. She was good."

His voice was calm, he wasn't crying anymore, and I wanted to get a question in while Devon completed his new-more-caring-manager mission. "Tell me again about going up to the door."

"Like I said, Sally—" I sighed but didn't correct him, "—I wanted to get him so he wouldn't miss the drawing. I had kind of a crush on Alicia, and I felt bad that her father would be out of the running. So I jumped down—oh, first I honked my horn. The good one, 'Never on Sunday,' not the blast."

Of course he did.

"I wanted him to know I was out there, and, you know, if Alicia was home she'd know it was me because everyone knows my horn."

They did.

"And I thought I heard the door slam. So I knew someone was home. And when I went to the door, like I said, the window was open, but he probably doesn't have AC or doesn't turn it on until July, like most of us because it costs so much so if it's not 100 we don't use it."

The sun had burned off the fog, and by now it was warm out, maybe eighty-five, but with dry air that temperature felt comfortable to any Californian. "Of course the window would be open," I said. "So you looked in the window?"

"It was the smell. I smelled something coming from inside—"

"Sal? I'll take over from here." Devon was back, and the look on his face was definitely not the gentler-manager one. "Out you go."

He held the door open.

"I'll just listen," I could hear the whine in my voice. I eliminated it immediately. "I'm reporting on the drawing for the truck spots in Edwina Sharp's place, for the *Quack*. I'm the press."

Devon didn't answer, but stood holding the door for me.

"Stop by later, August," I said. He nodded. "Ask him exactly how things smelled," I said to Devon as I went by.

He shut the door behind me and I heard the click of the automatic lock. I hoped that August wasn't in trouble.

If only this were two weeks later, I could have claimed to be his attorney. For now, with the suspension running its course, pretending to be a reporter was a lame second-best.

#

Outside in the sunshine, the Council members had regrouped in front of the flagpole. The truck owners and their friends were still across the street, being watched over by Sergio, and someone had started playing music on his phone. It was uncanny, listening to modern Mexican rap, complete with horns and guitars, while everyone waited for someone to tell them what to do—or what had happened.

Half the waiting folks spoke quietly in Spanish, the other half in English, and a friend of one of the truck owners returned with a huge platter of sweet rolls and bottles of Jarritos sodas for all. He even brought the rolls over to the Council members, though he didn't offer the sodas. I took a roll, and enjoyed it with my coffee as I observed the groups.

One benefit of folks not knowing I was pretty fluent in Spanish was their willingness to talk to one another without feeling hindered by me. I looked around for Carinna, but not seeing her—she did tend to vanish when trouble arose—I edged over to the truck owners. Close enough to hear, far enough to be insignificant, I took in their conversation.

"What's the big deal? If he just croaked, that's one less in competition." The women in the group crossed themselves every time someone said any version of *died*.

"Hey Sergio, if Silvestre died," cross, cross, "okay so that's sad, but why can't we get on with it?" Amparo asked.

Sergio shuffled his feet. He was still a kid to these folks, even to Siggy. "I dunno," he said in Spanish, colloquially. "Boss said we all had to wait. So maybe something happened."

Duh, I thought. If this had been deemed a medical emergency only, Luke Aureliano would be back, the drawing would take place with the four truck owners, funerals would be discussed, and that would be that.

My phone rang and all eyes turned to me. I checked the number, it was Ed at the *Quack*. I stepped away and answered.

"My pal at the fire station tells me one of the truck owners was killed," she said without preamble.

So it was more than just a medical emergency. "I'm down here at the flagpole, taking notes. Devon Plata kicked me out of the interview with Augustín Sanjusto, who found the owner, Silvestre Sanchez."

"Good job, you know more than I do. Stay as long as you can get away with it. It's chaos here: the nail salon upstairs, the one that was defunct but maybe not, well someone was trying to use their old dishwasher and it overflowed and leaked into the newspaper offices. Nightmare. I bet I'm paying their water and electric bills." She hung up.

All eyes turned to the police station as August emerged. He came straight to me. "Sally," he whispered. "I think Silvestre was killed. What should I do?" In the six short weeks it seemed I'd been here I'd become August's confidante and second mother.

"Let's see if they go ahead with the drawing," I said quietly. "Where's the Chief?"

"He said he'd be out in a minute, and that I shouldn't talk to no one."

I guess I didn't count.

Devon came out of the station, looked around, and rolled his eyes in clear exasperation when he saw August with me. "All right, everyone," he said. "Gather around."

Devon stood on the first of the two steps that led to the station, allowing him to look at everyone crowding close. I edged away from the center of the circle. I suddenly felt the need to keep an eye on the truck-owners. I kept Amparo, especially, in view.

Devon pushed the hair out of his eyes, squinting in the sun. He was in his element, and I could see some of the dramatics appealed to him. Not a big surprise that his son, who was currently building houses in Honduras with Habitat, had been studying acting before dropping out of college. "Sergio, want to translate?"

Sergio preened. "Yes, Chief," he said, swaggering forward.

"No ad libbing," Devon added, but he said it gently. "Now, we all know—" Sergio started to talk. "Not at the same time, Sergio. Just wait til I'm done, okay?"

Sergio nodded. "I saw this thing on YouTube where they were doing it at the same time, and—"

"No. Just wait. Okay. We all know that there are three spots for the trucks, while the city tries out the idea of food trucks downtown." He paused. "Now, Sergio."

Sergio did his thing, and Devon shot me a look. I nodded.

"Actually, boss, they speak English as good as I do," Sergio said.

"True," Devon agreed, though it wasn't quite true. He turned to the crowd. "Anyone who doesn't understand what

I'm saying, Sergio will translate. Okay, so there are three spots. There were five applications, and now there are four."

"Someone should tell Alicia," August said. Everyone began to talk at once. I picked up, *his poor daughter* in both languages, *oh my god that poor girl, first her mother and now her father, you should tell her, you're her father's cousin in law,* and more.

I wondered what happened to the girl's mother.

"We will tell her," Devon said sharply. "Just listen a minute. Okay, so here's the thing. We'll have the drawing now anyway."

That's disrespectful, in various iterations and languages. *We should, Silvestre's application was no good anyway,* in other voices. *Can we get on with it,* in English, from one of the Council members. Female. I couldn't tell which.

I watched Amparo. She said nothing. I noticed that Devon was also watching her.

"Council, please do the drawing now. No fanfare. Just get it done."

I looked over the group, and saw Justin bend down and whisper something in Ashley Sage's ear. She smirked and pushed him away playfully, then edged closer to the Council members.

Cindy took the Ducks hat, put the four slips of paper in the hat, and turned to Garth. "You didn't vote for this," he said. "You should draw."

"Doesn't matter, Garth. Majority rules, remember?" Cindy said.

"I'll draw," Ashley said.

"You're not a Council member yet," Cindy said acidly. "Matty?"

Jessica looked chagrined. She had put her hand up to volunteer, since after all, the drawing had been her suggestion, but

Matty Buono stepped up. He put his hand in, and pulled out a slip.

"Why don't we just make whoever you drew be the only one who doesn't get a spot?" Ashley said. "It'll save time."

Cindy sighed. "No, Ashley, because we need to allocate the spots. Now, this first drawing is for the spot in front of the Little Sisters of the Earth."

"Not downtown," I heard a voice in my ear. It was Mikey Charolais. I had forgotten all about him. I briefly wondered where he's been, but Cindy was announcing the name.

"Ernesto Carreras. Nate, you get the nuns."

"*Qué chin—,*" he said.

Mikey laughed. "Definitely not downtown," he said in my ear.

"Hey! No language!" one of the women said. "It's fair, it's fair."

Cindy drew the second slip. "Looks like *Happy Tacky* will be setting up shop by the bridge. Angelo DeVincenzi, it's your lucky day."

Amparo shifted her weight. The last spot, by the fountain where we stood, was all that was left. She cut eyes at Mark Segismundo. Siggy was bouncing on his toes, his hands behind his back. His light brown hair was flopping in and out of his face.

Everyone turned to them. "Last spot!" Cindy said.

We really didn't need the drumroll with the tension in the air. I glanced at Devon. He, too, was watching Amparo.

Suddenly a voice came from the back of the crowd. "No one is going to open anything until I go through each of your trucks, and your kitchens. Before you poison your neighbors and our guests, you'll be answering to me. You got that?"

"Justin March, health inspector, late to the party," Mikey said.

"Can it, Charolais. If you want your tasting rooms to stay open, and if you want that thug Arturo Buendía cooking for you, you'll shut your mouth. Where is that—"

"That's unnecessary," Devon said, striding into the crowd. His muscular shoulders and his authoritative stance parted the group. "Everyone who sets up shop will have an inspection, that's obvious, but you don't need to get aggressive." He looked Justin in the eye.

"Stay in your lane," Justin said, but he stood aside.

"What've you got, Cindy?" Devon said. "We've got a lot of work to do, I don't want everyone standing around."

Cindy Scott looked annoyed. Her star moment had already been ruined, and now she was being hurried. But the Chief of Police was the Chief of Police. She nodded. "Siggy, you got it. Sorry, Amparo."

"Be a Duck!" Siggy said.

Amparo looked around at the crowd. Every eye was on her, completely ignoring the winners of the drawing. She drew herself up, her eyeliner and shadow gleaming in the sunlight, her black bun's gray streaks shining. "You'll regret this," she said, and turned away.

Ashley started after her. "It's only the test period," she was saying.

"Let her go," Devon said. He looked at me. He didn't need to say anything.

Casually, as if all I had to do was write up a puff piece on the drawing, I eased out of the crowd. I would stay back, but I was going to follow Amparo.

A large hand gripped my upper arm. "What's this got to do with you?" Mikey said. I acted innocent.

"Going home, the show's over," I said.

"I'm not blind," he answered.

"Take your hand off the lady." It was Justin.

"Thanks, Justin," I said, though we hadn't actually been introduced at the level of first names. "Mikey's not bothering me. I'm good."

"Well, he bothers me," Justin said, but he turned away.

I looked to see if anyone else was watching. They were too busy badgering the Council members for the paperwork they'd need to set up the carts.

"Hey, really. I'm good," I said to Mikey.

"Have dinner with me tonight," he said. "Jack and Victoria are away, and we can have the pairing room kitchen to ourselves. This has been a very interesting few days, and I'd like to hear your thoughts."

I weighed the idea. Devon would probably be working into the evening if what I surmised, that Silvestre Sanchez had been murdered, was true, and wouldn't be stopping by for a glass of wine any time soon. I could probably get some information from Mikey. And he was definitely good-looking.

"Give me your number," I said. "I think so, but I've got some work to do first."

"Text me," Mikey said. He rattled off his number.

I did. "Hi," I wrote.

"San Francisco area code," he remarked. "See you later on."

Amparo was long-gone, and this distraction had put a spanner in my intention to follow her. I'd might as well make the best of it. "See you tonight."

I turned towards home, catching sight, in the distance, of the tall, slim, black-robed figure of Margo Schwartz, journalist, a.k.a. Sister Marigold, hurrying in the direction Amparo had gone, and most definitely away from the monastery.

CHAPTER FOUR

I typed up my notes from the drawing, and then looked at a map of Simpato, tracing where the taco trucks would be set up. The odd thing was that there were already two spots: first, Angelo DiVincenzo's *Happy Tacky* usually parked by the vineyards near Mount Santabella, and was a popular spot with vineyard workers. Second, Nate Carreras was already out by the hotel construction. Arturo had his job at Perdiz, and Amparo ran a small truck on her own, or with his help—I didn't know—that seemed itinerant. This would be Siggy's first truck. And Silvestre, where did he usually put his truck? When he was alive, that is.

I could understand why Angelo and Nate were eager to get downtown spots. The money would be good. But Arturo had a steady, well-regarded job. And why wasn't he at the drawing? Or at work? Amparo said he was sick, but it didn't seem that he'd called in to Mikey to report.

I made a notation: *ask Mikey where Amparo parks, and where Silvestre used to.*

Justin March, oddly, seemed to have a beef with everyone, even if that beef wasn't grade A. Or would it be a duck, here? I shook my head. Simpato, or Sin-Pato, was getting to me.

Justin's main target last night had been Nate Carreras, but today he was spreading his bad cheer more or less evenly.

I heard the blast of August's horn. Poor kid. I went to the kitchen door and watched the dust on the graveled parking area settle around his oversized black pickup truck. He honked once more before descending from the cab. Not his jaunty "Never on Sunday," just a noisy blast.

A constant presence in Simpato, August was considered *different*. A decade ago he'd been one of a trio of BMOCs of No-Duck High. August was never the prom king, but he was always the king's bodyguard. He was the one who put together the graduation stage, so it would have been unfair not to let him up on it.

I stepped outside onto the upper-most deck off my kitchen. Looking from the kitchen down to the driveway, I surveyed the series of redwood decks my father had built, decks that terraced down from the kitchen door to the parking area.

Normally, if anything could be called normal since I'd moved into the house, August would have bounded out of his truck and up the terraces of the deck in about three steps. Of course he was only twenty-eight years old and he loaded trucks for a living. He could lift practically anything, and knew to an inch how much would fit in the trunk of my Prius. That Prius had just winked at the pickup truck. "You know what you like," I muttered to the Prius.

This time, August was subdued. He actually walked up the decks, pulled over my good Brown & Jordan lawn chair, which was one of the few items of furniture I'd kept in the divorce, and extended himself gingerly into the chaise. "Sally," he sighed. "I'm freaking out. Can you hold a special Keeper session for me? Like right now?"

#

The Simpato Keeper of Secrets was role my mother had evidently created when they lived here, first in the summers when she was still teaching, and then, in the last two years before she and my dad disappeared at sea, nearly year-round. On one evening a week, my mom had placed her own chaise lounges on the deck, facing away from the drive, and folks came up, sat down next to her, and told her their secrets: secrets that they couldn't bear alone.

She neither gave advice nor granted absolution. She just listened.

I'd apparently inherited the position from her, even if ten years had passed since she'd been lost at sea, and within days of my arrival, post-divorce and at the start of my legal-suspension-caused-by-now-ex-husband, I had been pestered and bullied into starting up the Keeper practice myself.

One of the absolute rules of the Keeper was that I was to tell no one. My mother had broken that rule only once. I had broken the rule on my very first night.

I sat down in the chaise next to August's. "No, I can't. But tell me anyway. What did you see at Silvestre's?"

He turned towards me. "I told Devon that part already. I came to the window, the window was open, I smelled the stink, I opened the door, poor Mr. Silvestre was lying there in a whole mess of puke, with flies everywhere." He used the common respect-term of a title like Mister with the first name, in honor of the fact that Silvestre Sanchez was dead.

"It must have been horrible. Was the door locked? It couldn't have been if you just walked in."

He shook his head. "No one locks their doors, you know that. There's no crime in Sin-Pato."

"What do you want to tell me?"

He sighed. "It's just that when I was coming back from work last night, you know, since it was Thursday night and I'm off on Fridays, I went by their house, in case Alicia was visiting her dad, just because, you know, to say hi, because it's the big Duck Concert next weekend so I thought maybe she'd be home. She's way too smart for me, she went to UC"—the University of California, notoriously difficult to get into—"but she was always fun and nice to me. And she wasn't home."

I waited.

"And the window was open."

I waited.

"Don't tell no one." He looked at me expectantly.

"August. You know better than that. A man is dead."

He covered his face with his hands. "Please." I shook my head *no*. "Thursday night, when I went by, Señora Amparo was there. With him. They were, um, together." He looked at me, begging me with his eyes to understand enough that he wouldn't have to go on.

I nodded. "Did you just drive away?"

"Yeah. And today, when I went over because you told me to …" I nodded, to reassure him, "… when I went over and he was, um, you know, I just kept thinking of last night. But I didn't tell Devon about Thursday, because I was afraid he'd get mad at me."

"I may have to."

"Don't tell him that it was me who told you, okay? Because Arturo, her husband, he's only mean. But Amparo, she's scary. Definitely a *bruja*. And now I'm really scared."

#

August left, leaving me flummoxed. Amparo and this unknown Silvestre Sanchez, *together*, as August said. Amparo of the scary eyeliner, vicious glare, and mean husband.

August wouldn't lie or make something up, definitely not something that odd, anyway. I made a couple of notes. I'd let the thoughts coalesce on their own time.

I turned my attention to the evening coming up. As usual, my larder was well-nigh empty. Maybe it was a defense mechanism: if I didn't stock my pantry properly, it would mean I was just here temporarily, on vacation or on suspension, no commitment to Simpato. If I started buying things like flour and baking powder, or stocking up on canned tomatoes and broth, I'd have really moved in. But still, I needed food.

Naturally, the local grocery store was called the Duck Shop. I picked up my basket and went straight to the wine. I was currently enthralled with my Malvasia choices, since I'd never even heard of the white, crisp, slightly sweet elixir before six weeks ago. I grabbed a bottle, and made sure to pick a local label. Otherwise I was bound to get an earful from the checker.

I had a tough choice, deciding whether to have dinner and wine with Mikey—could one be interested in a man named Mikey?—or wine with Devon. I had finally decided to thread the needle, texting Mikey that I needed to attend to something later that night, and moved our, well, was it a date? to six thirty. I told Devon I'd see him at eight thirty. I was sure he'd have enough to do at the station to stay an extra half hour.

It also reassured me. In these fraught times, going to dinner at a stranger's place, especially one he had "all to himself," required a little back-up. Not bad when one's back-up was the Chief of Police.

And I had to admit, it felt pretty swell to have two dates, if either one *was* a date, in one night. I hadn't done that since college.

I also picked up a nice triple cream Brie from Marin County, and a seeded baguette. Strawberries were coming into season, and I had bought some at the farmers' market earlier in the week, so that made for a nice after-dinner plate. If Devon was super-hungry, he could get something before meeting me.

Last, I picked up a package of prosciutto. I had eggs, and could make a nice omelet if dinner didn't work out that well. I remembered that Arturo was sick, and Mikey hadn't said anything about his own culinary skills.

I got in line at the front of the store. Two women ahead of me turned and said, "Hola, Mrs. Keeper," and turned back to their conversation.

This was so typical of Simpato, the slide between the languages, and nearly everyone could say at least a few words in both. Among the younger generation, the teens and twenty-somethings, the slide was even more pronounced, with fluent conversations that started in one language and ended in the other. I wondered how long that would last. Would the kids in elementary school lose their parents' language, as my mother had? I only had the barest glimmers of Yiddish beyond jokes and food, and yet that had been my grandparents' primary language. I shook my head.

"What? What's wrong, Sal?" the checker asked. I'd reached the front of the line without noticing. Andie was at the register, her dyed red hair pulled into a tight, small bun. Her reading glasses hung on green-and-gold Simpato High lanyard, bouncing off her Duck Shop T-shirt as she moved the items across the scanner.

"Just miles from here, mentally," I said, putting the cheese and bread in my shoulder bag.

"Got a hot date with the top cop?" she said, holding up the wine.

An older woman in the next line giggled. "La Mrs. Keeper gets around these days, I hear!"

Had they heard already about my potential dinner with Mikey at Perdiz? That wasn't possible. I glared at her.

"Sorry, Sal," Andie said, handing me my receipt. "That was rude. I'm sure you're as moral as any other divorcee."

"I'm divorced too," said another woman, tall and graceful despite her baggy sweatpants and Duck sweatshirt. "Twice. Nothing to be ashamed of. And I'm a good Catholic. So there."

"Lots of people are divorced, Janice," a much-older woman said to the first speaker, whom I didn't even know. "Look at Ashley Sage. She's what, twenty-eight? And she's been married three times! And she's still running for Council. And I'm gonna vote for her, instead of that old battle-ax, Cindy Scott. Thinks she runs the whole city."

"Well, she's gonna be mayor, next. You know Garth, poor soul, doesn't have the cojones to run this town."

I picked up my wine and fled.

#

I walked back to my house, passing in the four blocks the Duck Bill coffee shop, the gorgeous boutique Feathers, a new, vintage and used clothing store called Teal, three wine-tasting venues, and an ice cream shop that somehow didn't have a Duck-related name. I turned up Second, and stopped.

In front of the narrow walkway from the sidewalk to my door there were two men, and while they were still on the public property of the sidewalk, it was clear they were looking and pointing at my house.

They didn't look dangerous, but they didn't look friendly, either. One wore pressed khakis and a collar shirt, the other was in jeans and a black sport coat, which meant that they were likely just coming from a Rotary meeting or something, but it put me on edge. I approached cautiously.

"Ms. DeVine?" the first one said. That branded him as an outsider right there. Though Ms. had been popularized as the appropriate honorific more than half a century ago, it was still used awkwardly in Simpato. Most used Mrs. for any woman who appeared to be over thirty, or Señora. And second, almost half the town called me Mrs. Keeper, reluctant though my role as the Keeper of Secrets was.

Or, of course, *Sally*, as August had named me. Sal was short for Salvia, and I'd never been Sally, but August was August and that was that.

I nodded at them. "Who's asking?" I said in my lawyer-voice. Not aggressive, not loud, not to be trifled with.

Khaki-pants took a step back. "I'm Conrad. This is Bill. We're with Pathways Development."

Pathways. Ah yes, the group that was putting a housing development up near Cragstown, with the investment of former mayor Sebastian Solis, who was now living with Cragstown's mayor. Simpato was not without its charm. I nodded again.

"And we'd like to take a look at your lot, if you don't mind."

I frowned. I didn't need that kind of complication today. "Why would you want to do that?"

Bill stepped back up. "You see, Ms. DeVine, you happen to hold a half-acre right downtown. That's mighty rare, you know." I could almost hear the suppressed *little lady* in his voice.

"And?"

He shuffled his feet. "Um. Well. Uh, Mr. DeVine, your, well, your former spouse, suggested we might want to talk to you about the property. Maybe, because you might want to sell it. We were going to develop here in Simpato, but that didn't work out."

I knew about that former, failed development. But wait. My former husband? "What? You mean Saul contacted you to talk to me about this property?"

Bill nodded. "He mentioned that you might be interested. Nothing firm, of course. But he said he'd told you we'd be coming by today?"

I shook my head. "No. And I'm not interested in selling. But thanks."

They looked at one another. "We've made this trip specially," Bill said. "No harm in letting us just walk the boundaries."

I stared at him, summoning all the iciness I could into my glare. Conrad got the message. He handed me a card. "If you change your mind. Call or email any time."

Bill nodded. "Absolutely. Any time, Ms. DeVine."

I dropped the card in my bag with the cheese, wine, and bread. "Have a good afternoon," Conrad said.

I moved around them, still standing in front of my walkway, and went up the path to my door. I let myself in, turning to shut the door. They were on their phones.

Phone. Right. I remembered that Saul had sent me about six texts that I hadn't read.

I put the bag down and reached for the phone. Before I could get to texts, though, it rang. It was Devon. He never called, he texted. Something had to be up. I slid the answer toggle. The texts would keep.

#

"Look," Devon said without preamble, "I need you to set up an emergency Keeper audience tonight. Just put it up on the WAD and people will come. Something is way off and that's the best way to jumpstart getting behind what's—I don't know, we'll have backup for you until I can get there later."

"Hello, Devon. Fine thank you, and you?" I said. "And no. I can't. I have other plans."

My phone binged a message. It was turning into a hand-held Grand Central Station.

"Sal, this is vital. We're pretty sure—this is confidential— that Silvestre Sanchez was poisoned. We don't know what kind of poison yet, or how he got into it, or maybe he took it himself but I don't think so—I'm sorry, Sal." Devon took a deep breath. For a normally cool Chief of Police, he was unbelievably excited.

"That's a horrible way to do oneself in," I said, buying time. "And like I said, I have plans. Although ..." I was intrigued. It was a chance to get in on the inside track of the investigation.

He waited.

"I could do it tomorrow night. Even though it'll be a Saturday night, if I do it early, like five to six, it won't interfere with peoples' plans. And it will give me a chance to get it up on the WAD and let folks know. Meanwhile, tonight you can bring me up to speed on what's going on."

Devon was quiet for a moment. He sighed. "Okay. Good. I'll probably be late, I'll let you know if I'm hopelessly delayed."

He hung up. No goodbye. No thanks. That's what happened when you semi-dated a cop, I guess.

I went to my computer, to access the WAD, since it was easier to get a full look at the site on my laptop than on my phone. I pulled the laptop out onto the small glass table I'd set up on my deck, and poured myself a little glass of that Malvasia wine.

The afternoon sun was streaming through the branches of the liquid amber tree that shaded the driveway, making a dancing pattern on the redwood decking. The air smelled of turned earth and grilling meat in the distance. The ridges that led up to Mount Santabella were sparkling with mica in the sunlight, and the dark holes of abandoned silver mines looked like cool caves full of invitation.

I opened the laptop and pulled up the WAD page.

Despite the fact that the group was both private and moderated, comments got out of hand now and then, and the moderators had to step in and shut things down. At least there *were* moderators.

There were already photos from the truck drawing at the flagpole. I clicked on them, one at a time, to enlarge them. I zoomed into the photo of the group of Council members about to start the drawing. Cindy was looking edgy. I hadn't really noticed that at the drawing. Here she wasn't looking at the hat with names, or at her fellow Council members, but off to the side. Could be a momentary glance, or it could be that something caught her eye.

I clicked on the next photo. Cindy was still looking away, but in this photo, I could see Ashley, notably younger and more fashionable than anyone else in the group, right in Cindy's line of vision. Maybe that was when she was telling Ashley that she couldn't be the one who drew the names. In retrospect that was pretty petty.

But then, in the next picture, Amparo was behind Ashley. Had she been there the entire time? Amparo, with her malevolent eye makeup, was looking right at Cindy.

In the corner of the photo, August was standing with his hands in his pockets, as usual, and was wearing his Ducks cap backwards. I stopped. Behind him, even though he was a big kid, I could see someone bigger. And just about the only person bigger than August was Mikey.

Mikey's hand was out, reaching, it seemed, towards—who? I couldn't tell whether it was Nate or Angelo. It wasn't Siggy, because Siggy wore chinos. This man was wearing shapeless jeans, a shapeless sweatshirt, and had pulled his shoulder away from Mikey.

I shook my head. I had no idea why this all was catching my eye, but it was. I scrolled down, to see if any of the comments enlightened me. Interestingly, since very few of the Latino residents were on the WAD, there was little comment on the trucks from the owners' point of view. The restaurants, on the other hand, were vehemently against the trucks downtown. In fact, their objections were at a level of intensity that was definitely not present at the Council hearing.

And then I stopped. Someone named Saint Jack-como Partridge posted the comment as I was scrolling: "What a bunch of cowards. These trucks are a blight on the entire landscape. No trucks should be allowed anywhere, except at the construction sites. Not outside the hotels. Not outside the wineries. And definitely not sullying our downtown."

His photo was a partridge. I clicked on it. So I thought. It was actually the owner of Perdiz, which as I mused I realized was Spanish for partridge. Cool name for a winery. And on his profile it said Saint Jack-como Partridge. So this was Mikey's boss, Jack, also known as Sangiacomo.

I looked around his page, which was obviously set to "friends of friends" because I could see plenty. He was not a bad-looking man, maybe fifty, with white-blond hair combed away from his forehead. He was white, and one of the close-ups showed that he had blue eyes. In some of the photos further back he was standing next to a very, very thin blonde woman, so thin I thought I could see her sinews. In no photos was he touching her. From the comments it was clear that this was his wife, Victoria.

I clicked her name, and came up blank.

I shook my head. I was there on Facebook to post my Keeper session on WAD. I made a short post. "If you want to talk about it, the Keeper will hold an extra session tomorrow, Saturday, from 5 to 6, maybe 6:30. Usual place."

Within less than a minute it had seventeen likes.

My phone beeped. Oh, darn. I still hadn't read Saul's texts. We were up to fourteen now.

I took another sip of wine. It had gotten a bit warm, so I poured some fresh from the bottle. Steeling myself I opened Saul's texts in first-to-last order.

#

I'm glad I had the wine. From the beginning to the end, Saul's story was simple. First, a sweet-talking *hey, let's talk.* Then, as it progressed, he mentioned the cat. When I still hadn't answered he called me a name that rhymed with she-who-flies-on-a-broom. Then finally, he cut to the chase.

I've got a tax issue on some of the money from the land sale. It could involve you. I'm sending a guy I know named Conrad to take a look at your folks' property. Maybe a development? It would solve a lot of problems. We could be rich!

It took more than a few deep breaths to calm down. I admit to uttering some pretty bad words of my own. First, it was May, so too soon for any post-separation tax problems, which meant any problems he was having were probably going to be my problems, too. Second, it was my parents' property, which was my separate property, not community property, so he couldn't touch it—but the IRS could. Third, well, how dare he send over a developer to look at my property? *How dare he?*

After about fifty deep breaths I was about to hyperventilate into passing out. Saul's shenanigans, both legal and extramarital, had gotten me suspended from the Bar, so in addition to not being able to practice for two months, it had meant that I'd had to send each and every one of my clients a notice that I was suspended. It was easily the most humiliating thing I'd ever had to do. And to top it off, Saul had been sleeping with our intern, and was now living with her in an elegant townhouse in Alameda. And he had tax problems? That might be mine, too? And he wanted a developer to look at My Separate Property?

Another fifty or so deep breaths, and the rest of the glass of wine, brought me down to some semblance of calm. I picked up my phone and texted Saul back. One word. *No.*

Tonight I had dates with two men. I was going to dinner with Mikey (really, couldn't he be just Mike?) Charolais, and then having a nightcap with Chief Devon. Take that, Saul.

CHAPTER FIVE

I dressed with care, to give the appearance that I'd just run a comb through my hair and always looked like this. I put on a pink silk top, paired it with a pair of black skinny jeans with pink piping, and flat sandals. Even if I was not quite five-three, and Mikey was a big guy, heels bothered me.

I brushed my hair until the auburn highlights in the otherwise honey-brown mop outshone the gray threads. I was going to have to find a hair stylist up here in Simpato. I put my amethyst earrings on, sprayed a bit of perfume, and grabbed an actual handbag, instead of my usual messenger bag, and packed it with the usual necessities.

The sun was just starting to move towards the western mountains, reflecting softly off the eastern slope. I loved May. I could smell the vineyards, their leaves now full, the little tiny buds forming. It was a particular aroma, one I'd never smelled anywhere else. If the smell of May were a color, it would be an acid green, with edges of earth-brown.

My GPS showed the Perdiz vineyards and tasting rooms to be less than two miles from my house. Nearly walkable, though not in the evening for my first visit. I smiled to myself—first visit indeed. I was planning more, I could tell.

Simpato was ridiculously safe. I could walk downtown in the middle of the night, and had, without any concern. People didn't lock their doors or close their windows when they left. My fine outdoor furniture sat on my deck, with no gate or even a latch to pose a visual barrier. But what it had in safety it lacked in street lights. This place was dark.

Fortunately it was a Friday evening, so even when the sun went down it would be pretty lively where I lived. That was one of the appealing and unusual features of my folks' home: a half-acre, within two blocks of the main street. It was also why developers were sniffing around.

I got into the Prius and started its silent engine. I listened for any comments from it. The car seemed to have thoughts, and occasionally made noises like sighs or hums, when it had opinions. I was sure it also rolled its eyes. But tonight it just started up and went into gear without discussion. That, in my opinion, boded well for the evening.

I turned down Second, and made my left on Main. I passed the police station, City Hall, and the fountain, its natural hot spring water steaming in the near-sunset. It was capped and controlled now, but photos in the town museum showed a full-on geyser in its heyday. Nearer the mountain in Crags county you couldn't dig a well, out of fear of hitting a stream of near-boiling water.

The restaurants were starting to fill up, and lights were on even though it was far from dark yet. Women in excessively summery dresses, not really suitable for the weather, fluttered about like shivering butterflies, with shawls or sweaters over their shoulders, as men, some in shorts, stood outside the bars with drinks in hand. Sure, that was illegal, but this was Simpato, our job was hospitality, and serving wine on the sidewalk was a principal activity of tourism.

I crossed the Valley river, and there, sure enough, was *Happy Tacky*. Angelo had set up folding tables and chairs, he'd strung his truck with fairy lights, and music was blaring from a speaker he'd mounted on the hood of the pickup he used to tow the food truck around.

There was a line of people waiting for the order window, and groups of others, holding paper cups that I was willing to guess held beer, were either eating at the tables, eating standing up, or were waiting for their orders to come up. There had to be thirty people there, I figured, as I stopped at the stop-sign at the end of the bridge.

There was a big trash can, and in large letters, a sign that said, *Put your trassh Hire*, and another with *Basura Stupid* on it. Okay, he was trying.

A honk behind me told me I'd been sitting at the stop-sign too long, so I moved on. The Prius snickered. "Quiet, you," told it. A month ago, at that very stop sign, the Prius had refused to move. I was in danger and didn't realize it, but the car sure did. Of course, it backfired. The car's plan, not the car. I ended up calling a mechanic, and he ended up being a psycho.

"You're not always right," I told the car.

But the car had a point. Would the trucks have beer-and-wine licenses? If not, they would be no competition for the restaurants, and further, there would be less noise and disruption. I was amazed no one brought it up.

The car snickered again. Okay, it was right. Maybe no one brought it up because everyone involved already knew that they'd serve beer, whether or not the trucks had beer-and-wine licenses, and I was probably the only one who didn't even know if they did. But I was on my way to see someone who would know.

I made two more lefts, into the stealthily growing darkness of the vineyards outside the main two streets of Simpato, and at my GPS's prompting, since I would have missed the small sign otherwise, I made my turn into Perdiz.

#

A small brass partridge marked the entrance, and a gate blocked the way. There was a keypad next to the gate, at car-window level. On it was a note:

Just hit 3333# and it will open up.

I wondered if the note was just put there for me, or if it was always there.

The gate swung open with a creaking sound, and I advanced up the rutted drive. This didn't look like luxury to me. And then the road turned, and a beautiful stone archway, decorated in wrought iron twining grapevines, ushered me into a cobblestoned courtyard. A graceful walkway led up to a building that was all cream-and-yellow stones, seeming both airy and solid at once. Large windows flanked open double doors, and Vivaldi's *Spring* was playing somewhere nearby.

I stepped into a foyer tiled in yellow and cream, mirroring the walls. There was a large red and gold rug in the center, which softened the entry and invited the guests to venture in.

"Sal?" Mikey called from somewhere inside. "Come on in, I'll be with you in a second. Had to get something from the oven."

Whatever that something was, it smelled intensely good, of yeast and mushrooms. I realized that it had been nearly ten hours since I'd eaten actual food. And the Malvasia's glow was long gone.

I walked a little further into the foyer, to large French doors that gave way into an inner courtyard, as the building's wings made up the inner walls. The doors were closed but in the last of the daylight I could see that it had the same cobblestones that the front courtyard had, and the yellow stones of the walls cast a warm, buttery glow over the space. There were wrought iron benches along the sides, lush plantings towards the center, and in the middle, a small bubbling fountain spilled over onto the stones.

The hall branched at the door, with one hall leading left, where the delicious aromas were coming from. To the right the hall ended in a rustic wood door with a large, ornate metal hasp. I guessed that would lead to the private areas of the building, though likely not the actual living quarters of the owners. Offices, maybe.

I turned towards the enticing bread smell as Mikey came around the corner. He smiled. "Sal—" He held out flour-covered hands. "Oh. Well, welcome to Perdiz."

He was wearing an open-necked white linen shirt in the style that used to be called a poet's shirt, with blousy sleeves that ended in elastic above the wrists, setting off his tan and broad shoulders without being the least bit tight. He wore skinny jeans, and at this moment he had a navy blue half-apron tied twice around his waist, on which the evidence of his baking was distributed.

He shook his head to get the hair that flopped over his forehead out of his eyes. "I got a little behind here. I was making us some empanadas and the kitchen was a little disorganized. I can usually get them together and into the oven in less than twenty minutes. Of course, not tonight."

"No worries," I said as my stomach gave a little growl.

"Says you," he grinned. "Here, let me wash my hands properly and open a bottle of, shall we say, house wine? The empanadas are just out of the oven now, and will be cool enough to eat in less than ten minutes."

He turned back and I followed him into what was, for most of Valley County, a tiny tasting room, but its size was not uncommon up here in Simpato. There were several seats at a high bar, and six tables that could each seat four. Most tasting rooms closed by six, and some even earlier. The tables were cleared and empty, so I was left to imagine them with glasses sparkling and filled with Perdiz's offerings.

We moved into what was a more traditional dining room, but with two long tables set parallel to one another, and maybe ten chairs on each side. "This is the pairing room, we do it by reservation only. It's like a private party, with six wines accompanied by small plates of the perfect pairing."

"So, no one tonight, obviously," I said, admiring the tapestry wall hangings that decorated the room. They showed stylized views of vineyards, and what could only be Mount Santabella, in warm colors, though one tapestry gave the impression of an ocean, in contrast to its terrestrial companions.

"Nice," I said, indicating it.

Mikey gave me another smile. "Jack's wi—maybe-soon-to-be-ex-wife, she made them. She's a pretty talented weaver. She used to say it was math and art in your hands. It's the water under the ground here."

"Not the ocean, then?"

He shook his head. "The water table is very, very high in this part of Valley, as I'm sure you know. The fountain in the courtyard is a natural spring, and the source is only twenty feet down. Makes for interesting farming."

We had arrived in the kitchen by then. As a combination working and show kitchen, it was set up in an alluring way, with the stove as far from the entrance as possible, the big refrigerators on the other side of the room, and a huge sink in between. A gleaming stainless steel counter ran the length of the room, and beyond that, a butcher block table, about the size of a dining room table for a family of eight, was set with two places.

"I hope you don't mind. We'll eat in the kitchen."

"It's gorgeous," I said. "And are those empanadas ready to eat? I'm starving!"

"Can you drink red?" Mikey asked. "House pinot noir."

I'd priced their wines on line, and the one he held in his hand retailed, if you could get it, for over fifty dollars. I nodded. He poured.

It was as if the gates of heaven had opened and wine had been brought out. Well, that was a bit much, but wow was that good. It made my fourteen dollar bottle of Malvasia look like day drinking. Which, of course, it was.

Mikey brought a plate of half-moon pastries to the table. "Here, try one. They're at the perfect temperature."

I took one, and he handed me a small plate with the Perdiz logo in the center. Steam escaped as I bit into the flakey, buttery pastry, and meat, flavored with cinnamon and something else, melted in my mouth.

"Swoon," I said after I swallowed.

"Now sip the wine and tell me how it changed," he said, slipping into his tasting-room voice. "Most experts wouldn't put such a fine wine with a rustic dish like a beef empanada, but it works, doesn't it." I was a statement, not a question, and he was right. The fruit notes of the wine came forward, the tannins receded.

The next sip brought the flavors back in reverse order. "How does it do that?" I asked. "It's like magic."

"Exactly. Chemistry is magic. That's what I studied in school, chemistry. My folks were surprised when I went into the hospitality business, but it's the perfect place for an outgoing, friendly scientist."

"A freak of nature," I said smiling.

He poured a bit more into my glass. "So, tell me what brought you to Simpato."

A nice, ordinary *getting to know you* question, innocuous on its face, was a loaded sack for me. What to say? How much to leave out?

"My parents bought the house as a summer home, about twenty years ago, to get out of the Sacramento summers."

"Oof," he said. "I went to Davis, I know how hot it gets out there."

So he was more than "just" a chemistry major. The University of California at Davis required plenty of smarts to get in. "So," I said, "chemistry at Davis."

"Uh huh," he said, "but we were talking for a moment about you. Don't worry, I'll monopolize the conversation soon enough. Get your share in while you can!"

I laughed at the refreshing honesty. "They moved here full time when my dad retired, and then, when they were lost at sea during a sailing trip to Hawai'i, they left me the house. I've been coming up to check on it yearly."

"I'm sorry about your folks," he said.

I nodded. "Ten years ago, but still, thanks."

"Of course," he said. "Now let's hear why you're living here now. Because this is Simpato, and there are no secrets in the Duck. I've heard stories, and I prefer actual facts. It's the scientist in me, I guess," he added, softening the comment.

"No secrets," I replied. "Got divorced, wanted a fresh start, and besides, it's only temporary."

Was it? It was supposed to be, but somehow …

"And your law practice? Going to open up here?"

Might as well bite the bullet. "My ex-husband—also a lawyer—was involved in a shady real estate deal. Well, more than one. He was also involved with our intern, also more than one. He forged my name to some documents, the intern notarized them, the client complained—but only when they didn't make as much money as they thought they would, by the way—and the State Bar didn't like it. He was suspended for two years, I was suspended for two months because, and they were right, I should have known about it given some peculiar facts, and my suspension ends in two weeks. So I haven't really decided yet. There. Those are my skeletons. How about yours?"

Mikey nodded. "Okay, most of what I heard checks out then. And your mother was the Keeper, and now you're the Keeper."

"Also true. Your turn, Mikey. And start with why you go by Mikey instead of, say, Mike."

"In a minute," he said. "I need to take care of some dinner items."

#

Dinner consisted of about ten different little dishes. The empanadas gave way to a little salad of the tiniest greens, with a light, herbal dressing. "Don't drink any wine with the salad." He poured some sparkling water.

Followed by rice balls with burrata at the center, oozing cream. Then four small slices of perfectly medium-rare steak. A dish of shrimp in garlic butter, but I passed on that. "Allergic?" I shook my head, "No, just a strong personal dislike."

"Sorry," he said, and ate all of them.

Tiny yellow potatoes topped with sautéed mushrooms, "See what that does to the wine," he said, and then fava beans, first of the season, lightly dressed in the same vinaigrette as the salad, but giving a completely different effect.

All the while we chatted, while Mikey got up and got the dishes, returned, put a finishing touch on something, cleared plates.

"It's Mikey because my real name isn't Michael, it's Michel. French. And I was Miché as a kid. Mikey sounds more natural to me. And folks remember it. You know Charolais, my last name, is a type of cow?"

"I was too polite to mention it," I said.

The second bottle of wine had been a somewhat more intense red, with deep berry flavors and stronger tannins, to stand up to the food. But as far as my standing up, that was looking dicey. I declined another glass.

"How long have you been with Perdiz?"

"Three years. Bounced around a bit, did lab work, analyzed grapes for wineries, that's a big part of Davis's viniculture courses, worked in another winery on tastings and pairings, got a Masters degree in it at Davis, and landed here."

I looked around. "Do you live on site?"

He nodded. "The owners, well, now just Jack, he lives here. You probably didn't see it, but there's a really nice house just in back of this building, and that's Jack's house."

"The house that Jack built," I giggled. No more wine for me if was going to be able to drive the two miles home.

"But you saw that oak door when you came in? That leads to the offices and the caves, where the wine barrels and the bottles are stored. Air-conditioned, climate controlled, all that good stuff. I'll show you. And beyond that, there's a little apartment. That's mine."

Unspoken was, *I'll show you that, too.* Not tonight, he wouldn't. But I could feel that it was quite a possibility for the future.

"Restrooms?" I asked. After all this was a business, not a house.

He indicated the direction, and I made sure I walked with confidence. Any time you have to make sure you're walking with confidence, you're not. I stumbled over one of the cobblestones, grabbing the corner of one of the tasting room tables to keep from falling. I must have had a lot of wine on an empty stomach.

Once I found the bathroom, and after splashing water on my face, I felt better. I looked at my phone. It was almost eight.

Devon would be at my house by about eight thirty. I was going to have to drink and run. And I really didn't want to drive.

I considered texting Devon to cancel. He would cancel on me without a qualm if his work required it, that I knew. And I hadn't even gotten to ask Mikey anything about the food trucks.

Stay? Go? Ask? Don't ask?

I walked back to the kitchen, steadier than when I'd exited. "Could I have coffee instead of more wine? I am going to have to drive home," I said.

Mikey winked. "Of course. I'll make espressos for our desserts. And I know that you did say you had an engagement tonight later. Much as I'd like to, I won't keep you."

What a gentleman. "That's really thoughtful," I said.

Mikey got up and went to a big, gleaming copper espresso-maker. I watched as he put the coffee in, put two little cups under the spouts. Then he stopped, took the cups out, and looked at them. He shook his head, took the cups to the sink. "Not clean," he said. He was frowning. He got two other cups from a cabinet, looked them over, and put them under the spout.

"I don't know what the hell is going on with Arturo. He missed work today, as you know. The kitchen was left a mess last night. I couldn't find the rice. There was half the amount of shredded beef I thought there should be. There were dishes in the sink. That's not like him."

I stood still. He didn't know what I knew about Silvestre, and Amparo being at Silvestre's the night before. "No?" I said casually.

"No. And it's weird. You know how everyone was all crazed about who got what spot downtown? Even Arturo and his wife? But Arturo almost never handles the truck, it's Amparo. And half the time she parks it right outside our gate, so even if he was doing the truck, I would have seen him. Luckily I could handle the tastings, since we didn't have a full-on pairing today."

"That's a good thing," I said, taking the espresso from him. "Delicious. I'm sure you did just fine without him. But I wonder what kept him?"

"Amparo said he was sick, at the flagpole," Mikey reminded me. I nodded. "But it was unlike him not to call in."

"Was it unlike him to leave a mess in the kitchen?" I asked as we carried our cups to the French doors.

"Completely unlike him. He's neat as a pin. Unlike his wife."

"Amparo? How do you know what Amparo's standards of cleanliness are?" I stopped walking, the thought of August's horrified sight of Amparo with Silvestre freezing me. Was Mikey a frequent visitor to her home? Maybe when Arturo was here working?

"Sometimes she parks her truck outside the gates to our winery, just during the lunch hours," he said, not noticing my stop. "About three days a week, the men in the fields look forward to it. I'm pretty sure that's where some of the meat goes. Arturo takes it home for her to serve in the truck. At least I wouldn't be surprised."

"Then we're going to fire his ass," said a man's voice. I jumped, spilling the hot espresso on my hand.

"Jack," Mikey said. "When'd you get back?"

Jack wasn't even looking at Mikey. He was staring at me. "I know who you are," he said, and his voice was not friendly. "You're the gal that was involved in that gossip columnist's murder."

Out of the corner of my eye I saw Mikey take a small step back.

"That's right," I said, in my best lawyer voice. I'd taken on more jerks in my twenty years of practice than this guy could guess. "And I believe I saw you at the clothing store, Feathers."

He opened his mouth to say something. I beat him to it. "I'm Sal DeVine. You must be Jack Partridge." I didn't smile, but I did wipe the espresso off my hand before offering it.

He stepped forward. He was a little over average height, quite slim, maybe fifty. Oddly enough, he was wearing a tuxedo jacket, with neither shirt nor socks. He had a T of brown hair interlaced with a bit of grey on his chest, though the hair on his head was nearly white blond. His blue eyes glittered in the light from the sconces around the courtyard.

"Sangiacomo Partridge, and yes, I go by Jack." He shook my hand as briefly as decency allowed.

He turned to Mikey. "So, if we fire Arturo for stealing meat, do we fire you for stealing wine? And coffee? Or using my home for your own private playground?"

I felt for Mikey. As a man, he couldn't just cave. As an employee, he had to. I stepped up. "I so wanted to see the winery. It's beautiful. I hope that was okay."

Jack smiled a thin smile. "Of course. Always looking to increase local appreciation of our lovely place."

"And I am very glad to have met you," I lied. "But Mikey knows that I've got to be back by eight-thirty, I have an important matter to attend to, one I can't miss."

"I'll see you out," Jack said. "You just clean all this up before you pass out," he added to Mikey.

I threw Mikey a quick wink, and was facing Jack before he caught it. "I'll get my purse from the kitchen, and be on my way."

Mikey followed me into the kitchen. "Sorry," he whispered.

"Cocaine?" I whispered back. He nodded. That explained the glitter in Jack's eyes. I'd seen that plenty among lawyers with more money than sense, and I'd recognized the aggressive talk.

"I'll see myself out," I told Jack when I found him pacing the foyer. "I'm just parked right here by the door."

"The Prius? That's what got me to come in and check who was here. But before you go, let me show you the caves. It's the best part of the tour." He took me by the upper arm.

"Oh, I sure wish I could," I simpered. God how I hated the way we had to placate an out-of-bounds man's ego. "But that matter I'm expected at won't wait."

"On a Friday night?"

I drew a trump card. "*Shabbat*. Waits for no one."

He let me go like I was on fire. I quickstepped it out the door before he could formulate an answer. And now I knew something else about him, something that it would behoove me not to forget.

#

I knew better than to race home, even though it was almost eight-thirty. Devon could be late for all I knew, and I'd had enough wine that even with only two miles to drive I could do something that could catch the eye of the Highway Patrol. And unlike the local cops, who at this point all knew my car, the CHP didn't care one bit why I was hurrying.

Besides, even if the interaction with Jack had knocked the wine high out of me, my blood alcohol level hadn't changed.

The Prius snorted when I started it up. "Really?" I said to it. "Like you would have done any differently?"

It was too short and too dark a drive back for me to do anything but concentrate on getting home. I wanted to sort out everything I'd learned tonight, but this wasn't the moment.

It was pitch black when I pulled into the long drive behind my house. I hadn't thought to put the outside lights on. Devon's Jeep was already there. He was sitting on the deck, and didn't move when I parked. I frowned. I know the Prius was silent, but he would have seen my lights.

I got out and in my rush I didn't even close my door. That gave me enough light from the inside of the car to see my way up the three decks. "Devon?" I said.

A loud snort responded. "I'm awake," he muttered, proving he hadn't been. "Sal! Oh, of course," he said.

I smiled. He'd fallen asleep in my lounge chair. "You must be exhausted," I said. "Come on. Let me close the car door and we can go inside."

But I'd been scared.

Once in and settled into my little living-dining room, I asked him, "It's not even that late. Did you have a long night last night?"

He looked away.

Oho! I thought. Well, I'd feel less bad about having dinner with Mikey, then.

"Wine?" I asked. "I've got some nice white, but I'm having coffee, if you don't mind."

"Same here," he stretched his arms. "So, how was Perdiz? They have an amazing pinot noir, I'm told."

"It is," I said smugly. He didn't look fazed. I felt like I was in middle school. Were we going out? Was I trying to make him jealous? *I'm forty-freakin-five years old, this is absurd.*

He looked at his watch. "It's even later than I thought. Let's compare notes, and then I'll probably go home and hit the hay."

"No long night tonight?" I said. Middle school.

"Hope not."

I made coffee, missing the delicious espresso I'd spilled most of on my hand. I handed Devon a cup and sat down across from him.

"What do you know about the owner of Perdiz? Sangiacomo Partridge, goes by Jack?"

Devon scratched his chin. "Not much. I do know we were called out there a couple of times when he and his now-ex were having some issues, but he never pressed charges."

"He? *He* never pressed charges?"

"It's not the norm, I know, but there are plenty of instances of spousal abuse perpetrated by women. Again, not the norm, but it happens. Most of the time the men are too embarrassed to call us. Especially given the size disparity here: Vicki is a skinny little thing, as short as you—"

"Hey!"

"Well, you're pretty small," he said. "And she's, like, ninety pounds or something. But you don't have to be big when you're holding a gun."

"She shot him?"

He shook his head. "Threatened him. She's got a license for it, she practices at the duck-hunting range near Benicia. I told him, if he gets a restraining order she'll have to give up her guns until they straighten things out. He still said no."

"Even though he called you?"

"That's the thing," Devon said. "He didn't call. A lot of guys would rather die than call us to tell us they're afraid of their wife. Someone else called. I don't remember who, but it wasn't him. Might have been Mikey, but somehow that's not what rings a bell."

"Can you check?"

"I guess. It was a couple of years ago. Not sure that's relevant to anything now. I just thought of it while I was waiting for you. So, did you pick up any information that would help us figure out what happened to Silvestre Sanchez?"

"Not there," I said. I thought about what August told me. It was in confidence, but if there was a murder investigation, there were no secrets. Even as the Keeper. "But August told me something that may or may not be relevant. First, though, did you figure out if Silvestre died of natural causes or not?"

Devon looked at the ceiling. "You are in a special situation," he said. "You seem to attract information. Otherwise, I wouldn't tell you."

"I know."

"He was poisoned. It looked like some kind of terrible stomach disease, but the coroner said it wasn't. Or at least he didn't think so. It looked like it would have taken some kind of poison to kill him like that. But to be exact, we'll have to wait for the tests."

"Any idea when he died?"

"Again, not yet. But sometime this morning. Early, maybe? But today."

Wow, was it only today? All the events at the flagpole, the *Quack*, Perdiz, all today?

"August said he drove past Silvestre's house last night, well, more like evening, on his way home from work. He thinks he saw Amparo there."

I waited.

"That wouldn't be that odd. They're some kind of cousins."

I frowned. "You'd think August would know that. It seemed from what he told me, they were, I don't know, canoodling."

"Canoodling?" Devon burst out laughing. "Wow, I haven't heard that word in a while. Was he specific?"

"No. He was embarrassed to be even telling me."

Devon thought for a minute. "Maybe not first cousins. But what was August doing driving by there anyway? He works at the loading docks, and the way home sure doesn't take him out by Sanchez's home."

"Alicia. Sanchez's daughter. I think he was hoping to see her."

Devon shook his head. "If so, he's barking up an empty tree."

"Kill that metaphor!" He smiled. "Also, explain."

"Look, Alicia went to college. And not just to college, she went to UC. And now she lives in San Francisco, *with a boyfriend,* and is working at a tech company, making good money. She's not going to be interested in August."

Poor August. "Has she been told?"

Devon nodded. "That's how I know what she's doing. I spoke to her on the phone today. She's really upset. Seems she lost her mom to breast cancer when she was in high school. Now this. Poor girl. She's coming home tomorrow. There was nothing she could do tonight, and she decided to stay with her boyfriend."

"I don't blame her. So, Amparo's his cousin?"

"Some kind of relative, anyway. Sometimes I think half this town is related to the other half. And besides, if Silvestre Sanchez was poisoned by someone, we'll know soon enough what they used. And then we can start looking."

I stretched out in my chair. If I was going to stay here in Simpato, I was going to need a couch. I guess, no matter where I went I'd need one.

"Did you post on the WAD?" Devon asked, working his way to standing. Looks like this definitely wasn't a date. I nodded. "For tomorrow night?" I nodded again. "What?"

"Nothing," I said. Total middle school. "I'll check in with you tomorrow."

He nodded. "Stay safe."

And he was gone.

I woke up around four a.m. to the sound of banging on my kitchen door. There was no peep-hole at the back, so I flipped on the back light and looked through the window, but even before I did I knew who it would be.

I opened the door to August, who rushed in and slammed the door shut. He was breathing hard, his big eyes were wild, and he was sweating. He loomed large over me. "Sal, Sally, oh my god …" he panted.

Even in my sleep-fuzzed state I noticed that his truck wasn't outside. "Come inside," I said, moving into the living-dining room. "Sit down."

He shook his head. "No! I can't. You need to come with me, you need to hide!"

I took a deep breath and watched him imitate that. I did it again. It was funny how that type of mirroring always seemed to work. Briefly. "August. It's four in the morning. What's going on?"

He took one more breath. "I'm sorry, Sal. I usually get up right around now because I have to be at work at six, though I know it's the middle of the night for you. We got a phone call at our house. My ma was freaked because no one calls us at this hour, and if work wants me, they just text me. But the person wanted to talk to me. And they said some really scary stuff. And now you need to hide!"

I walked back into my bedroom and pulled a sweatshirt over my sleep shorts and T-shirt. "That's ridiculous, August,"

I said sharply. "If someone wants to scare me, they need to tell me."

I was angry, and it showed.

August looked at the ground. "But what if they told me instead?" he asked quietly.

"Why would they?"

"Well, maybe they have to work or something, and can't tell you later on."

I shook my head.

"What if they're in danger?"

I looked at August sharply. "If they're in danger, they need to tell the police. Who, by the way, are open twenty-four-seven. Unlike me."

"They can't. The police will arrest them."

It was hours before dawn. I had been out at a winery the night before. I had a headache and I was not completely sharp. But I could tell that there was something, maybe something important, going on. "What time do you need to leave for work?" I asked him.

He folded his thick legs under him. He was still sweating, whether from anxiety or his run over to my house. He pulled his No-Duck High Class of 2015 sweatshirt off, shoved it under his chair. "I don't. It's Saturday. I'm off Friday, Saturday, and only have a half-day on Sundays because ..." I glared at him and amazingly, he took the hint. "I just, oh Sally, I'm so scared. I'm sorry I woke you up. It was stupid, but that's because I'm stupid sometimes."

I got up and went into the kitchen. I put a capsule in the coffee maker. "Do you drink coffee?" I called back to him. I thought of his untouched cup at the police station.

"No, but if you have a soda I'll take that."

I didn't. I poured him a glass of water from the dispenser. The water in Simpato was horrible, and only those who couldn't afford to buy bottled drank tap. I brought it to him with my steaming mug of coffee.

We sat in silence for a bit, while I waited for the caffeine to do its job. As my brain fog began to clear the issues came into focus.

"Okay, August. Let's take this from the beginning. But only true things, okay?" This big child of a man nodded. "Did someone actually call you?"

"Yeah. Amparo called my ma. But I heard the phone ringing, and when ma came in to tell me she was on the line, I was kinda ready. I know that it takes an emergency for people to call in the middle of the night, even if that's the time they're up."

So Amparo had called. "What did Amparo say?" August looked at the floor. "Come on, August. I can't help if I don't know."

"She didn't say what I said earlier. I'm sorry. That was just the first thing that came into my head."

"Okay," I said, sipping my coffee. "Now, tell me for real. What did she say?"

"She said, but she said it in Spanish, okay? She said that she heard my truck the other night—I can't remember if I honked my horn when I went on Thursday or not, but I almost always do, right?" I nodded. "And she said that if I told you I'd went to the Sanchez house on Thursday night—and then she called you some bad words—she was going to put a big knife so far up—but so far up that my duck wouldn't quack again as long as I lived."

I laughed. He looked at me, appalled. "How do you say *quack* in Spanish?" I asked.

"*Cuac*, but that's the sound, not the word. I don't know the word for, like, quacking. She said *cuac*."

I looked up the actual word on my phone: *Graznar*.

Of course. Same word as to babble. Made sense. "Okay, that's horrible. But you're not really afraid of Amparo Buendía, are you? I mean, you're twice her size, half her age, and strong as an—" I changed the word. He had probably been called an ox in an unflattering way a few times. "As a bull."

"Yeah, but she's a *bruja*. That's why I ran over here. Because I was afraid to get in my truck, in case she'd put a spell on it or something. Cursed it. She was sure cursing you."

Great. "Well, now you've told me. So, you made up the part about the caller wanting to talk to me?"

"Not really, sort of. It was confusing. She told me that if I told you I'd been at Silvestre's, well, you know. But she also said that she had a few words she wanted to tell you, and that she was thinking she'd go to your house tonight and carve you up and serve you as tacos."

My eyes got wide.

"So I was thinking, oh, Sally, I don't always think all the way through, I was thinking I had to come and warn you, and maybe you shouldn't do the Keeper thing tonight, and that I needed to take you to my house to hide you and keep you safe, and all that is just so stupid. Like me." He looked down, kicked the leg of the chair he was sitting in. "Always stupid. I get everything mixed up. Only good for loading trucks."

#

As soon as it was light I called Devon's cell. He answered on full alert. I gave him the rundown.

"Okay," he said. "Cancel the Keeper session. It's too dangerous."

I blinked. I was totally awake, and clearly he wasn't. "Duck no!" I said. "What better way than to flush out Amparo's real motives?"

He chuckled. "Proper police procedure, maybe? I can have her brought in for questioning. We have a witness who saw her with the victim, the night before Sanchez died, and we need to know what happened."

"Right," I said, "and Amparo sticks a knife into August. You know those food trucks have giant knives."

"We'll do it without telling her that we know about August. Look, Sal. Just because you were helpful in figuring out what happened to Georgiana Noyes doesn't mean you should get involved in police matters. And since we're pretty sure that Sanchez was poisoned—"

"Pretty sure? You mean there's a chance that he just, what, got stomach flu and died of it?"

I could hear Devon sigh. "Tell you what. I'm off until four today. Why don't I come by and we can sort this out. Three, maybe?"

I acquiesced.

"And until then, can you stay out of this?"

I knew he was right. "Sure."

"Oh, and wait. Where's August now? Did he go home or is he still at your house?"

I laughed. "No, he's gone."

"What's funny?"

"Just that it took you so long to ask. He went back home about an hour ago. It took that long to calm him down, tell him that nothing was going to happen to him. There's no such thing as spells, *brujería*, curses, what have you. I told him to watch himself and stick close to home. No power of Amparo's was greater than his massive strength."

"And he went for it?"

"Nah," I said. "But his mother needs some furniture moved and he couldn't deny her that. I did tell him to watch his surroundings, though."

Devon was quiet for a moment. "I'll send Sergio by to make sure he's okay some time today."

"Oh, Sergio will love that. Protecting the big guy. High school never dies. I have to write the story up for the *Quack* anyway. That will keep me busy."

I finished with the tag line of No-Duck-High: "Be a duck."

#

As soon as I'd sent the draft article to Ed Sharp she answered. "Get a photo of one of the food carts. Can you take a decent picture?"

Embarrassingly enough, the answer was "no." Even with the fancy phones I still managed to get blurry, headless photos of my subjects, with perhaps their feet in full focus. "I'm terrible at it," I answered. Maybe she could get someone else. "When do you need it by? This may not be the best time to find one open."

It was Saturday, and the trucks that were usually at the construction site and the vineyards wouldn't have customers, and the newly awarded spots wouldn't open until about noon.

"I need it more or less now. Or, if not now, by eleven a.m. Today. Do your best. Maybe they're selling breakfast burritos somewhere. The writing's pretty good," she added. I warmed to the praise, now willing to take a photo of anything she wanted. I was that easy.

Then I remembered that Mikey had told me that Amparo sometimes parked her truck outside the gates to Perdiz, when they weren't doing a tasting. That presented all sorts of opportunities.

In fact, the more I thought about it, it was a rich vein of trouble to tap into: I could observe and possibly talk through whatever was troubling Amparo, show her I wasn't the enemy, see if Arturo had shown up to work, and yes, have a reason to text Mikey. After the non-date with Devon last night, and his warning to stay out of trouble, I was pretty willing to look at

Mikey in a new light. Besides, it would also give me a chance to see what had happened with Jack Partridge after I left.

I hadn't mentioned the dust-up with Jack coming back early. For rational reasons I hadn't really told Devon much about my evening at all. I wasn't going to be some comic-book heroine who keeps information from the police, but there was no reason to tell Devon anything about my personal life, as long as he was playing it so cool.

Ugh! There I was again, reduced to middle school. Well, I wasn't going to let that happen, either.

I texted Mikey. "Is the A's food truck parked outside Perdiz this morning?"

"Good morning," he answered. "How are you today, Mikey?" he added a smiley-face.

"Sorry," I texted back. Oh, the heck with it. I pushed the phone icon. He answered on the first ring.

"Hey. I'm sorry. It's just I've been up since four this morning, and you caught the tail end of a conversation I'd had most of in my mind." He laughed. "So, good morning, Mikey."

"Good morning, Sal. Beautiful day, isn't it?"

"Yeah. Okay, so now, are they?"

"Relentless lawyer," he said. "I haven't gone down to open the gate yet. We open at ten, and it's not yet nine. If they do set up, they won't do so until ten at the earliest. Amparo makes amazing breakfast burritos and churros."

So my hunch was right.

"I can check when I open up and let you know," Mikey added.

"Would you? That would be great. So, no pairings today?"

"Actually, we do have one, a party of fourteen, so a pretty substantial one, at three this afternoon. And that's a good reason to check. I haven't heard from Arturo, he's not answering his phone, and he better be here today to cook."

"That's odd, isn't it? Is he usually pretty reliable?"

"Yeah, he's come in reeking of drink from the night before, but he's always sober enough to work. He, um, feeds off the energy of cooking, I think. He doesn't drink on the job that I know of, and the few times he's missed in the three years I've been here he's texted."

I thought about it. "Maybe we should have the police do a wellness check."

"That seems a little extreme, don't you think? I mean, his wife was at the flagpole drawing yesterday, so if he had gone missing or something she'd have said something. But yeah, I'll check when we open, and let you know."

We disconnected, and I called Carinna. "Hey, do you know anyone who can take a decent picture with a phone?"

"Anyone can," she answered. "It's impossible to mess up."

"Says you," I told her. I explained that I needed to take a photo of one of the food trucks, and my unusual facility with messing up photos. "I think that the A's park at Perdiz sometimes, so I thought I'd get that, since I don't have time to get one of the trucks that are at the new spots."

"Sure you do. The one in front of the Little Sisters is already there setting up."

"At nine in the morning?" I guess their supplier of leaf and butter for their cookies would be there first thing in the morning, but a food truck?

"It's Saturday, remember? They have their services on Saturdays, just like your people do."

My people. I rolled my eyes, grateful that she wasn't close enough to see, or for me to wring her neck. "Right. A good reason not to come down. Mother Sassafras will snag me and make me sit through one of their sessions."

"Services," Carinna corrected. "But they don't start until noon."

"Tell you what," I said. "Why don't you meet me at the gate to Perdiz at ten, and if the As are there, take a photo for me. And I'll go back with you to the monastery for their noon …"

"Service."

"Service. This way, if Arturo and Amparo aren't at Perdiz, I can get a photo of Nate at the monastery. Even if it's late, she may be able to use it."

"Let's do it the other way around. Since Nate's already setting up, why don't you come over and let me take a photo now, and then we can head over to Perdiz afterwards. This way you can send her both. And we can still go to the service together after Perdiz."

I gave in on the logistics, mostly because if I kept insisting on the less practical way around it would give away my rather odd—to anyone other than me, of course—interest in going over to Perdiz. I wasn't going to be roped into a service at the monastery. I'd been to one the prior month and one was enough for me.

"They're trying out a new flavor of cookie!" Carinna added.

"Not my thing, but thanks."

"There'll be plain ones too, silly. See you in forty-five."

#

I was still in my sleep shorts and T-shirt, though I'd taken the sweatshirt off once August left. I caught a glimpse of myself in the full-length mirror August had put up for me soon after I'd moved in. It was a good thing I'd put the sweatshirt on, I realized. Not just because it was cool in the morning, given the revealing nature of the loose shirt.

I pulled on my usual yoga pants, and pondered my collection of tops. Since I'd moved to Simpato, and out of law practice, I'd lived in jeans and yoga pants. Maybe I should level up a bit, I thought. I selected a raw silk top, with wood buttons. Too rustic? Maybe the black top with the crisscross straps. But with the black yoga pants I'd look like I was in mourning.

The grey chemise top? It was clingy in the right places, draped in the others nicely. I slipped it on, its smooth lines rippling down. Good. Now hair. And then I had to laugh. Yes, this was what a new interest could do. Notably, I'd not dressed up for Devon.

I polished my black heeled open-toed shoes with a sock. I limited myself to the lovely foundation I'd bought online and a touch of mascara.

I gathered my notebook, pens, phone, and looked down at my shoes. No. I needed to be sensible here. I went back to the closet, and chose my pink leather dance sneakers. Flattering, yet functional.

Heavens above, I really had returned to middle school.

#

I walked the three blocks to the monastery in what had to be a hormonal daze. The sun was shining in Simpato, a beautiful May morning was warming up nicely. The liquid-amber trees had leafed out, and the little balls of what could be seeds looked like holiday decorations. I identified the calls of blue jays, crows, and a mockingbird. If I were the singing type, I would have burst into song. *The hills are alive …*

I pulled myself together. But still, I had to smile.

Up ahead I could see the red outline of Nate's taco truck, with the yellow lettering identifying it as *La Sabrosa*. The Tasty. There were several people milling around on the sidewalk where the window would be. Excellent, there would be business at the truck, and I could get Carinna to take some photos of people buying and enjoying the food.

I could only make out Carinna, by her height and her white outfit, and one of the nuns, by her eco-green full habit. I wasn't sure which nun it was, as this one was taller than Sister Sorghum and stockier than Mother Sassafras or Sister Marigold, a.k.a. Margo Schwartz.

There were three men, and as I got closer, I heard them talking in raised voices. One was Nate, whose English was strongly accented and mixed with Spanish. As I joined the outskirts of the group I saw that a second man had his hand on Nate's shoulder, not quite holding him back but definitely trying to calm him down.

The third man, his slim-muscled frame leaning casually against the food truck, was Justin March.

"Sal's a lawyer," Carinna said. I froze in my steps. "Hi, Sal. We've got a problem here. Can you sort it out? Being a lawyer and all?"

My rosy mood took a dive. "Hi, all," I said. "I just stopped by to see Carinna, but if you want to tell me what's going on?"

What could I say? I'm suspended for two more weeks? That I had to take the Professional Responsibility exam again before I could practice? That I wanted nothing to do with this problem, whatever it was? Probably I'd have to say all three things eventually.

"She speaks Spanish," Carina said helpfully. Not.

Nate turned to me, and in rapid-fire speech told me that Justin had it in for him—which was obvious at the Council meeting—and that he just wanted to shut him down because of—and here I wasn't sure what he said but something about a donkey.

"*Buey*?"

"Made him look stupid," the man with Nate said.

"He's the fool," Justin said. He pushed back his straight brown hair with what looked like a practiced gesture. "Man can't follow the rules. I don't make them, but I sure as heck enforce them. And Nate here can't keep his kitchen clean, can't keep his knives off the blocks, doesn't sanitize his hands. And I'm not gonna let him open until he does. You got that, *buey?*"

Justin took what looked like an order pad out from his plaid shirt pocket, along with a pen. He flipped the pad to a new page that had a yellow and a pink page underneath, wrote a few words, and tore off the yellow sheet.

"You're closed until you fix these things and I reinspect. And I won't be out to reinspect for, hmm, two weeks. But I will be driving around, so if I see you open before re-inspection, you won't ever be opening again."

Justin shoved the yellow sheet at Nate, who stood glaring at him. The paper fluttered to the ground. Justin smirked and shook his head. "Good luck, Nate. *La Sabrosa* is shut."

Nate's shoulder twitched. He looked at the paper on the ground, and at Justin. And then he spat.

The gob landed on Justin's shoe.

"You just signed your death warrant," Justin growled and turned away.

Nate shouted a foul word and moved to go after him, but his friend's hand tightened on his shoulder.

"Let him go," his friend said. "Just let him go."

We all breathed a bit as the county inspector's pickup truck rolled by. To my shock, Justin threw me a wink as he passed.

"I'm opening up anyway," Nate said as soon as the truck was out of sight. "He's gonna shut me down anyway. He's been saying that for months, and now he's got an excuse because of the new rules. What can he do to me now, lawyer-lady?"

The attention was suddenly on me. "This isn't my area," I said. "But if you've been shut down, temporarily, you probably shouldn't open." That much was obvious.

"Okay, so how am I going to pay my rent? Put the food in my kids' mouths?"

I didn't have an answer. Or maybe I did.

"Sister ..." I said to the nun.

"Sister Calendula, dear. We met when you came to the service during your first few days in Simpato."

I nodded. I remembered her now. She had a sweet voice and a sweet disposition to match. It was proof of how used I had gotten to the funny names of these eco-sisters that I didn't even snicker at "Sister Calendula."

"Sister, would it be possible for Nate to use the monastery kitchen? It's certified for baking, right?" She nodded.

"And they'd never shut you down, anyway," Carinna added.

She was right. "If Nate uses your kitchen while he fixes up whatever the citation is for, and he's selling here in front of the monastery, that will give him a way to stay in business."

Nate's friend translated. "I understood, father," Nate said.

"I'm Jim Avila," the man said to me, holding out a hand. "Father Jim Avila, of St. Cuthbert's, patron saint of ducks, locally known as Santo Cubierto." I smiled. *The covered saint.*

"I've passed the statue," I said. "Sal DeVine."

"I know. The Keeper. Nice to meet you in person. That's a good idea," he added. "Calendula, do you think they'd go for that?"

I noticed that he didn't call her Sister. After all, they weren't real nuns.

"I can ask," she said. "Thank you," she added to me. "We were all looking forward to tacos after the service. Along with the cookies," she said to Carinna, "of course."

CHAPTER SEVEN

"I don't think I'll be using a picture of *La Sabrosa*," I said to Carinna as the group dispersed. "Except maybe to write up this little contretemps."

"Fancy French word," Carinna said. "What's *buey* mean in Spanish?"

"Donkey, but apparently, well, obviously, dummy, but from the context it seems like Nate made the inspector, Justin March, look foolish at some point, which is why Justin's got it in for him. I guess."

I took a couple of pictures of *La Sabrosa* with my phone anyway. I think even I could photograph a stationary truck, without people.

While I was taking the photo my phone dinged. "Dang. It's going to be blurry now," I said as I looked at the message. I had to stop myself from smiling. It was Mikey. "As truck is here. Come by?"

So Amparo and Arturo's truck had parked in front of Perdiz. "Let's go over to Perdiz," I said casually. "Looks like we'll have a chance to take some action shots after all."

"Want me to drive? I have my truck here," Carinna said.

No way. Her pupils were as dilated as this bright day would allow. "Nah, let's take my car. The three block walk will do me good after that dust-up."

"Better than whatever French word you used."

We walked along the uneven sidewalk, me walking carefully, Carinna strolling without a care.

"Oh yeah, I remember something about that now," she said suddenly.

"About what?"

"About a year ago, or a little more, Nate's daughter, Ernestina, was at the truck with her mom one day after school. It had to be at least last year, sometime before Nate's wife had the newest baby, and Nate and his wife used to park just outside the hotel. Ernestina got bored and went outside, and Justin was behind the hotel pool with some lady, and Ernestina saw them. Ernestina told her mother, who told Nate, who then confronted Justin in front of the hotel. Everyone heard about it, and for months Justin couldn't come around to inspect without guys jeering at him."

"Do you know who he was with?"

"Not to swear by, but the story goes that he had his pants down, and he was with Victoria Partridge."

"That seems unlikely. She's got the whole Perdiz Winery, her house, enough money to get a suite at the fanciest hotel in town, why would she be getting it on, one, with a health inspector, and two, outside behind a hotel pool?"

"Excitement?"

"Or a lie."

"Either way, he started coming down hard on the tiniest violations of standards, in the trucks, in the kitchens, until folks stopped making fun of him to his face."

A little power can be grossly abused.

#

If the Prius could be said to grin, it was grinning when Carinna got in. "Your car likes me," she said.

Carinna also talked to her pickup truck, so she understood.

It took a few extra minutes to get to Perdiz. It was now late enough on this beautiful spring Saturday morning that tourists were out in force, and I drove slowly, watching for pedestrians crossing mid-block, parents with strollers, elders with jaunty, decorated canes. Sure enough, there was *Happy Tacky*, music blasting over the bridge, and a line of contented patrons waiting for their tacos al carbon, al pastor, and "the happy vegetarian" with rice, beans, guacamole and if you wanted, *queso Oaxaca*. Whether the beans were made with pork lard was an open question.

Once out of the four-block downtown, I turned onto the through road, and made my first left. "It's a lot darker at night," I said.

Carinna laughed. "And I'm the one who's high!"

"You know what I mean. And there are no lights on this road at all."

I slowed as I neared the Perdiz gate. Sure enough, across the road from the gate was the red and green food truck with "*Buen Día*" in gold script along the side.

"I wonder if Arturo is better," I said.

"Who?"

"The owner's husband. Amparo Buendía runs the truck, and her husband, Arturo, cooks at Perdiz. Arturo's been sick, evidently."

"I don't know this truck," Carinna said. "Mostly *La Sabrosa*, and everyone knows *Happy Tacky*. There's a third, parks over by the old Little League field, where the new hotel is, but I don't know that one either. Mmm," she added, breathing in. She'd opened her car door and the aroma of frying food wafted in.

"I'll tell you what, go ahead and get something to eat. I'm going to text Mikey Charolais. I think Amparo hates me—"

"What? How? I mean you've only been here what, five or six weeks? How can some food-truck lady hate you?"

"I don't know," I said. "But according to August, Amparo has put some kind of curse on me."

"Oh for crying out loud, is August at it again?"

"Uh, what?"

"He gets that way. Every now and then, he sees ghosts. He thinks he hears voices. Tells someone they're cursed. Poor kid. He's not right, you know."

I nodded. "But he came over at four this morning, and was absolutely beside himself, saying Amparo had called his mother and told her she'd put a curse on me. He ran over to my house to tell me ..." It really sounded wacky in the telling.

Carinna nodded. "So if you believed him, why are you over here taking a picture of her truck?"

"Um ..."

"Let me guess. Charolais?" I felt myself blush. "And what happened to Chief Devon? History already? Girl, you get around!"

I shook my head. "It's not like that."

My phone dinged. Mikey. "Coming to the gate. Let's grab a breakfast burrito. No sign of Arturo, but I'm going to see what Amparo has to say."

I thumbs-up'd the message.

"He's pretty full of himself," Carinna said. "Musclebound, if you like that sort of thing, but it's all Mikey all the time," she added. "Well, here comes your newest knight in short-sleeved armor."

Carinna got out of the car. Mikey stopped when he saw her, then looked over at me. God I was slow. There'd been a strong chill at the Duck Bill when they'd crossed paths Wednesday— was that only Wednesday? And now it was clear they had some kind of past together. And I was oblivious.

I got out on my side. "Hey, Mikey." I put out my hand. He shook it very briefly, his eyes going from me to Carinna. "I brought Carinna, so we can get some photos of the food truck for the *Quack*."

He nodded to her, and looked back at me. I had only met him this week, but somehow his silence seemed uncharacteristic. He'd certainly been talkative enough when he'd cooked me dinner, and at the Duck Bill.

"So, what's good?" I said, walking towards the truck. There were two men chatting by the pick-up window, and no one at the ordering one, so I went right to the opening.

A menu, beautifully calligraphed in Spanish and English, graced the side of the truck next to the ordering window. Burritos were king here, but there were tacos on offer as well, in beef, chicken, and carnitas. There were empanadas, though the beef ones had been crossed out, but pork was still available. And surrounded by decals of mallards in flight, were *tacos de pato*—duck tacos (after eleven a.m. only, while supplies last, thank you.)

Amparo was facing away from me, at a counter that ran along half the back of the truck. Beneath the counter were pull-out drawers, some half-open, with rolls of foil, paper plates, napkins. At the back of the counter there were bins of several different colors of salsa, lettuce, slivered cabbage, pickled peppers, and other toppings, along with a large vat of guacamole.

Amparo was putting salsa on a huge burrito and rolling it up inside a sleeve of foil. A second burrito was already waiting. Above her, on a magnetic strip, hung a series of glistening knives, in sizes from rain-forest-path-slashing to a slim, silver paring knife at the end. To her left, closer to the ordering window, was a flat grill, and I could feel the heat from it where I stood.

I thought of the rules. Food was prepared in certified kitchens, and then brought to the truck. It would be reheated on demand, on that griddle, as would the tortillas, and then assembled to order.

Amparo grabbed a couple of paper plates, forks, a handful of napkins, and the burritos, and shoved them out the pick-up window. "Gracias, *chula*," one of the men said. The other laughed. Amparo neither spoke nor smiled, only turning away to face the order window.

And stopped.

The name she called me could best not be translated, but if I had to I'd put it somewhere around doubting my mother's virtue as well as mine by virtue of my parentage.

"And your mother, who birthed you," I answered her in Spanish.

Her blackened-in eyebrows rose.

Her eyeliner was pitch black and extended about a half an inch beyond the corners of her eyes, and the shadow was a lurid mint green, with mauve under the brows. One false eyelash threatened to come loose, though the other held firm. The malevolence in her eyes was all natural.

Behind me, Carinna spoke. "Can I have the *Buen Día* Special, please? No lettuce." Amparo's eyes never left me.

Then Mikey put his hand on my shoulder, gently moving me from the center of the window. "Hola, Amparo. Where's Arturo?"

"In his underpants," she answered.

Carinna laughed.

"You sure about that, Amparo?" Mikey said. "Because I want his underpants, with him in them, in my kitchen in the next hour. We've got fourteen people coming for a tasting in less than four hours, and I haven't seen or heard from him in three days."

Amparo looked from Mikey to the back of the truck kitchen, and back to Mikey again. Although her makeup and glare hadn't changed, I could see that she was nervous.

I switched to Spanish. "I don't know why you're angry at me. I never even saw you before Tuesday night. But if there's something wrong, tell us. Maybe we can help."

"Daughter of a whore," she answered.

"Hey. Really. What did I ever do to you?"

"I saw you at the City Council meeting. Talking to everyone, taking notes. You're the Police Chief's girlfriend, and you're his spy. And you don't know anything about this town, or about how we do things, or all our hard work. You just go running to the cops, and all my hard work, you just undo. And now, weaseling your way into Mr. Mikey's bed, right?"

I just shook my head. She was ranting, raving. My Spanish was good, but maybe not good enough to counter this deluge of false accusations.

But Mikey had his own agenda. "Look. All I want is Arturo. Jack Partridge wants his chef. I want my job. You know where he is? Unless he's dead, get him here."

"Tell the cop's girlfriend—" she didn't use the word *girlfriend*, "—to back off. I'll call Arturo. But if he can't come—"

"Why wouldn't he be able to come?" Mikey asked.

"If he can't, I can cook as good as he can. I'll cook for Mr. Jack tonight." To my eyes, Amparo looked scared.

Mikey shook his head. "I sure hope we don't come to that, Amparo. Call him. Now."

"*No puedo*," she turned to me. *I can't.* So I was an ally now? The switch was too fast for me. "Explain to him, I can't call Arturo. But I'll cook."

"You just told him that. It won't make any difference to him if I say it or you do. But why can't you call him?"

I had a dreadful feeling.

"He's sick. Really sick. He can't talk on the phone."

"Take him to the hospital, then," I said.

"No money."

"They'll treat him anyway," I said. "It's the law."

She closed her eyes, and the evil fury was banked for the moment. "I'll cook for you, Mr. Mikey. I'll be there in an hour."

"What's with the Mister Mikey, Mister Jack stuff? Didn't Lincoln free the slaves?" Carinna said. "Can I have my *Buen Día* Special burrito, please?" she added, to Amparo.

We all turned to her. "So you can get your picture. And," she giggled, "I'm hungry." She pulled her wallet from the back pocket of her jeans.

Amparo turned away, grabbed a large flour tortilla and slapped it on the grill. She threw a handful of shredded meat on next to it, and as it sizzled she tossed in a few onion slices, a bunch of chopped tomatoes, a big, big handful of what looked like spinach, and an extended shake of seasoning salt.

"No lettuce," Carinna called out.

Amparo took the tortilla off the griddle with her bare hands, laid it out on a foil sleeve, and dolloped beans, rice, salsa, cheese, and stopped herself as she reached for the lettuce. She grabbed a handful of herbs and threw them on top, and in a smooth motion grabbed a spatula and flipped the meat from the grill to the burrito.

She rolled it up and handed it to Carinna. Carinna put a twenty on the pickup windowsill, and with a big grin, bit into the gigantic roll.

I lifted my phone, and snapped about ten times.

"Hey, I hope you didn't get me with salsa running down my chin!" Carinna said with her mouth full.

"Don't worry, I probably cut your head off anyway. But I got my photo."

Behind us, Amparo was slamming the windows shut. "I'll be back in an hour," she said to Mikey.

I heard her turning off the grill, the gas, and closing all the drawers. In less than five minutes she was starting her pickup truck, the attached food truck lurching to a start behind her.

As she was pulling away I caught sight of her face, the makeup streaming down her cheeks. The trailer rocked as it went from the dirt to the road, steadied, and she laid on the gas. In a minute she was out of sight.

"What a nightmare," Mikey said.

"With you, always," Carinna said. So there *was* some history.

"At least you'll have someone to cook," I said to him.

He shook his head. "Jack's gonna shit a brick."

#

I sent my photos to Edwina, with a short article about the dust-up between the health inspector and Nate's *La Sabrosa* truck. The pictures weren't half bad, with a nice view of *La Sabrosa*, along with Sister Calendula and Father Jim Avila. Nate was definitely not in the picture.

The photo of the *Buen Día* truck was a bit more interesting, with Carinna taking a big bite out of the *Buen Día* special. Mikey was leaning into the order window, and as I enlarged the view I could see that Amparo was handing him something. It looked like a mini-taco of the hard, rolled up type, a small *flauta*. It was a nice picture.

Edwina thought so, too. "But I can't run the article about Nate's truck running into trouble with the health inspector. We'd need to vet the story more, actually interview the inspector and Ernesto Carreras, because just saying the health inspector shut him down in the first minutes of operation, without a reason, would be really damaging to Nate, and all we know is that you saw it. I'll put the photo in, since it looks so nice, along with the *Buen Día* truck." I'd made the deadline for the Monday edition.

I shrugged. I'd done more than my part. Girl-reporter life had its ups and downs.

I checked the WAD, made sure my Keeper announcement was in, showing that I'd be available from five to six tonight, if anyone wanted to share a secret. It wasn't likely, but I hoped someone would stop by and tell me where Arturo was.

I texted Devon, asking when he was coming by. He'd said he didn't go on until four today, so he was planning to swing by around three this afternoon, but my six weeks worth of experience told me that confirmation was always a good idea. No answer, but that wasn't unusual. A cop's life wasn't as predictable as, say, lawyer's. Which reminded me ...

Was it only yesterday that men from the development company had come by? I had finally read through all of Saul's texts. There were seventeen of them, of which I'd answered one. In the next-to-last text, this one from me, I told him to take his tax problems to my lawyer. I hadn't seen his answer, which had come in sometime today. *We were still married in the last tax year. My problems are your problems. A little cooperation goes a long way, with me and with the IRS. I'll call you tonight, around five-thirty.*

Well, I'd be the Keeper right about then, so I wouldn't be picking up. Besides, my prior answer stood. *Talk to my lawyer.*

I looked around the little house. I was getting pretty comfortable here. Would I be staying after my suspension ran, in two more weeks? I'd ordered a coffee table and an end table for the living-dining room, and found a set of lace-lined curtains at one of the many antique stores in town. There was only enough fabric for two of the three windows, and my homemaking skills didn't extend to curtain-making, but the owner of the shop had directed me to the less commercial end of town, where the laundry and dry cleaners were. The woman running the cleaners doubled as a seamstress, and she had promised me a matching set, as close as we could get, and if I'd order the fabric she could do the whole new set in a week.

Now Saul's additional chicanery was threatening to take this from me. I needed to put my lawyer brain back on, and consider how I'd defend against this new threat. But first I needed to understand the nature and extent of the problem.

That analysis also held for the problem of the taco trucks. What did I know? What did I need to know? And how did it affect me, or anyone I cared about?

It struck me hard. Whom did I care about in this little duck town? I had no dog in this hunt, as my dad used to say. Or did I? Devon? We were still getting acquainted. I'd only just met Mikey. Carinna? No, but there was one person I wanted to make sure came out okay. August. The King's Bodyguard, the *a little different* August.

My text went off. Devon had to go on duty early, but he could come after my Keeper session. He'd give me a bit of leeway so it wouldn't look like telling the Keeper a secret was like telling the police.

It was only one in the afternoon. Plenty of time for a nap, a list, and a plan.

#

The nap came easier than the list and the plan. Once I was up and snacked, I sat down at my computer.

First, to make the list, I needed to figure out what the issue was. I made a note: *I don't know what the issue is*. But it centered around the "As" as Mikey called them. Amparo and Arturo Buendía, owners of the *Buen Día* taco truck.

Here's what I knew:

Ernesto (Nate) Carreras owns *La Sabrosa*. It scored a spot in front of the monastery. Justin March, the health inspector, shut *La Sabrosa* down within two minutes of opening. It looked like he (Justin) had planned that in advance.

The "As" own the *Buen Día* truck. Arturo is also the chef at Perdiz Winery, and is renowned as a great cook. Amparo wears vicious eye makeup. She's hostile to me, to August, to Justin March, to Angelo, and really everyone else. Except maybe Silvestre Sanchez.

They did not get a spot downtown for this trial period.

No one has seen Arturo since the City Council meeting.

Silvestre Sanchez owned a taco truck—did I know the name?—and he was dead. He didn't complete his application.

Devon and the police think Sanchez was poisoned.

August found Silvestre. August has a crush on Silvestre's daughter, but she lives in SF with her boyfriend and works in tech.

August thinks he saw Amparo at Silvestre's house when he drove by the night before.

Angelo DeVincenzi owns *Happy Tacky*. He got the bridge spot. He is a big flirt. He also suggested that Amparo stick a knife in Arturo, but he even flirted with me. He's open for business downtown and is very *Happy-Tacky* about it.

Mark Segismundo (Siggy) got the spot by the fountain in front of City Hall and the police station. He hasn't opened yet, and by all accounts doesn't even have his truck ready—he who was a stickler for rules. Why did he apply, then?

Mikey Charolais works at Perdiz. Amparo treats him with respect. Carinna doesn't. Do they have a history?

Sangiacomo (Jack) Partridge owns Perdiz Winery with his estranged wife, Victoria. Someone called the police at some point, accusing Victoria, who can't weigh more than 110 pounds, of hurting Jack. Who's about six foot and 180. But I shouldn't discount it based on preconceived notions about spousal abuse—odd suggestion of a gun being involved.

Jack seems to do coke or something. And is vaguely antisemitic but that probably doesn't play into this.

#

Okay, so that was a lot of facts. I read them over. I guess the two main questions, with one sub-question because I'm a lawyer and that's the only way that I could think, were:

One, was Silvestre Sanchez poisoned, and if so by whom and why?

And two, where was Arturo, and by extension, why was Amparo so hostile to me, and basically everyone else?

As to what was or wasn't my business, question one was strictly for the police. Though poor August was somewhat in the middle of it, since he both saw Silvestre and Amparo the night before, and by his mortified account, they were in what the Victorians would have called a compromising position, and he found Silvestre dead the following day. I doubted that August had anything to do with whatever happened to Silvestre, but I would keep an eye out for him, as far as I could.

As to the second question, it was really only my curiosity. If Amparo was hostile to me, I was hardly being singled out for a unique honor. She was a piece of terrifying work. But there was a personal aspect to her animosity: she'd cursed me, apparently and again via August, and I think she was trying to tell me to stay out of all this in her *you don't know anything about us* rant.

Tonight, as Keeper, I would turn my lawn chairs away from the driveway and see who came up my deck to confide. Although I'd inherited the role from my mother, to my surprise and dismay, I had somewhat molded into it. In one limited way it was like Shirley Jackson's "The Lottery," the story of a perverse community ritual that let the pressure escape and prevent explosion in a small town.

In "The Lottery," as I remembered it, a small town gathered annually to draw stones. The unfortunate resident who drew the unlucky white stone was stoned to death, in a horrifying and cruel community scapegoating. And for the most part, the townsfolk were satisfied by the blood-chilling ritual, as soon as they drew the black stones.

Here, the community operated a more benign custom. In a town where everyone knew everything about everyone, having a secret was both intensely difficult and gratifying. Accustomed to living in a mode of amplified openness, the Simpato residents cherished their shards of privacy. But carrying an unshared secret could be a burden, especially if one was unaccustomed to such weight. And so, the role of Keeper of Secrets was born. Did my mother create it? I didn't know, but she certainly perfected it. And may have died because of it.

At an appointed time, my mother would set out her lawn chairs, turn them towards the house so her back was to the driveway where people lined up to speak to her, and put out a pitcher of water or lemonade, some cups, and a box of tissues. One by one, those with secrets came up and confided in her. She did not dispense advice, she didn't counsel or console. She listened. And she didn't tell.

Rather than dial back the magnifying glass nature of the town, instead they instituted, or supported, a steam-valve that allowed individuals to have a private thought, but share the weight.

Tonight, at five p.m., I would take my place on the deck, with my lawn chairs turned away from the driveway, and await confidences. But in my case, if anything came up that related to Silvestre Sanchez, I was to tell Devon Plata, Chief of Police.

My confidants didn't know that I was not a sealed vault, though everyone seemed to know that Devon and I had a mild sort of relationship. Perhaps I had become, not just the Keeper of Secrets, but also a safe way to let the Chief know something without having to go to the station, risk being seen, and have everyone know they'd, perhaps, squealed. It was an uncomfortable role to begin with, and had been definitely made more complicated by this change.

Again I reviewed the list I'd made. I had no business with this particular death, disappearance, or conflict. I didn't even like tacos all that much.

#

Of course, everything happens at once. At five p.m., my text went off. Mikey was reporting in. *Thank god for Amparo. She cooks as well as her husband, and doesn't drink while she's at it. Best tasting ever. Want to come over and eat leftovers before I clean up?*

Devon had his say as well. *I think you should call off the keeper tonight. No one is going to tell you anything. I'll be by at 8, right after work.*

I had just turned my chairs around, put out the pitcher of water and a box of tissues, and I could see a line forming at the end of my drive. Devon was wrong. And with this line, no, I couldn't go eat leftovers with Mikey.

Going ahead anyway. Long line, I texted to Devon.

Sorry, duty calls, I texted Mikey.

I sat down in my Brown & Jordan chaise, one of the only things I kept in my divorce, and poured myself a glass of water. It should have been wine.

"Mrs. Keeper?"

"Have a seat," I said to the young woman with a blonde braid nearly to her waist. She wore the usual jeans with holes at the knees, a spaghetti-strap tank top, and had tied around her neck a thick green sweatshirt with "Be a Duck" printed across the chest. A No-Duck High grad, no doubt.

"Can I tell you a secret?"

I nodded.

"My math teacher asked me out."

My heart stopped. My Keeper job wasn't to give advice, or even probe deeper into confidences. I looked at her again. She had to be in her early twenties, so not a current high schooler. "So, how do you feel about that?" I asked. I'd learned why therapists asked that. It was the most neutral way of probing.

"I think it's gross. Because, you know, he's like, at least forty. That's disgusting."

I had to ask. "Do you want to tell me more?"

She shook her head. "Nah. I'm just, like, so grossed out, and he, when I was in his class, I mean, a million years ago in eleventh grade, I was repeating geometry, he used to wink at the girls, and we all would wink back at him, just to drive him nuts, but to ask me out, well ..."

I waited.

"So, I don't have to go, right? Even if I said okay, because we were at El Pato Loco and drinking and doing Jell-O shots, and he wanted to go to dinner with me, and I said okay, and today he texted me and said to meet him at *Happy Tacky* tonight and he'd buy me dinner, I don't have to, right?"

I looked her in the eye. "No. You don't have to. And you can text him and say you are not interested in him. And if he insists, tell him that you'll report him to the school board."

Her pale face turned a bright pink. "Wow. And I thought the Keeper didn't tell you what to do. I guess I was wrong."

She got up, and without saying bye or thanks, just flounced off. No good deed goes unpunished.

"Hey Sal," came from behind me. I turned to welcome Andie, the checker I knew at the Duck Shop. Andie was wearing a Simpato High baseball cap over her dyed red hair, and her usual track suit, this one a difficult shade of orange—not coral, not tangerine, but something in between. Under the zip-up jacket, which was open given the pleasant temperature of this May evening, she wore her Duck Shop T-shirt, "Where shopping is a Quacking pleasure!"

She sat down on the chaise, which creaked a little, and poured herself a glass of water. "I got a secret to tell you," she said. I nodded. "Don't tell your boyfriend, though."

I shrugged. "Don't have a boyfriend," I said.

"You know who I mean. Don't tell Chief Devon."

"Not my boyfriend." I hoped he wasn't early.

"You want to hear my secret or not?" Andie said, exasperated.

"Sure, if you want to tell it," I said. One thing I'd learned, with the long-time residents of Simpato, the less I pushed the better.

"Fine, have it your way," Andie said. "After Nate Carrera's truck got shut down earlier today—" I raised my eyebrows, "—yeah, everyone knows about that. That creep of a health inspector, you know who I mean, Justin something-or-other, too bad he's so good-looking—" like I hadn't noticed "—anyway, that's not what I was going to tell you. You know Mr. Partridge? Jack Partridge, he owns Perdiz, and Mikey's his manager?"

I nodded. "What about him?" This might be a piece of plain old gossip, but I'd take it.

"Well, Mr. Partridge himself, he came into the Duck Shop and bought ten pounds of pork. The butcher had to cut it special, because he don't usually have that much cut up on hand, but ten pounds of shoulder, cut in chunks, and sold to Jack—you know his real name is Sangiacomo, that's his name, I kept forgetting, right around ten-thirty this morning."

I waited.

"So, that's my secret."

Not much of a secret. "Maybe he's having family over tomorrow and is making carnitas for everyone," I said.

Andie snorted. "And maybe he's opening his own taco truck, huh? Not duckin' likely."

"So what do you think it means?" I asked.

"Darned if I know," she said, pushing herself out of the chair. "But I just thought that your boyfriend ought to know about it."

"Not my—"

"See ya," she said, and nearly scampered down the deck steps, something I would not have thought possible.

I listened through two more pregnancies, both purportedly joyful secrets, and they just couldn't wait to tell the baby-daddy, won't he be surprised, and one guy who thought he saw another construction worker steal a bag of cement but wasn't going to rat him out because sometimes you just need a bag of cement, and all he wanted to do was tell someone so it wouldn't weigh on his conscience and Father Jim over at Santo Cubierto would give him too many prayers if he told him.

Finally, I looked at my watch. It was nearly six-thirty, later than I'd intended, and as I glanced back the line was down to two people. I didn't think I recognized one, and the other looked familiar but she had her back to me. I felt disappointed. What had I expected? Amparo to come and confess that she'd done away with her abusive husband? That she was carrying on with Silvestre Sanchez and that he'd gotten a bad mushroom or something?

A pretty girl, early twenties, with glossy, completely straight hair that fell loosely to her shoulders in a stylish cut, approached my chaise. She smiled a bit but her eyes were red, and she took a tissue from her jeans pocket and dabbed them as well as her nose. "Mind if I sit?" she said.

"Please do," I said. "Water?"

She nodded and poured herself a cup. "Thank you." She sipped quietly for a moment. "So, how does this work? I tell you my secret, and you tell me what to do?"

"Uh, no, that's not how it's supposed to work, though I do tend to give a bit of advice sometimes, it's not always welcome. I'm supposed to just listen. So, you're not from here?"

She laughed a little, and her face went from sad to cute to beautiful. "Oh, born and raised. I'm Alicia, Silvestre Sanchez's daughter."

"I'm so sorry," I started to say, but she went right on.

"But I was too young for the last Keeper, and my friends who've come to talk to you just said, oh, you just go tell her your secrets! No one knows why! So I thought I'd try it out."

I waited. She sat back and sipped her water. I glanced at the end of the driveway. The one other person was still waiting. "So, you just want to talk?" She nodded. "Well, tell you what. Do you want to wait, I will chat with the last person in line, and then you and I can just have a conversation after?"

She looked at the drive. "I guess," she said. "But maybe I just should go back ..."

"No, please. Stay. You can even wait inside," I said.

She shook her head. "I'll just walk around some," and she got up. "Do you need me to wash the cup?" I smiled and shook my head. No one had asked that before.

"Your turn," Alicia said to the woman waiting at the end of the drive, and she walked away towards Peaches Street and the mountain. I really hoped she'd be back.

I was surprised to see that the last woman was the owner of Feathers, the local overpriced boutique. She seemed to be about my age, and wore long, spangly earrings that nearly brushed her collar. Her hair was a true, deep chestnut, nearly matching her eyes, and if she wore makeup it was so artfully done as to be invisible.

She sat right down. "I remember your mother," she said. "I'd just opened the store, didn't know what the hell I was doing, and I was sure the girl I'd hired for after-school help was stealing from me. Your mom was great."

"Glad to hear it," I said. "I miss her," I added, to my own surprise. I sounded warm and real.

She patted my arm. "Of course you do. I wish she were here now."

"Well, now we have me," I said. I was eager to move her along, but didn't want to be rude.

"Okay, well, my secret? You know when they were drawing the cards to see who got what spot for the taco trucks?"

I nodded. So this might be interesting after all. Not some high-school girl filching over-priced earrings.

"The one who's running, Ashley Sage?" I nodded again. This was someone who ended her sentences with a question. "So Ashley? She was telling that fake nun, Sister Marigold, who's no more a nun than I am, for more than one reason," she winked at me, "to keep an eye on the health inspector, that bastard, Justin, who thinks that just because he's good looking and has a job with actual benefits that women should be falling all over him—but that's not what she was saying."

She stopped to breathe. I waited, silence being one of the best encouragements to speak. "So Ashley was telling Marigold, whose real name is Margo Schwartz, by the way, that the wife of the guy who cooks at Perdiz, the one with the vicious eye makeup, was sleeping with Justin Marsh to keep her truck open, and she was sure to get a spot. Then she didn't. So, that's my secret. What do you think of that?"

I blinked at her. "Well. Um, quite a secret."

"So, Mrs. Keeper. How do you think Ashley knew that?"

"I have no idea." I was flummoxed.

"Because Ashely is sleeping with him, too! Because Ashley sleeps with everyone!"

"Really?" I said. It was not my role as Keeper, but as a lawyer I had to ask. "How do you know that?"

She grinned. "Because Jack Partridge told me!" She licked her lips. "Good, huh? You gonna write that up in the *Quack*? I mean, we all know that you're writing for that rag since Georgiana was killed, so isn't that something juicy?"

God, could I ask it? I had to. "Are you sleeping with Justin Marsh, too?"

She threw her head back and laughed. "Oh my ducking god. No! Are you kidding me? No! He was in, buying some trinket for Victoria Partridge, now there's a piece of gossip that you should know, even though it's a bit stale, right?"

"Wait. You mean Jack was buying—"

"Ha! No. Justin Marsh was. And he told me that Victoria, that skinny ice queen, was a lot hotter than Ashley-the-masseuse. Though you'd think it would be the other way around—magic hands and all."

I had to push my mouth closed.

I caught a glimpse of Alicia coming back around the corner. I had to talk to her, but I couldn't let—I didn't even know her name—the Feathers owner get away.

"I didn't get your name," I said.

"Oh, of course. Tiffany." She put out her hand.

"Sal," I said.

"I know. So, you want to have coffee tomorrow? Or a glass of wine? We have so much to talk about!"

I hadn't even had to ask. She pulled out her phone. I gave her my number and she texted me, putting herself in my phone. "See you tomorrow!" she said.

"Hi, Alicia," she added as she passed her at the drive. "Back to give the Keeper another secret? I didn't know you could go twice. Sorry about your dad," she added, not sounding sorry.

Alicia nodded. "No, I just forgot to give Mrs. Keeper something for my dad's obit," she added, and headed up the deck.

So now I was in the obituary business, too. My brain was swirling. "Come inside," I said to Alicia. No need to sit outside in plain view.

CHAPTER EIGHT

Alicia perched on the edge of the folding chair in my living-dining room. Well brought up, she would not have chosen the other chair, upholstered and comfy-looking, while her elder was left with the folding one. Little did she know that the folding chair was easily the most comfortable seat in the house. She glanced around, taking in the two lace curtains and the sheet tacked over the third window.

"On order," I said, nodding at the sheet. "I found someone to make a third matching curtain."

"Señora Rosa? At the cleaners, over by the feed store?" I nodded. "She does nice work. But you know, Dagmar Rubin is a lot cheaper and a lot of folks say she's even better."

I smiled. "Well, they're on order now. But Dagmar Rubin, you say?"

"Yeah, she works out of her house, but she made my quinceañera dress, and a couple of years later she fixed it for the prom for me, and it's really something."

I took a little yellow pad from the magazine rack that doubled as my filing cabinet, and noted the name. Chitchat completed, I turned to Alicia. "Listen, dear. I'm really sorry about your dad." She nodded. "But tell me, tell me what's on your mind. I don't judge, and I don't tell." I crossed my fingers behind my back.

She sighed, a sound far too old for such a young girl. "I don't know where to start. I mean, most or maybe none of this is a secret, but I need to tell someone." She giggled a choked kind of giggle, nearly a gag. "I guess that's why you're here, right? Like a therapist?"

I nodded. "Like a therapist but free."

"Okay. Here goes. Okay. You know my dad, right?" I'd never met him, but she wasn't waiting for an answer. "So, my mom, she died almost a month after my quinceañera, I can't ever be grateful enough to her for living that long. Breast cancer. I already get checked, and I'm only twenty-three."

She stopped, waiting for an answer. "I'm glad you get checked," I said.

"So, my dad kind of fell apart. I was the only kid. Well, I used to have a brother, but he died in elementary school, he got hit by a bus. We're kind of the bad luck family around here."

Poor kid. And now her father.

"And now my dad. I don't know, Mrs. Keeper—"

"Sal. Call me Sal."

She nodded. "It seems weird. I talked to the police chief, Mr. Plata, and he said he thinks my dad was poisoned. I mean, who would do that? Like, why? It doesn't make any sense. He never hurt anyone. I know he was going to do the application to get his taco truck downtown, but he didn't even know if the Council was going to pass it, and you know, with our family luck, he wouldn't get it anyway. He asked me to help him with it, but I hadn't done it yet, and he said he'd wait to see if it was passed."

Interesting. "I'm glad you were going to help with it. He had no idea that they would come up with this trial period," I said. "And it was only for three months. If it worked, he had plenty of time to put in the application."

I was reassuring her, I thought, about feeling bad that he didn't have the application in on time, but I had it wrong.

"No! That's not it!" She looked around my little sitting area. "No. You don't get it. It's—he wasn't ready. We're different from the other families here, we're bad luck—And my, oh how do you say it, god-mother, my *madrina*, Amparo Buendía, she has a truck, and she was going to get a spot because one, she's a witch, everyone knows that, and two, she and her husband, Arturo, who, forgive me, is an asshole, are like the best cooks in the whole valley, and not to give her a spot will bring hell down on our town."

It had.

"And so why would anyone poison my dad? He's like, nobody, except we know we're cursed. I told Mr. Plata that. He just said, well, it looks like someone did. But you know what I think happened?"

So this was it. "What?" I said softly.

"I think that Arturo poisoned him. Because he's jealous of the fact that Amparo loves him. Loved him. Loves him. I don't know. It's not fair." She started to cry. My box of tissues was outside on the back deck. I got up quietly, so as not to spook her, to get it.

When I came back in, the chair was empty, the front door was open, and she was gone.

#

I looked out the front door, down the road in both directions, but there was no sign of Alicia. Why had she run off? My non-suspicious mind said that she was likely overwhelmed by the events of the past twenty-four hours, and had realized that here she was, confiding in a perfect stranger.

But my emotional heart said something else had scared her. What had she seen, or thought of, or heard, that made her take off like a jackrabbit?

I gave the living room a once-over, trying to see it from a grieving, scared young woman's eyes. The furniture was dull and old. There was minimal art on the walls. My bookcase had few volumes except novels. Even my law books, now retrieved from storage, were up on the top shelf, since we mostly did on-line research anyway.

There was nothing I could see that would have spooked her.

With an hour before Devon would be here, at the earliest, I wrote up my notes. Was this for a story for the *Quack*? Or to tell Devon? I didn't regard my promise as Keeper of Secrets as including him. He had no interest in the surprise pregnancies, but anything having to do with Silvestre Sanchez was, in my opinion, fair game.

By the time Devon's Jeep pulled up in front of my house I felt I could give him a coherent rundown of what I knew. I watched him as he stepped down from his Jeep, and I could see the tense set of his shoulders. He was wearing a gray button-down collar shirt with blue stripes, and his usual khakis, which I knew had a great deal of elastic in them, to facilitate quick movement. His brown hair was brushed to the side of his broad forehead, and he was frowning.

"Hey," I said, opening the door for him. "Long day, huh?"

He nodded, put his hand on my upper arm, and moved past me. We didn't yet know whether a kiss on the cheek was the right greeting, or a handshake, or a hug. We were still in relationship limbo, edging in one direction or another. It struck me that the edging was based on his work, his moods, and his needs. I was a stolid obelisk in the swirling eddies of his life. I cringed at my own metaphor, and stepped aside. "Wine?"

I brought out a Perdiz red. He raised his eyebrows a bit, but said nothing as I poured. I had put some soft triple-cream cheese and some slices of fresh sourdough baguette on a wooden board, and I put that down in front of him. He slathered a slice with the cheese and downed it in two bites. "Hungry," he said unnecessarily.

Almost all the restaurants in Simpato stopped taking orders by eight thirty, another casualty of small-town life, so I offered to scramble us both some eggs and slice more bread. "I didn't have time to eat at six, when my dinner break came. I ate a power bar, drank a Monster. Not the best for the digestion," he said.

I hadn't eaten either but that was just because I'd forgotten to. I had no high-level police work to excuse myself.

The wine was very, very good.

"How was the Keeper tonight?" he asked as he scraped the last of his eggs onto a slice of baguette.

"Complicated. I tried to put it all in context, but it won't fit neatly. Listen to this: I told you on the phone that this morning, and it seems like a lifetime ago, around four a.m., August came pounding on my door, saying that Amparo Buendía had called his mom and said she was going to put a bad spell on me. Then, when I went to grab a photo of the food truck in front of the Little Sisters—*La Sabrosa,* Nate Carreras has that one—the health inspector shut him down."

"Wow, that was quick," Devon said. "What were the grounds?"

"I have no idea," I said. "But then the Sisters said that he could use their kitchen—my idea—and sell from the truck. Okay, so then Carinna and I went to Perdiz—"

"Really? I thought she hated the guy."

"I noticed there was no love lost between her and Mikey Charolais, but I have no idea about their past."

Devon chuckled. "Everyone else in town does. Seems he was trying to date her daughter, but that didn't work out. Publicly. At the fountain. She pushed him in. Nearly boiled him alive."

"Oh gosh. Well, they aren't friends, but they were cooly cordial to one another, if you know what I mean. And it turned out that Amparo Buendía's truck was parked at the Perdiz gates, and we got some photos for the paper. Then Mikey talked Amparo into cooking at Perdiz today, because Arturo is still MIA. He says it went fine, she's as good as her husband, only sober."

"Glad Charolais's problem got solved," Devon said dryly. I smiled. "No, it's just that his boss, Jack Partridge, is a real SOB, and if it didn't work out he would be hell on wheels."

"Yeah. He does coke and is an antisemite, too."

Devon looked at me. "How do you know that?"

"It's like the wind. You can feel it even when you can't see it. Besides, he jumped like a cat on a spring when I told him last night that I had to leave the winery because it was Shabbat." I laughed. "Got him to stand aside, but quick."

"Doesn't make him antisemitic," Devon said

"Says you," I replied. "Anyway, at the Keeper session, you were wrong, by the way. Plenty of people showed up. A couple of pregnant girls, as usual, and a guy who may have taken a ten-finger employee discount, and the checker from the Duck Shop, who told me that Jack Partridge had personally come in and bought ten pounds of pork from the butcher—and I can't see the relevance of that—and then Alicia Sanchez, Silvestre Sanchez's daughter showed up."

"That would be right after she left the police station, then. She was there until six or so."

"I guess. I talked to her briefly, then invited her in. She was nervous, and, I guess, grieving. Oh, and the lady who owns Feathers told me that Ashley who's running for City Council is sleeping with Justin March."

"You're kidding."

"No, well at least that's what she said. Um, probably slander but she said that Ashley sleeps with everyone. Which for a woman is damning, right? But apparently our health inspector is a regular Lothario, himself. I mean, he *is* attractive, in that kind of way, you know, thin, menacing, good features, but still.

Because evidently, according to—gosh I can't remember now which of these people told me—Amparo slept with him too. And, get this, Amparo is, well, *was*, carrying on with Silvestre Sanchez, and is also Alicia's godmother."

Devon sat back in the upholstered chair. "Wow. Simpato, without a duck but with plenty of ducking ..."

"Oh, don't. I don't think I could stand another duck pun right now."

"That's quite a haul of information for one day," Devon said. "You should come and work for us."

I poured us each a bit more wine. "Good stuff," Devon said, swirling the deep garnet liquid in the wine glass. "I'm worried about Alicia, though."

"Me, too. She took off running from here as soon as I got up to get a box of tissues. I don't know what spooked her."

"Besides her father being murdered?"

"So we're sure?"

Devon nodded.

"Poison?"

"Yeah, but we still don't know what or how. If we were in a big city we would have our answers, but the samples had to be sent from the little hospital here to Sacramento, to the forensic lab, because they can only eliminate some of the obvious stuff here: meth, alcohol, acetaminophen ..."

"Like Tylenol? People get poisoned with it?"

"Yeah, big time. But mostly, I mean I've only seen it as an accident. But it can destroy your liver in no time, and you need a transplant, which, you know, is nearly impossible up here."

"I had no idea," I said.

"Interestingly, I do have an idea. When I was in school I took a class, actually I took two, in toxicology, and this is pretty strange. I sent some requests in with the lab order, let's see what they come back with."

We finished our wine. "Want to go for a walk?" I was daring him to move beyond our one "date," a dinner after the arrest in Simpato's only murder in a decade. Until now, anyway.

"We can check out the food truck sites," Devon said.

"All work and no play," I replied.

"Sorry," he said.

I interrupted. "It's okay. Let me put on some real shoes. If this isn't social, these pretty shoes won't work. Sneakers it is."

He took my hand. "We can make it be both. But yeah, change your shoes."

#

We'd only gone as far as the fountain, where the steam from the underground geyser wafted through the control valves that kept the near-boiling water from spewing all over the little plaza, when Devon's phone rang.

"Got it," he said. "I'll be right there. I'm right outside right now."

We were right outside the police station, so it was obviously work. "I've got to go," Devon said, already striding away.

"Wait, what?"

"I'll have to tell you later. But go home. And call me right away, day or night, if anything happens."

He was going up the steps to the cop shop, his hand on his phone and the other one pushing the door open.

"What do you mean, if something happens? Tell me!"

But he was gone.

#

I stood and stared at the door, until I heard the police car come around the back of the station, lights and sirens blaring.

I saw Devon sitting in the passenger seat, talking into his hand, and a young woman I didn't know was driving. If she weren't a cop she would deserve a fat ticket, I thought, as she blasted through the stop sign, turned on to Central, and from what I could see, ran an orange light as she headed away from town, towards Valley.

Slowly, I walked back to my house. There was nothing I could do.

But that wasn't true. I opened my computer and found Edwina Sharp's email and direct phone.

"Do you have a scanner?" I said.

"Hello Sal. Yes I do. And how are you, this gorgeous evening?"

"What's going on?"

"You're taking this girl-reporter thing rather seriously, aren't you?" Her gravelly voice came through the phone. "Why? Do you want to cover this newest Simpato disaster?"

"Ed. What is going on. Tell me please." I was short, emphatic.

"You got bitten by the bug. Okay, Valley Hospital has asked for police presence. I don't know why. But they want it, and they want it now. So maybe there was a shoot-out in Valley, or a drunk husband waving a knife around in the ER. I don't know. But we don't cover this stuff. We're a weekly. We are absolutely after the fact. So settle down."

I took a deep breath. "Who would know?"

"Your cop boyfriend?"

"Not my boyfriend."

"As you wish."

Devon wouldn't have had to rush off if was a drunken husband. First of all, the county sheriff's office would have been called, since Valley Hospital was outside the Simpato city limits, and second of all, they would have just sent a couple of officers, not the off-duty Chief.

"I just think it might be important," I said.

"Okay, you want to play Lois Lane? Fine. I'll pick you up in twenty minutes, and I'll use my press pass to get into the hospital. And you can take notes."

I thanked her profusely, then sat down to wait for her. And as I waited, I started to wonder why I had even jumped on this. It wasn't to play Lois Lane. I knew in my bones that the emergency was related to the food trucks. I only hoped that it was no one I knew, that it wasn't August who was hurt.

#

I heard a soft knock on the back door just as a red Fiat pulled up in front of the house. I saw Edwina's grey bob in the driver's seat of the car. I knew that the knock on the back door wasn't August because he honked and pounded, and his footsteps on the deck made the house shake.

I opened the front door, waved, and raced to the back. Luna had chosen the back door to push against, meowing loudly. I slid my foot around her to get her away from the door and opened it. On the deck outside the kitchen stood Alicia, her perfect black hair disheveled, and a long gash dripped blood off her cheek.

I pulled her into the house and slammed the back door shut.

"A kitty!" she exclaimed.

"You coming?" called Edwina from the front.

Alicia turned to bolt again. I grabbed her upper arm. "Hold on. It's a friend. Hold on!"

Edwina came into the living room, and I nearly dragged Alicia in as well. "Who's this?" Edwina said.

"Don't tell her," Alicia said in Spanish. I don't know how she knew I spoke it.

"It's okay," I answered in English. "She's the owner of the newspaper. We were about to leave—" I stopped. "What happened?"

"I can't tell you if it's going to be in the newspaper," she said.

"It won't be. Can you give me a moment?" I asked Edwina.

"Fine, I'll be in the car. Five minutes, max."

Alicia stepped into the living area, and her eyes strayed to the folding chair, under which was a balled-up sweatshirt. "Whose is that?" she asked.

"August's."

She looked at me, wild-eyed. "That's what I thought. Is he here?"

"No," I said. "He was here early this morning. Now, what's going on? We have five minutes before my friend drives me up to the hospital."

"Why—"

"No, Alicia. Just tell me."

She sat down hard in the upholstered chair. Luna jumped into her lap, and she caressed the cat mindlessly. "I'll try to make it fast. Okay. I told you that my dad and Amparo are close, like third cousins or something, on my mother's side, of course. She's my godmother. She was also, well, after my mother died, she was consoling my father, especially when I went to college. And her husband is an absolute jerk. Mistreats her, beats her, everything. And she won't leave him, but she definitely, oh, I don't know, if she were younger, I'd say she gets around."

I nodded. "Go on."

"But she's really powerful in our community. And even though we called her an old slut," she giggled, stifled it, and went on, "no one will say it to her face. Besides, with a husband like that, who wouldn't."

She looked at me, checking for judgment. I kept my face neutral. "Well, she came to the house tonight, and she said, oh my god, that she and my dad had been, um, having sex, when he started to get sick. And that ..."

She started to cry. I put my hand out, unable to reach her from my chair. She shook her head, she didn't want my comfort.

"And August ..." she sobbed.

"August?"

"August has always had a crush on me. It's sweet. But he's not for me, right? I mean, I went to college, I live with my boyfriend in San Francisco, I work in tech, I'm only half of this world, you know? And August? He's really sweet. But, well, no."

I nodded. "Of course. I totally understand."

Edwina honked her horn.

"I'll fast-forward. That's why I ran away this afternoon, I saw his sweatshirt ..."

I looked under my seat. "It's a Simpato High sweatshirt. It could be anyone's."

She shook her head. "No. I can see, it's got the class on it, and it says at the bottom, *Always Be a Duck*. No one who graduated ten years ago would wear a class sweatshirt like that, especially one as big as that, except him."

I acknowledged that he probably left it this morning.

"But then, she said that August saw them. And he honked his stupid horn, 'Never on Sunday.' And if he told anyone, she was going to curse him like he couldn't imagine. Because my dad was poisoned, and if he got sick while they were, you know, and she had brought him her amazing *empanadas de res*, beef empanadas, because he can't eat pork, and he died from poisoning she was going to get blamed."

Wow.

"So I asked Amparo, *why are you telling me?* And she said, because that August is hot for you, so you're gonna go get him in bed, and make him understand that he should tell nobody."

Oh my god. I shook my head, speechless.

"And so I called her a *puta*. And she laughed, and said if I didn't do it, she was going to make me so ugly no one would want me. And to prove it, she scratched my face."

She was crying. I got up and put my arm around her.

Edwina honked twice. I needed to act.

"Come on with us. We're going up to the hospital. Something has happened and we need to see what it is. Edwina is with the paper, she actually owns the paper, so we'll have press credentials. I don't want to leave you here, and you need to tell the police—"

"No! Amparo will kill me!"

"We'll only tell the chief, Devon Plata. He'll make sure you're safe. Now, come on. At least when you're in the car with us, you'll be safe. Even if you don't talk to Devon."

I went to the door. "Hold your horses," I yelled to Edwina. "And maybe while we're there the ER can see if you need stitches for that thing. It looks like a lot more than a scratch."

"Have you seen her nails? They're scarier than her eyeliner."

"Then you'll probably need an antibiotic or something, anyway," I said, hustling her out the door onto the walk.

"We have company," I said to Edwina, pushing the front seat forward for Alicia to climb into the vestigial back seat.

"Sorry there's only room for a kitten back there, not a person," Edwina said. "Fill me in. I'm sure it will be good.

CHAPTER NINE

Edwina drove up the winding road to the Valley Hospital Emergency entrance while Alicia and I clung to the sides of the car. "There's no fire," I said one time to Edwina. "Whatever it is will still be there when we get there."

She just shrugged. "Get used to it, girl-reporter."

Alicia giggled in the back seat, but other than that, it was too hair-raising a ride to talk.

We pulled into *patient short-term parking* and Edwina yanked the parking break so hard I thought she'd break it off. I realized, to my surprise, that she was nervous. Of course, she'd been running a sleepy weekly in a sleepy town in a sleepy county for over a decade. Her chops for real news were probably pretty rusty.

"Before we go in, we need a plan," I said. "We can't just waltz into the ER and say, *hey, we're the press, what's going on?* Besides, I want that cut on Alicia's face looked at. You're so young," I added. "No disfigurement, okay? Do you have insurance?"

She nodded, wide-eyed.

I turned back to Edwina. "We're here. How do we go about finding out what brought the cops up here?" I could see two of the three Simpato police cars parked right out front ("we serve and protect [duck emoji]") including the one I'd seen Devon ride out in. I could tell by the badly dented fender, no doubt from the unfettered driving of the cop who drove him.

"Well," Edwina said, shuffling through her purse, "first I take out my press card, where the hell is it?" She pawed through the handbag. "I put it in here before I—here it is." She took out a bedraggled, laminated piece of cardboard. I took it from her.

"Nineteen ninety-seven? This card expired nearly thirty years ago!"

Edwina, the commander in chief of her little paper, looked sheepish. "It's all I had."

"Oh, for crying out loud," I said. I pulled out my wallet. "Here. This will probably do more good." It was my California Bar Card, and since I'd paid the twenty bucks extra, it was the plastic kind. "Valid until March of next year," I said. "Though, of course, it isn't. But at least it doesn't say so."

"Why isn't it valid?" Alicia asked.

"Long story, involving my divorce. It will be revalidated next month." I hoped. "Just a temporary glitch." She nodded, either satisfied or incurious. "Let's go in and talk to someone, see if we can find out who was brought it, and why the police were called with such urgency. They may not tell us, HIPAA and all that, honored more in the breach by the way—" Edwina grinned, "—but at least we have some questions and we'll be there when the cops come out. And besides, like I said, I want Alicia—"

She held out her palm in a *stop* motion. "I'm fine, let's go. Duck, you old folks spend a lot of time talking and not a lot of time doing."

Edwina and I bristled, but I took the lead and walked us all through the sliding doors of the ER.

This was not Oakland's Highland Hospital, or San Francisco General, where the seats would be filled with the bleeding, the vomiting, the crying, and the people surfing on their phones. There was one woman with her foot on a chair, and I could see from here that it was broken, and a receptionist behind glass at a small desk. I was disappointed, having thought that the chaos

I had expected would be more beneficial to us than this nearly empty room.

We approached the desk, and a young woman with light brown hair in a messy bun, rectangular glasses, and bubblegum-pink lipstick raised a finger. I noticed she had an earphone in, and we waited until she disconnected. "Can I help you?" she said, with about as much enthusiasm as a dental patient.

"We'd like to have this woman seen for this cut," I said, gesturing at Alicia. "We think that the cut was made by a septic instrument, and needs an antibiotic."

She looked at Alicia. "Seriously? You come into the ER with a scratch when we've got a guy dying back there, and cops swarming the place?"

"A guy dying?" I said innocently.

"Yeah. Probably poisoned, just like the other guy the other night the cops brought in. At least this time we know what to do. You shoulda been here then. It was a madhouse. I mean, he was dead when he got here, so we couldn't do nothing, but no one knew what had got him."

So much for HIPAA, they'd only withhold information if you asked them.

"That was my dad," Alicia said softly.

"Oh my ducking god!" said the receptionist. "I'm so sorry. Oh my god. Wait. Are you Alicia Sanchez?" She nodded. "Sylvia Cordell. I was a couple of years ahead of you. I remember you, though. You went to UC. Never gonna forget that! I'm sorry about your dad."

Alicia gave a little acknowledgement of the condolence.

"So that's why we want this cut—" I would not call it a scratch, "—looked at. There might be some toxin or something."

"Wow, yeah," Sylvia said. "Let me tell the doctor. But the guy in there now, he's not dead. I think they might, I dunno, might be able to save him, though it sure don't look good."

She pressed the button on her earphone. "I got the daughter of guy who died day before yesterday here in reception. She's got a gash that might be septic." She gave Alicia a wink. "Can you send someone for her?" She waited, nodded. "Okay, I'll just send her back. She's got some aunties with her, she's not alone."

Aunties?

"Go on back," she said as she pushed the door buzzer under her desk. "Let's go to room four, at the left end of the hall. But don't look at room one. It's way gross."

"Hey! I was here first!" said the woman with the broken foot. "I've been waiting almost an hour!"

"Triage," said Sylvia. "Emergencies first. Your foot ain't gonna get unbroken in the next half hour."

#

Devon emerged from Room 1 just as the four of us, Edwina, Alicia, Sylvia and I, paraded through the hall toward our cubicle. He was wearing a hospital gown over his clothes, and whatever it was spattered with did not look nice. "Sal. What the hell are you doing here?"

Not *are you okay?* Not *who's hurt?* Though common sense told me that since the four of us were walking under our own power it wasn't dire, whatever it was, and though honesty compelled me to realize that he'd likely seen through whatever excuse I was going to offer before I even could try it, I was just a wee bit hurt.

"Alicia got cut. She needs stitches."

He looked beyond me to Alicia, and nodded. Whether she needed stitches or not, she was a major player—daughter of the victim—and not to be dismissed.

"Come on in here," said Sylvia, ushering us into the cubicle and pulling the curtain. "I'll get the nurse."

As soon as she was gone I edged out of the room. Edwina made to follow, and I shook my head. "He'll talk more to me, I think."

"I'm the editor in chief of the newspaper, Sal. I'm press. He can't ignore me."

"You're press with an expired, thirty year old card. Just give me a few minutes."

She shrugged and I escaped.

Devon was waiting for me. "What are you really doing here?"

"Trying to find out what's going on. Alicia is scared to death."

"Right. How'd she get the scratch?"

"It's more than a scratch, and Amparo did it."

Devon froze. "Wait, what?"

I did not preen. I'm better than that. "Yeah, Amparo, who's her godmother, who was her father's lover, who was also, according to local gossip, practically everyone else's lover, whenever it suited her, including, like I told you, that power-drunk health inspector—"

"Stop. Stop. Don't say another word."

"Why? Don't you need to know—"

"Be quiet." He bent his head down close to mine. "You didn't hear it from me. That's who's in there. Justin March."

"Oh my god. No!"

He nodded. "And I don't think he'll make it. He hasn't regained consciousness. And," he spoke even more quietly, so I could barely hear him, "he was poisoned. Just like Silvestre Sanchez."

I stood back, aghast. "Amparo," I said softly.

"Probably so," he answered. "I'm glad you brought Alicia in. That scratch, or cut—how did she get it?"

"Amparo's nails," I whispered.

"We'll need to test it," he answered. "And maybe take her into protective custody. This is nuts. I'm going to send out an officer to bring in Amparo for questioning. Now. And Arturo, too. If they can find him."

"If Amparo hasn't killed him too."

#

Justin March did not make it.

"Do they know what the poison was yet?" I asked.

We were standing outside the ER, next to the police truck Devon was going to go back to Simpato in. Edwina and Alicia were still inside, while the paperwork was processed to release Alicia. It was nearly eleven at night, and it had been a really, really long day.

"Sort of," he said. "The first report on Sanchez came back late this afternoon, but it's really preliminary. It looks like arsenic poisoning. We used Sanchez's results to try to save March. All the symptoms were the same: severe abdominal pain, vomiting everywhere, unchecked rice-water diarrhea, loss of consciousness, blood pressure in the tank. Kidney failure. But it was too little too late. Valley Hospital doesn't have the means to do what they call 'chelation,' and they had to send to UC Davis to get what they needed. And like I said, too little too late. I've seen drug deaths. I've seen gun shots. But this, it was terrible."

I put my hand on his arm.

"I'm sorry," I said. "But don't tell Alicia. Please. I don't want her imagining her father in those throes, all alone in his house."

"Of course. Of course. I mean, unless she asks. And she has the right to see the lab report. And anyone can look up what death by arsenic poisoning looks like."

"But that's so weird," I said. "It's like an archaic poison. *Arsenic and Old Lace*, where these nice old ladies poison some man by putting arsenic in his tea. It used to be in cosmetics, and in rat poison. I mean, anyone could get it. But now ... how would—I guess Amparo—get ahold of arsenic?"

"I guess we'll find out. They're holding her at the station now, and from what the officer at the desk tells me, she's none too happy about it. I need to get back. Will I see you tomorrow?"

"Sure," I said. "I mean, you were going to see me tonight, right? So sure, we can plan for tomorrow."

I stopped myself from saying, *though you'll either not be able to come over, you'll be distracted or exhausted if you do, or, like tonight, you'll have to leave after a half hour.* I didn't say it because I knew it was a painful reminder of how his marriage fell apart, his daughter barely spoke to him for five years, and his son had abandonment issues that were still, ten years later, wreaking havoc with his psyche.

"I'm sorry about tonight," he said, reading my mind.

"Goes with the territory," I said, uninflected.

"Here comes Alicia. Do you think you can get her to stay overnight at your place?"

I blinked at him. "Where? The place is tiny."

"She's young, she can sleep on—no, you don't have a sofa yet, do you? Maybe Edwina?"

The two approached, Alicia with a couple of butterfly closures on her cheek. "So it doesn't scar," she said as she noted my gaze. "And some antibiotic ointment." She glanced at her watch, an Apple Watch, I noticed, testament to the earnings of a tech gal in the big city. "Wow, only two and a half hours. That's got to be the fastest ER visit in history."

"Thanks to Sylvia's greasing the skids," Edwina said. Alicia looked at her. I guessed that *greasing the skids* wasn't a common phrase in her crowd.

"Hey Edwina," Devon said, "can I talk with you for a sec?"

Edwina raised her penciled eyebrow and followed him around to the side of the police pickup truck. As he moved with her, Devon threw me a glance.

Oh, so it was on me to talk Alicia into staying with Edwina. Thanks. I decided to go straight to the point. "Chief Plata is worried for your safety tonight. Amparo is at the police station right now, waiting to be questioned—"

"About my scratch?" She was shocked.

"No, no, not really. It's just that there are a lot of things going on right now—" I realized she didn't know that the man in room one was Justin Marsh, that he was dead, and that he'd died the same way her father had. I wasn't sure what I could tell her. Figures Devon had left this one to me.

Well, she was young, but not a child. "He's worried that Amparo may have been involved, somehow, in your dad's death, and in the death of the man who was in the other cubicle here tonight, and he wants you to be safe."

"My godmother wasn't involved in my dad's death. That's crazy shit. And yeah, she's a witch, but I'm not afraid of her. Besides, didn't you just say she was in jail?"

"Not in jail," I said. "She's at the station, going to answer some questions. And when they're done asking questions, they may send her home, or they may arrest her if they have enough evidence. And if they send her home she may be pretty furious. And he doesn't want it taken out on you."

"Fine. I'll go back to the city tonight."

"It's almost midnight, Alicia. No, I'm suggesting you stay with Edwina Sharp. Just one night. Devon is talking to her right now."

"The newspaper lady? How's she gonna keep me safe? She's, like, sixty." Alicia's city-girl veneer had worn off. "I can drive back to San Francisco tonight. My boyfriend doesn't have a car so he can't come out here, but I don't need rescuing. I can take care of myself."

"It's all set," Devon said, as he and Edwina approached us. "Alicia, you can stay at Ms. Sharp's tonight, just to be on the safe side."

"It's not all set," I said.

At the same time, Alicia said, "Oh jeez, what a ducking mess. Okay. One night. I'm going to go home and get my stuff as soon as we're back, though."

"Of course," Edwina said. Devon nodded and went back to the truck.

"Why did you say it wasn't all set, Sal?" Edwina said to me.

I rolled my eyes. "Never mind."

"Because I don't want to stay with you, but as long as the chief cop is standing there I'm gonna pretend I will. I don't want police trouble."

"Let's go," Edwina said. "We can talk it over in the car. But it is for the best."

#

Once in the car, Edwina made short work of Alicia's protests. "The guy in the other cubicle, the one where we could smell the puke? You know who that was, Alicia?"

"No, because no one tells me anything."

"It was Justin March. You know who he is? Was?"

"Did he die?"

"Yep. Poisoned, just like your dad. Probably the same poison, probably the same poisoner. So, you know who Justin March was?"

"Of course. He's the health inspector, the guy who kept shutting down my dad's truck, for no reason, just to get a payoff. He shut down my godmother's truck, same thing, but not money. Duck only knows what he was getting from *Happy Tacky*."

We all digested this.

"Wait," Alicia said. "So he's dead? He's the guy who died?"

"Yeah."

"Oh my ducking god. Dad's gonna be so—" She burst into tears.

Edwina drove the last five miles in silence.

#

"Do you want me to drop you off first, Sal? Before we get Alicia's stuff?"

Alicia sniffed in the tiny back seat where she was curled like a cooked shrimp, a seatbelt, likely ineffectively, crossing her torso and shins.

"It's close to Sal's house, but from here we can stop first at my," she swallowed, "dad's house and then take the left off Peaches onto Second. I'll be a minute, at most. I haven't even unpacked much of my bag. All I did was clean."

That poor girl.

We pulled up in front of one of the small stucco houses that lined the streets well away from the tourist area. Often two or three to a lot, they had dry dirt yards, some with gravel, an occasional old palm tree shedding its skin and fronds onto the sidewalk in front.

The Sanchez home was in the front part of the lot, and I could glimpse two other houses behind it, all three of them white with blue shutters, all well-tended. The shutters to her home were open, as were the windows, just as August had described. I could smell the vomit from the car.

I frowned. How had no one in the other two houses smelled it? Heard anything?

"Yeah, it's bad," Alicia said, climbing out from the back after I opened my door.

"Yeah, it is," I said. "But how come none of the neighbors noticed?"

She stopped. "Good question. Since Maribel and Pat live in this one, here, so close, didn't they smell anything? I mean, I can see not calling the cops, we never do, you know, even with some of my classmates on the force, it's still a pretty ingrained habit from before, back when the old chief was here." She shuddered.

"I'm sure that Luke Aureliano has interviewed them," I said.

"But at least they would have called an ambulance. Maybe that would have saved him."

She opened the door, not using a key. I glanced back at Edwina, sitting in the car looking at her phone. For a journalist she wasn't exactly curious.

That reminded me.

"Where do Amparo and Arturo live?"

"If you go out Second, where your house is, and before you get to Peaches, you make a left, away from town, about three blocks. A block from August and his parents." She looked distracted. "Like, three blocks from here."

The geography of the town, with its bending roads that snaked to avoid the Valley River, still eluded me.

"You're two and a half blocks down that way." She pointed in the opposite direction I would have guessed. "But of course, you can cut through on Peaches."

Of course. No matter where you were going, you could cut through on Peaches.

Alicia went into the bathroom to get the few things she had taken from her bag. She had done a good job of cleaning, but there was a big, man-size stain on the carpet in front of the TV and of course, the place reeked. The bathroom must have been a nightmare, as Silvestre Sanchez struggled with the onset of symptoms, before returning to the small living room and collapsing.

I looked out the window. Although it was now past midnight, there were street lights that lit the outside. Streetlights off the tourist drag were a rarity in Simpato, but there was one just to the left of this set of houses. The front yard was lit fairly well, and anyone outside would have been pretty visible.

I thought back: August had rolled by around six on Thursday evening, while it was still light, and rang out his horn. He said he looked at the window, which was open, as, no doubt, were the shutters. There he saw Amparo and Silvestre, and while he hadn't been detailed, he had suggested they were either having sex or at least making out.

The living room, smaller than mine, was much wider away from the window than it was long. The couch was along the wall next to the window, facing the TV, as would be expected. The TV faced the window. They couldn't have been on the couch, then, because they would have been shielded from view from the window by the wall that ran along the front, even if August had gotten out of his truck and walked up the drive.

What would have been visible from the window was *not* the couch, it was the floor in front of the TV.

Silvestre and Amparo had to have been on the floor.

These were not young people.

I tried to imagine myself making whoopie down on the carpet, a greenish, short-pile wall-to-wall, with, no doubt, a concrete slab below. Nope. Especially not with a couch handy.

Alicia emerged from the bathroom, pale and sad. "Pretty awful, isn't it?" I nodded. "The cops or whoever did a decent job of getting the worst of it, but it was gross. I guess I'll have to hire a service or something."

Something about that comment bothered me. I tried to tease it out but it was after midnight, and it had been a very long day.

I went with the obvious. "Or rip out the carpet."

"That. I'll have to paint it, too, before I sell it, so I might as well do it all."

"Your dad owned, then." I said it as a statement, hoping to avoid my surprise. "I wonder how the parcel is divided for ownership."

She shrugged. "Some kind of homeowners' association. I don't know, I'll ask my—" She stopped. Then she swore, a real, non-duck-substitute obscenity.

She sighed. "I guess that's another thing I'll have to find out."

"Come on, let's let you get some rest."

She nodded passively, and pulled the door shut behind me.

"Not locking it?"

"Nah, there's no crime in Simpato.

CHAPTER TEN

I awoke to a beautiful Simpato Sunday. The bells at Saint Cuthbert were ringing, and the big campana at the monastery was answering back. Though the Little Sisters of the Earth held their unusual services on Saturday, they rang the big bell almost as an assertion of their validity on Sunday. Except, of course, that they weren't really a religion. Or, depending on how you defined religion, anything was.

I could see the liquid amber trees outside, glowing in the morning light as the sun illuminated their tops. It had taken a few weeks for me to adjust to the trees and western-facing bedroom, as my old room in my beautiful, spacious, and luxurious condo in San Francisco had faced east, with a distant view of the Bay Bridge.

A condo bought with Saul's fraudulent activities, I reminded myself. Fraudulent activities that had not only gotten me suspended—only twelve days left to go—but had possibly saddled me with some horrific tax liability. As soon as I got up I'd make a note to call one of my colleagues, a specialist in family law taxation. I was not, repeat *not*, losing my parents' house because of him.

All that thinking got my blood pumping, and lying in bed, looking at the blue, sunlit sky was no longer an option. Once showered and dressed, I took a legal pad and started making lists.

On the first, I put Legal: *tax lawyer, how is Sanchez property owned, how you get ahold of arsenic*. Things I needed to look up, maybe send an email.

On the second I put People I needed to see: *Sister Marigold, Amparo, Mikey.*

I made a third list: *Devon, Carinna*, and oh! Feathers. What was her name? *Tiffany.* People I actually wanted to see. Smiling, I put *Mikey* on that list, too.

And then a fourth: *Ashley, Victoria, Amparo.* People Justin March was known or presumed to have slept with.

There was someone missing from the list, but I didn't know where to put him. Jack Partridge seemed to weave a common thread among the groups: married or divorced or divorcing Victoria; Mikey and Arturo's employer; had a beef with Justin March because maybe March was sleeping with Jack's wife, and March allegedly reported that Victoria was abusing him—Jack, that is. Also, a nasty, antisemitic coke user. So no, definitely not going on the want-to-see list. But he was important somehow. I added him to the Legal list, for lack of a better placement.

Oh, Alicia. I needed to add her somewhere.

And Ernesto (Nate) Carreras, shut down by Justin March, amazingly just yesterday.

To be consistent, I also listed all the Council members and all the truck owners. Odd, I thought, Siggy Segismundo was the only "winner" not yet in business, and with a prime spot by the fountain outside the City Offices, no less. Surely without a truck he should not have been given a spot. It should have gone to Amparo and her Tacos *Buen Día.*

In the Venn diagram, nearly anyone could end up in the center.

#

I reviewed my list while I sipped my coffee. Now that I got coffee from the same source that the police station used, the father of young officer Sergio Gallego, I was well-supplied with delicious brew every day. Gallego Roastery definitely had the richest beans in the county. And best of all, there were no duck puns involved.

Luna had found a shaft of sunlight that conveniently crossed my thigh, and had curled herself onto me, efficiently both sleeping and shedding long white cat hair all over my pants.

I pulled my phone to me and texted Devon. He answered right away, *we let her go this morning around four*. I looked at the time, just barely ten. Too early to go badger Amparo. *Get anything interesting?*

I'll see you at four, he replied. I thumbs-upped the answer, and I got a "recipient has turned off notifications for text messages." Okay, politely blocked.

After checking on Alicia, who apparently was deep on the phone with her boyfriend and showing no signs of wanting to talk to Edwina, I thought about who had useful contact with Amparo besides Alicia and, of course, August.

Right. Sister Marigold, who, as Tiffany from Feathers said, was no more of a nun than either of us were. She had rushed off right after the drawing at the flagpole on Friday, taking unfair advantage of her long legs to follow Amparo, while I'd been waylaid by August.

And Tiffany, who wanted to have a glass of wine, seemed to have a scoop on Marigold.

#

I unceremoniously dumped Luna off my leg, brushed half a cat's worth of hair off, and put my shoes on. A walk to the monastery to track down Marigold, nee Margo Schwartz, was in order. And I was going to get her cell phone number this time.

It was truly gorgeous out, nearing the mid-seventies this morning, with a perfect blue sky. I looked over at Mount

Santabella, to the northeast of town, its sides still green from the winter rains but showing streaks of yellowing as the grasses dried. Pock-marked with old mining entrances, it could loom with menace on an grey day, but not on this brilliant May morning.

At the bottom of the mountain, lying like a carpet at its feet, were rows and rows of grapevines, deep green now, and rising a little way up the foothills. On the right I could see a bit of the main road to Cragstown snaking up the side of the mountain, and the path across the mountain where the vines stopped.

I slowed my stride, taking more care with my steps, as so many of the sidewalks here were treacherous: narrow, with roots growing up under the paving, making shards of cement stick up like palisades in some places, and leaving holes for ankle-turning in others.

I picked my way up the rest of the block and approached the Little Sisters of the Earth home. Sure enough, open for business, marginal though it was on this Sunday, was *La Sabrosa*, with Nate and his daughter, Ernestina, diligently making tacos and burritos for those who wanted them.

Ernestina smiled at me. "You're the newspaper lady, right?" I nodded back. "I want to be a reporter," she added. She wasn't the least big apologetic, as I would have been at the age of, what, thirteen?

"Looks like you're off to a good start, then," I said, quickly adding in case she thought I was being sarcastic, given that she was rolling a burrito as she spoke, "translating at the City Council meeting. Civic engagement is a great way to start." I sounded like a clueless, childless, middle-aged spinster lecturing a "young person."

Well, I wasn't a spinster, anyway. But she took it well. She handed the burrito to a waiting customer, a man in shiny pants and a collar shirt, who thanked her in Spanish and continued his walk back home from the "real" church, St. Cuthbert's, on the other side of downtown.

"Lot of people come after Mass," Ernestina volunteered. "It would have been nice to score the spot at the fountain, since it's only two blocks up from the church, so there's business all week. But oh well."

Perceptive kid.

"Anyone from the Little Sisters buy anything?" I asked.

"A few, earlier. This is a better spot, we're finding out, on Saturday when they have their Mass."

"Live and learn," I said. "Take care."

"Be a duck!" she replied.

At no point did Nate even look at me. And nowhere was the shut-down tag that Justin March had forced on him yesterday.

#

I faced the massive front doors of the monastery, a full-block-long dark green building only minimally set back from the sidewalk, placed for greater dominance and grandeur. This had once been a real convent, with an elementary school attached, but had served the Little Sisters of the Earth for over a decade. I knew the doors would be locked unless the Sisters were open to visitors. Otherwise the preferred entry was around the side, by way of the gardens.

The doors to the monastery were indeed shut and locked. Perhaps they were enjoying a day of rest. I slipped around to the right side of the building. I was familiar with the side entrance, and it wasn't, technically, wrong for me to try it, but I felt eyes on me the whole time. Guiltily, I looked over my shoulder. Sure enough, Ernestina was watching me closely. I waved.

The path on the right side of the building was lined with flower beds. Purple and pink hyacinths, blooming in a carpet of sweet alyssum, gave off an overwhelmingly sweet aroma. Behind the screen of trees up ahead, I could faintly hear the gurgle of the Valley River, but only if I listened for it.

An iron bench flanked by two little wrought-iron chairs painted white, and a matching table, marked the end of the path. From there I went left, and as I neared the back patio the river was totally drowned out by the screeching of children on a playground, invisible thanks to plantings, just beyond the fence that marked the edge of the monastery's territory. I knew all this, having explored the back of the building with unfortunate thoroughness earlier in the spring. Now there were no signs of the frightening events that had transpired barely steps from here.

At last I came to the little back entrance to the building, an unassuming single door with a standard knob and fading light green paint. On either side of the door were windows, now with proper drapes, that I knew from prior visits hid the kitchen on the left, the baths on the right.

I tried the knob, and to my surprise it turned and I pulled the door open. I was greeted with a squeal. A woman, presumably one of the Little Sisters, emerged from the bath area with only a towel and her glasses on.

I jumped back. "Sorry," I said. "The door was open ..."

"Of course it was," she said sharply. "No one locks their doors in Simpato. What do you want?"

She held the towel up with one hand, and gestured at the door with the other. She was inviting me to leave.

"I'm looking for Sister Marigold," I said.

"Not here."

"What do you mean? Is she out?"

"Look, I know who you are. You're Sal, the Keeper, and Mother Sassafras is crazy about you, but we don't need you letting yourself into our house. Marigold is out, she isn't here, and you aren't going to be, either."

I was nonplussed. "I'm sorry," I said again. "I should have knocked."

"Yup," she said. "Bye."

"Could you at least tell Marigold that I —"

"Bye."

I heard the lock click when the door shut behind me.

#

As I came out the front of the building, Ernestina was still there, still watching me. "Are you going to be one of those pretend nuns too?" she asked.

"No," I said. Then, in spite of my conscience, I asked, "Did you see the tall nun, the one that calls herself Sister Marigold, who's also a reporter, did you see her go out?"

Ernestina giggled. Nate shot her a quelling look and she stopped. "You mean the Jewish lady one?"

It was my turn to be quelled. Or dumbfounded.

"Sorry," she said, mistaking my surprise for offense. "I'm not sure how you're supposed to say that. I didn't mean to offend."

"No, no," I said. "That's perfectly fine, I know that it's awkward." She looked shy. "Uncomfortable," I added. "When people are different. I'm also a Jewish lady."

"I know," Ernestina said. "Can I still be a reporter if I'm not? My dad says all the newspapers are Jewish."

My heart fell. *Even here.* "You can still be a reporter. And your dad is not correct." I didn't want to say *wrong*, I wanted her to learn. "That's just something some people who don't know anything about Jewish people say."

"Yeah, I know. We learned about prejudice in school. We're not supposed to judge, but, you know, people still feel it. Like with Señor Silvestre, his ancestors—"

"*Callate*!" Shut up. Nate grabbed Ernestina by the shoulder. "Go away, lady," he said to me in English. "Leave my girl alone."

I stared a moment, then realized that I would cause more trouble for Ernestina if I stayed. "Okay, I'm leaving," I said in Spanish. "Your daughter is very smart. She'll do well in the world."

I was walking away but I heard him say, "Only if she keeps her mouth shut.

CHAPTER ELEVEN

I walked back home, the desire to text Tiffany ebbing as I contemplated Ernestina's comments. So I was the "Jewish lady"? I didn't realize anyone had noticed. And that nasty old trope about the media was alive and well, even in this small town. But—and this was the strangest thing of all—how did this relate to Silvestre Sanchez?

Unless, and it *was* possible, he was a descendant of Crypto-Jews, those secret Jews in Spain, Portugal, and throughout Mexico and Peru, who maintained their religion despite superficial conversions to Catholicism "at the point of a sword" during the Inquisition. This had been a topic of much study recently, and I had learned about it in passing in college, but I'd never really given it much thought.

At the moment I couldn't see how it was relevant to delve into anyone's religion. I took out my phone and texted Tiffany.

#

We met outside of the Duck Bill, which, being Sunday, was open until three. We grabbed one of the sidewalk tables, and I ordered a tuna sandwich and an iced coffee. Tiffany, dressed today in a lime-green shift dress that was a little tighter than it needed to be, adjusted her seat to accommodate her short skirt. She wore grey flats, and her earrings, again dangling almost to her shoulders beneath her warm brown hair, were grey and green stripes. I suppose that owning Feathers made her a fashion icon.

Tiffany ordered a glass of chardonnay and a bagel with smoked salmon and cream cheese.

"I'm so excited to finally meet you," she said. "I mean, not as a customer, not as the Keeper, but, you know, as a human!"

"Likewise," I agreed, though I had ulterior motives. I sipped my iced coffee. "It's hard to get to know folks here. They're all friendly, but they're not particularly welcoming. Unless you went to Simpato High or have been here for twenty years, you're a *new* person."

She nodded. "I know. I've been here about thirteen years or so. I came with my ex, when he got a job at one of the wineries, and after about three years I was bored silly, and lonely to boot. My husband's job kept him late every night, well, more than his job but I didn't know that until later ... That's when I opened Feathers. Just to do something. And your mom was so nice."

I took in what she said. "If I stay—I can see why I'm not being actively befriended, I mean, I may be gone in a month—it will be a while before I'm accepted."

"Why wouldn't you stay? I mean, besides that compared to San Francisco it's boring as heck here."

I smiled. "I may miss the nightlife and culture of San Francisco, but I'm sure not bored. So, your ex worked at a winery? Which one?"

She named a large, world-renowned one. "That was right after Jack Partridge left to run Perdiz."

Here was an unexpected opening. "Really? I thought it was his family's vineyard."

"It was. His dad, old Sangiacomo the first, inherited it from *his* father, and it was just growers then. They didn't make wine, just grew the grapes and sold them. After the *Judgment of Paris*, you know, where a Napa wine won the competition, everyone in all three grape-growing counties got into the act. Napa, Sonoma, and Valley all went nuts. Sangiacomo Senior opened Perdiz, and when he died, he was nearly eighty, Jack took over. He still sells most of his grapes, but he makes about 5,000 cases of wine a year. So, by winemaking terminology, a 'very small winery.'" She made finger-quotes.

I filed all that away, careful not to show excessive interest in Jack, or, by extension, Mikey. "Well, it's pretty good wine. I think I saw Jack in your store this week? I was buying a gorgeous scarf."

She laughed, and I could see a little blush on her cheeks. "He was just reminding me of the winery dinner. There's a few of those in-the-industry dinners at different wineries, some of them really big, but he holds one twice a year, with select invited guests, and he was reminding me to RSVP. I guess I'm select now."

I nodded. "I haven't gotten an invite. But of course, I just got here. When's the dinner?"

"Oh, not for another month."

"Well, no harm then, I may not be here anymore by then. So, you said you had something you wanted to tell me about? When we had that silly Keeper session last night?"

"I don't think the Keeper sessions are silly," she said, frowning.

I tried to reel it back in. "Not silly, no, you're right. It's just the ritual, you know, turning the chairs and putting out the tissues …"

She nodded. "Okay, I can see that. Well, nothing really that important. Just, you know, I was worried because I heard that the cops think that the food truck guy was poisoned, so I was wondering if it was safe to eat at them, if they're poisoning one another."

That was a quick way to ruin a business. I hadn't thought of that. "I haven't heard that. Just that he may have died of a poison, but I have no idea if it was an intentional poisoning or he was experimenting with mushrooms, or what."

"Really?" Tiffany raised her lovely eyebrows. "So maybe no one poisoned him? Boy the rumors do fly."

"I guess we'll know more when the police finish their investigation." I sounded prim. "Rumors run wild in this town." Now I sounded like a schoolmarm.

"Some rumors are true," she said a little self-righteously. "I'm not sure how to say this, but you know that there are rumors that the health inspector is demanding bribes from not only the trucks, but also—it's just a rumor—but from Jack Partridge, too. To keep his tasting and pairing room open. And like I told you, Justin March bought a present, and he said it was for Victoria, Jack's wife, at Feathers. I helped him pick it out. I mean, why would he tell me that, unless he was doing it to get at Jack?"

Obviously, the news of Justin's death last night had been kept quiet. Tiffany was still talking about him in the present tense. She was looking right at me, daring me to ask. So I did. "Did you tell Jack?"

She smirked. "No. I think Justin took care of that himself. Kind of twisting the knife, you know what I mean?" She held her hand up in horns.

"How did you hear that?" This was beyond rumors.

"Like I tried to tell you, Marigold, Margo Schwartz, who is definitely not a nun, is trying to get the story on Jack. What's he running there? And she came across the bit about Jack, and Victoria and Justin, and she asked me. But that was a couple of years ago, not now. So who knows?"

"Margo's been here that long?"

"Oh gosh, no. The supposed affair was a few years ago. And then, I think that Victoria told Justin to go duck himself, and he called the cops and said that she was abusing Jack. To embarrass Jack, since men are all about their pride."

That much I'd heard already, but now it fit in. "I guess Justin left Jack alone after that."

Tiffany laughed out loud at that. "My goodness, for a lawyer you're sure innocent. Margo's still investigating Jack, and so she's also talking to Justin. You know, you should talk to her. Straight from the horse's mouth, right? Or get the straight quack, right from the duck."

#

Back home, I settled into the big chair and swung my legs over the side. Luna jumped right up, meowed cat-food-breath into my face, and settled into my lap.

Sunday afternoons tended to drag, but I had plenty to think about. I was not some amateur sleuth in a novel trying to solve a murder ahead of the police. I was an outsider in a town in which my parents had been important and beloved residents. I was the Keeper of Secrets despite my best intentions. And I knew things because people talked to me.

They always had. It was an incredible asset in my profession. Saul used to marvel at it. "Why do they tell you these things? And they don't tell me?" For one thing, because I asked questions. For another, because I listened to the answers. Though no one knew how to make money like Saul.

I checked my email. It was Sunday, so of course there was no answer from my tax lawyer. Did I want to stay in this town I'd never really be a part of? Did I want to be the Keeper of Secrets, Sal DeVine, girl reporter for a weekly local paper, estates lawyer to the landed gentry, occasional date of the Chief of Police? Or did I sell up, take the money, go visit my sister in Hawai'i, and learn to read Tarot cards?

I woke up in my chair, sweaty from the afternoon sun streaming in the gap in the window with the sheet on in. Luna dug her claws into my thigh, then jumped down like she'd never met me. As she walked away with her tail in the air, I remembered what I had been thinking of just as I fell asleep.

Arsenic.

I spent the rest of the afternoon researching what arsenic poisoning looked like. Evidently it was relatively rare now, but had been quite common before arsenic was banned as a rat poison and eliminated from wallpaper, dyes, and cosmetics.

Yes, ladies had used arsenic for that strawberries-and-cream complexion, for those limpid, pupil-dilated eyes, and for the Paris Green wallpaper that graced bedrooms and boudoirs.

Arsenic also occurs naturally in our soil, our drinking water, and our wine. And it was quite the popular insecticide in the grape-growing world until the government put its kibosh on it. That wasn't to say it was no longer used, just no longer allowed.

Rice, wine, beer, water, all those staples, contain permitted levels of arsenic, I read, so determining poisoning wasn't as simple as a blood or urine test for its presence. The amount certainly mattered.

Arsenic and Old Lace, that popular film and staple of community theaters for a generation, involved a number of homicidal maniacs in an old Mayflower family, including the charming Aunties who poisoned elderly men with a cocktail that weighed in heavily with arsenic—though it included cyanide for good measure as well as efficiency and speed. As in speed of death. Arsenic was imprecise, and took a while.

Most people who were poisoned with arsenic evidently survived, because rather than being instant, like the Aunties knew, hence the cyanide, it could take multiple attempts, it involved unpleasant reactions that were bound to draw attention, including, as Justin March and Silvestre Sanchez displayed, rice-water diarrhea, vomiting, and time.

This overt display of being poisoned allowed hospitals to figure out what it was, and to institute the extraordinarily unpleasant treatment of chelation. That was a nasty-smelling injection into the muscles every four hours, and the contents would apparently bind to the arsenic and shepherd it out of the body.

Arsenic poisoning being rare, not every hospital knew to test for it, not every hospital *could* test for it, and finally, most small hospitals couldn't treat it. Luckily, unless the poisoning was strong, a healthy human could process it, ugly though that would be, and survive.

I was pushing far beyond my high-school knowledge of science, as well as my tolerance for anything more about excretion, but it looked like Sanchez and March, healthy though they may have been, had gotten quite a dose.

My appetite thus completely squelched, I opened a bottle of wine. Yes, it may contain arsenic, but it also contained wine. I smiled. It was one of the Perdiz bottles I'd gotten after my visit to Mikey. They did make a mighty fine cabernet.

I stopped before I took my first sip. Of course. Any old, old vineyard would have arsenic-laced old, old rat poison, ancient mold suppressant, probably lying around in a run-down shed somewhere. Not in the gorgeous winery's tasting room, with its fountain and its gold stone patio, but in some outbuilding near the fields.

What about that fountain? It was natural, Mikey had said, a local spring like so many in the area. I pulled open my computer, and after some extensive digging found the average mineral composition for the local groundwater. Sure enough, there was plenty of arsenic in it already, so most local folks probably had a resistance to it, to a degree. I mean, enough arsenic would kill anyone.

And wine had it, too. I drank it anyway.

All this information bounced around in my head, along with the business of Margo Schwartz, Jack Partridge, Justin March, Amparo and Arturo, Silvestre Sanchez and his daughter Alicia, Nate Carreras and his daughter Ernestina, Carinna and her daughter, whose name I didn't know but had once dated Mikey, Mikey himself, and of course, August.

Oh, and Ashley. The rest of the Council couldn't be involved in this, could they? Why would they want Silvestre Sanchez dead? I could see how they might not want Justin March sticking his unpleasantness into the trucks, if they were in favor of the trucks, but even if they were against them? Not worth killing him over this. Cindy Scott was against the trucks but in favor of the temporary permits, and Garth Mendez was against the temporary measure and I hadn't gotten a read on his view of the trucks in general, and they were both running for mayor.

One other fact stood out: no one seemed to know that Justin March was dead.

I checked the time. It was three thirty, too late to go hunting Amparo, since Devon was dropping by at four. Better would be to tell him all this, and see what he learned from interrogating her himself.

#

Devon's Jeep was pulling into my driveway when my text went off. Mikey's name and number popped up. *Busy tasting again today, but I'm off tomorrow. If you'd like, we can go somewhere. Maybe out of Valley County!*

Who cooked? I texted back.

Wow. So I guess the answer is no?

Sorry! Sure. Tomorrow sounds great.

I'm glad. And I did. Amparo left enough from yesterday's feast, so I made some knockout pork carnitas. Easy enough to do once the hard work is done. I'll save some for you tomorrow after I eat my fill for dinner! You do eat pork?

I sent him a piggy emoji with a heart. I stood my ground on shell-fish. *When it comes to bacon the spirit may be willing ...*

Glad to know the flesh is weak, he replied with a wink. Hmmhmm.

But no time for that now, as Devon tapped on the door.

#

We couldn't have wine since Devon was going on duty at eight tonight, but we could actually go out to dinner, for once. "Let's get out of Simpato," I said, and felt my color rise as I thought of Mikey's suggestion that we go out of Valley County. I hoped he didn't mean Crags County.

Devon mistook my blush. "Don't want to be seen with me locally?"

"Don't be an idiot," I said. "Everyone in this town refers to you as my boyfriend—"

"They do?" he was astonished.

"And I think I've said *not my boyfriend* more times than I've said my own name. Going out of town for that reason would really be closing the barn door. I just thought, in the six weeks I've been here I've left Simpato maybe three times, and one of those times it was to get a burner phone up in Cragstown!"

"Okay, okay," Devon said, holding up a hand. "Point taken. There's a really nice restaurant on the mountain road towards Santa Florita. I'll call them."

We left shortly afterwards, seeing as Devon had to go on duty at eight, and would be on the all-night shift. In a small town, even the chief took Sunday night.

Devon drove. I hadn't been in his Jeep before, and where I'd expected it to be uncomfortable it was actually reasonably smooth, and the plastic windows kept the cab relatively warm. It was noisy, though, and I had to raise my voice to be heard. That kept the conversation to a minimum. I looked out the window instead, seeing the other side of Mount Santabella.

There were vineyards up here, too, steep as it was, but also sheep, horses, and eventually, as we crested the mountain and started down the other side, there were cows and cheesemaking farms. "It's pretty up here," I said.

"Closer to San Francisco, too," Devon answered.

"Really? How so?"

"The freeway is right down there." Sure enough, the freeway that went straight to the Golden Gate Bridge appeared, a thick grey snake through the green. "Here we are."

We pulled into a gravel driveway, and up to a red barn-like building. *Matanzas* it said on the awning. "Killings?" I asked. "Odd name for a restaurant."

Devon shook his head. "Is that what that means? It's the name of a river."

The owner, a short man with iron-grey hair and a long mustache, greeted Devon by name, clapped him on the back, and then looked questioningly at me. "This is Sal," Devon said, and in his voice it was clear that he wasn't going to say more.

"Okay," said the man, "Sal, come in. I'm Steve."

"Nice to meet you," I said, and followed him to a table for two by the window. We were the only patrons here, though there were about eight or ten other tables that I could see, set with white tablecloths, heavy silverware and sparkling wine glasses.

"You have the whole restaurant," Steve said. "We don't open for another half hour."

He handed me a wine list, and both of us menus. My eyes widened at the prices.

"Have whatever you want," Devon said. "Everything here is delicious."

I ordered the veal, with a glass of Riesling. Devon chose the beef Wellington, with a glass of sparkling water. Neither of us picked the duck.

"So where's Alicia now?" I asked him as we sipped and waited. We spoke quietly. That was one disadvantage of an empty restaurant.

"She's decided to stay at your friend Edwina's until her dad's body has been released. I'm glad, because she's safer there than alone."

"You think she's in danger? Because I don't," I added.

I could see Devon suppressing the urge to tell me that I wasn't entitled to an opinion on the subject. Maybe he was right.

"I don't know," he said finally. "Something about this whole situation is so wrong—not just poisoning, of course—"

"Poison?" Steve arrived at our table holding two plates.

"For a class Sal is taking," Devon said smoothly. "This looks delicious."

As Steve put Devon's beef Wellington down before him, in its golden pastry crust, I thought of the empanadas Mikey had served me. Not so different, in that empanadas had been the result of European influence, for sure.

Where else had I seen beef empanadas?

"Sal? Dinner's going to get cold."

I tucked into the veal, prepared in a classic piccata, with tiny, crisp potatoes, and baby carrots. It was divine.

I looked around for Steve, but fortunately it was now five-thirty, and the first reservations were arriving, some with bottles of local wine to be opened, others dressed for a special night out. I looked down at my unremarkable clothing. I was glad I had thought to take the lovely scarf I'd gotten at Feathers with me.

That reminded me. "Do you know the lady, Tiffany, who runs the clothing store? Feathers?"

Devon smiled. "Oh yes, we all know Tiffany. She's, um, very friendly. Outgoing, if you will."

I took that in. "Well, I had lunch with her today. And she gave me an earful about Justin March, along with Jack and Victoria." I filled him in.

Now his dinner was getting cold.

"That changes the perspective on March's death, doesn't it?" he said. "But I can't see how it's related to Sanchez."

Nor could I. Unless … "What did you get from Amparo last night?"

"That she wants a lawyer. The only thing she'd tell us was that she's Sanchez's wife's cousin, not his. I guess otherwise it would be incest, if she was messing around with Sanchez."

"If it was first cousins, I guess. But the term is thrown around pretty liberally, in many cultures. There's brother-cousins, which are close cousins, first cousins, children of your parents' siblings, but there are others, more like second or third or once-removed or whatever, that are still cousins."

"Back to Justin March, though," Devon redirected the conversation. "It was odd," he dropped his voice, "but while both he and Silvestre Sanchez had arsenic in their blood, and lots of it, and even though Sanchez had very little left of anything in his digestive system, what they did find was beef, and remnants of some bread, in his intestines—"

"Jeez, Devon! At dinner?"

"Sorry, you've been talking about the murders so I didn't think you'd turn squeamish on me. Anyway, March had pork."

CHAPTER TWELVE

Monday morning was newspaper day. Eager to see my story in the *Quack*, with my own by-line, I jumped out of bed full of energy. I threw on some sweats and nearly skipped the four blocks to the Duck Shop, where the papers were available for free in a bin outside the store.

I grabbed one and bought a French cruller donut while I was at it. Not as good as the coffee shop across from the library, but at eight in the morning it would do. "Nice writing," Andie said from her check stand. There was no privacy in Simpato.

I sat on my deck, coffee, what was left of my cruller, and the paper in hand. We'd gotten a whole page. There were the photos, with my two-part story underneath. The tale of the Council meeting was under the photo of Nate's truck. It looked shiny and clean, the monastery's door and cupola were in the background, and the silhouette of Sister Calendula on the side gave the shot a charming, churchy quality.

The drawing at the flagpole, complete with mention of the tragic death of one of the applicants, was contained in the second story. There were no photos of the flag pole event—I had not thought to take one, and in any event, I had no confidence that I would produce anything more than headless Council members, their feet near the fountain.

Beneath the two stories was a terrific shot of the *Buen Día* truck. Carinna was holding a giant burrito in her hand, and had a mouth-full-grin on her face that radiated enjoyment. At the window, even clearer in the sharpened enlargement by the paper, you could see Mikey leaning into the window, and Amparo handing him a taco. In the background, the vines stretched to infinity, and on the far left the sign for Perdiz Wines was just visible.

I was so proud, prouder than I was of the stories, which of course left out all the excitement over Nate being shut down the first day. No one's head was cut off, nothing important was blurry. Maybe I could have a new career.

My elation slammed into a wall when I turned the page. There, looking out from the paper, was the photo of the deceased truck owner, Silvestre Sanchez. His straight black hair fell into his face in the picture, and his dark eyes, large and sad, looked into the distance.

I had seen him. He was the man I didn't know, on the bridge, with Nate Carreras, Siggy Segismundo, and Justin March. In the photo I could see the resemblance to Alicia, not just the hair but the intelligent, soulful eyes. Alicia, being a girl in her early twenties, had smooth skin and a softer jaw, but it was clear this was her father. I felt my heart wrench for her.

"Never on Sunday" blasted in my ear and I jumped up, spilling what was left of my coffee as August roared nearly up onto my deck in his truck.

"Sally!" he said, taking the leap from his truck and nearly onto my deck, in one step. "I saw your story. I was waiting to see you out here to come over!"

He was up next to me, sitting down in the chaise lounge, before I could say hello. "I'm glad you saw it," I said.

"Yeah, good job with the pictures. I didn't read the whole story," I knew that already, "but the pictures ... Did you see the picture of Alicia's dad? He looks so sad." I nodded. Not much more was needed from me. "Do you know where Alicia is?"

"I know she's safe," I said. I hoped that wasn't too much.

"I checked every day, she's not at home, and I went over to Amparo's to make sure she hadn't captured her."

"August. This isn't a video game. No one is capturing anyone. And please, please don't go peeking in anyone's windows. You gave yourself a lot of trouble from the last—"

"I wasn't peeking last time. I was looking for Alicia!" He was outraged.

"No, I know. Just stay away from Amparo, okay?"

He huffed. "Well, she wasn't home either. And I knocked politely on her door, I didn't peek. I'm not a pervert."

I soothed him down a bit, and eventually he said, "Are you going to eat the rest of that donut?" I shook my head *no,* and he wolfed it down.

"But I did see that nun, you know, the tall fake one, also go up to Amparo's door, and no one answered her, either."

I sat up straight. "You did? Sister Marigold?" He nodded. "And Amparo didn't come out?"

"Not then, anyway. That Sister hung around a while."

"When was this?" I asked, trying to sound casual.

"Yesterday morning. After I went to try to see Alicia. I know she doesn't always go to church, after her mom died, but if she wanted to I was going to take her …"

Right. "August, do you know why no one is helping Alicia?"

"I'm trying to!"

"I mean, none of the aunties. No one is doing a vigil, or helping her clean, or bringing her food—and Amparo's her godmother. Or trying to set the funeral," I added.

August looked away, out towards Mount Santabella. "No. I don't know the real reason. But like me, everyone always said, *Alicia's different. They're a bad-luck family.* Because of her dad. You know he came from New Mexico, Santa Fe, right?"

I didn't know, and didn't see the relevance, but I let him talk.

"My mom would know. But the people from New Mexico, they're not like us, some of them. And her mom, she was from, you know, California but originally from Mexico, real Mexico not New Mexico, I know they're both real but ..."

"Her mom?" I prompted.

"And Father Jim, he said Alicia could be baptized so I don't know."

#

I helped August get going, encouraging him to stay away from Amparo. Then, as he was pulling out of the drive, I stopped him.

"How come you're not at work?" I asked. "It's Monday."

He grinned. "Parent-teacher conferences! School's closed."

"You're not in school," I answered.

"No, but everyone who can takes it off, because how does your boss know you don't have a kid, and have to go to the kid's school, even if you're not married!" He laughed and honked his horn, both the regular and the "Never on Sunday," and backfired down Second Street. Maybe he *was* a kid.

#

If Amparo had taken off, too, or if she'd poisoned Arturo, along with Justin March and Silvestre Sanchez, it wasn't too big a reach to guess she was going to poison someone else. And that someone else would either be August or Alicia. Or, I realized with a chill, me.

Devon needed to stop her. He said they didn't have the evidence to arrest her, but I knew who would. Margo knew what was going on, I was sure, and of course, all she would think about was her story. I knew that from our last encounter.

I put on some decent clothes, fixed my hair—I had to find a stylist soon—and grabbed my notebook and pen. I needed to talk to Margo, and I needed to do it now.

#

Out in front of the monastery, no surprise, Nate Carrera was parked, his window open, and the aroma of frying tortillas filled the air. Ernestina was with him. Didn't she have school? Oh, right, legit parent-teacher day for her.

"Hard at work, Ernestina?" I said with a smile.

"Hey Mrs. Keeper," she said. "Or maybe Mrs. Reporter, right? I saw the pictures and the stories in the paper! You really got the whole thing, even me translating for my dad!"

She looked so proud, I ignored Nate's near-snarl. "You're a smart girl. You are going to go far. Just take every chance to learn something," I said. "I know it sounds like just teacher-talk, but you know I'm a lawyer, too?"

Her eyes got big. "You're a lady-lawyer, a lady-journalist, *and* the Keeper?" I nodded. "Is that why you don't have kids? Cuz you don't have time?"

Nate looked away but I could see him smirk.

"You *are* smart," I said, determined to ignore him. "And you know what, lots of ladies have kids and do all that. But having kids is up to the ladies. Remember that!"

Take that, Nate Carreras.

I turned my back on *La Sabrosa* and walked to the door of the monastery. If I had to brave the dragon at the back door so be it, but I was going to start at the front. The doors loomed large, and without much expectation I pulled hard on the handle of one of the oak masterpieces. The door swung open on its well-oiled hinges, nearly sending me backwards onto the sidewalk.

I stepped inside, onto the inlaid tile on the floor showing a huge conifer entwined with roses, and sprouting a compass rose, or maybe a clock face, with grapes at noon or north, and green olives, another important Valley crop, at six o'clock south. The atrium and main room soared three stories in front, though I knew that the rest of the building was of simple, two-story standard stucco construction that ran nearly the length of the block.

I looked around for any sign of the Sisters, or of Mother Sassafras, the Superior of the order. Their old-fashioned eco-green habits, complete with wimples and veils, were hard to miss. With very few exceptions, the Sisters were short older women, some as tiny as four-feet-ten. They all bore the names of plants, some more hilarious than others.

At the back of the foyer there were two halls and several doors. One door, I knew, led to a media room, where the Sisters prepared interviews or filmed videos for their socials. No, this wasn't a normal nunnery. They existed to foster ecology, as they saw it, and made films, radio, television, and TikTok style reels to spread their message. That they were also a refuge for older lesbians was really beside the point.

What looked like a rolling pine tree emerged from the media room, too big to be Mother Sassafras but too small to be Sister Marigold. As she trundled towards me I recognized Sister Sorghum, my initial introduction to the sisterhood. When she lifted her powder-white face, light from the cupola reflected off her glasses, and her smile was even more radiant.

"Salvia Divinorum!" she greeted me with the Latin name of the plant I was named for. It was a pun she relished, playing on my married last name of DeVine.

"Sister, how nice to see you," I said.

"Are you here for the press conference? You're early," she added. "It's not till eleven, but you are always welcome here. Your dear mother ..."

I nodded. Yes, she was a fan of my dear mother, the original Keeper, may her memory be for blessing, but Alta Grossman had been lost at sea ten years ago, and very few people still referenced her. A lot of memory was tied up in this town.

But no, I knew nothing about the press conference.

Of course I'd stay for it. "I was hoping to see Sister Marigold, um, before it started."

Sorghum looked troubled. "Yes, Sister Marigold. I was hoping that she was going to get back in time for the conference, as our embedded journalist, you know."

"Oh, did she go out?"

Sister Sorghum looked away. "Perhaps Mother can brief you …"

Something was wrong. "When did you expect Marigold?"

"That's the thing, dear." She pronounced it *deah*, like a real nun. "We didn't know she was going out. She wasn't at dinner last night, and we're not a terribly strict order, as you may recall, though we do have our immutable standards, but we do, of course make exceptions, when the situation warrants it …"

"About Marigold?"

Her eyes narrowed at me behind her goggle-level glasses. "I was getting to that, *deah*. Don't interrupt."

Chastened, as even a nice Jewish girl like me knows we're in the wrong when we're chastened by a nun in full regalia, even if it's a fake nun. I nodded. "Sorry, Sister," I said as well as any properly-raised Catholic, sibilating the esses.

"As I was saying," Sorghum continued, a bit more pointedly than I felt was warranted, "Sister Marigold is freer to come and go than many of the Sisters. We aren't cloistered, of course, and she is a professional journalist who may have to go out chasing a story."

She was giving Marigold more credit than she deserved, but I didn't interrupt this time. We'd get there eventually.

"So when she failed to appear at dinner yesterday, although she hadn't signed out, or told anyone where she was going, which is, indeed, contrary to our customs, I was not worried. But her bedroom was empty last night at eleven, when I retired, and Sister Calendula, who did Matins this morning, said that she had not returned at six."

"Have you tried calling her?" I asked the obvious.

"Straight to voicemail," said another voice, clear and emphatic. I turned to see the aforementioned Sister Calendula, the nun who'd been outside with the food truck on Saturday when Justin closed it down. She was tall, skinny, and much younger than Sassafras, and she held out her cell phone. "I tried a few times, and texted as well. Nothing. So either she doesn't have her phone on, or it's out of juice, or she's just not responding."

"Or something's happened to her," I suggested.

"Oh, don't be silly," Calendula said. "Like what? There's no crime in Simpato."

"Who said anything about a crime? She could have fallen into a mine shaft," I said. Both women looked at me, horrified.

"What an absolutely vile thing to say," Sister Sorghum said, blaming the messenger.

I was glad I didn't say, *maybe she's with a man somewhere, having a good time.* Since I knew from Marigold herself that she didn't play for Team Sappho. Not that she was trustworthy, but in this case it wouldn't have been worth the lie.

"Well, I came to see her, so I guess I'll be going," I said.

"Oh no, please stay for the press conference," Sorghum said. "We would love to have a friendly face in the crowd."

"If there is a crowd," Calendula said.

I had to come clean at this point. "What's the topic?"

Sorghum chuckled. "I could tell you didn't know. It's the food trucks, of course. Since we're practically sponsoring the idea of having them downtown, we're going to make a presentation on how food trucks are good for the environment."

I didn't say, *that will be a stretch.* I did say, "Sounds like something I'd like to know."

I was surprised to learn that the Order was practically sponsoring the move to have the trucks downtown. I would not have guessed that. I pulled myself back to the immediate present. "Sister Calendula, perhaps you can give me Sister Marigold's phone number, so if I can reach her I can get the particular questions I had for her today answered."

"I don't know," Calendula said. "That's kind of like a HIPAA violation, isn't it? To give out a phone number without permission?"

"No, not legally." HIPAA, the Health Information Portability Act, was used as a shield for all kinds of things it definitely didn't say, all the time. No, the receptionist at the doctor's office didn't have to call an elderly lady by her first name; no, burying a phrase in a five-page, single-spaced disclosure document that allowed a hospital or doctor's office to sell your information for ads to their subsidiaries wasn't based on HIPAA.

"Well, you're the lawyer."

"I'll defend you if Marigold sues."

Calendula still looked affronted, but she did give me the number. I entered it into my phone. "If I track her down, I'll ask her to call you right away," I assured her. "And if anything's wrong, I will definitely let you know."

She appeared mollified, and I quickly texted Edwina to let her know I would be covering whatever was about to happen at the monastery.

Thanks, she texted back. *I'd forgotten all about that, what with my babysitting job.*

Sorry, I texted. *Blame the police. How is she?*

Sleeping again. I think she's more traumatized than she knows.

Let her sleep, I replied. *Devon may call you and he'll definitely need to see her.*

Way ahead of you. He called at eight this morning. He said he'd be here at noon. Have fun with the Sisters.

I sent back a green-faced barf emoji, not because of the barf, of course, but the color. And then I thought of all the vomit, and felt a little sick myself.

#

To my relief I saw a couple of men walk in, one holding an old-fashioned steno pad and a pen, the other an e-tablet. I didn't recognize either of them, but Sister Sorghum approached them happily.

"Welcome, gentlemen. Let me escort you to the men's balcony." They must have known the drill, because they didn't object. It was sort of the opposite of an Orthodox Jewish arrangement: instead of a women's balcony, with a curtain for modesty, so they could enjoy and learn at the service without distracting the men from worship or compromising their purity, the Little Sisters of the Earth had elaborate balcony seating for men in their "chapel," a converted Catholic lady-chapel or shrine to the Virgin Mary. Up above the women, the men could sit and listen to a service, but could not speak. The women all sat below, on the main floor.

"I thought you'd have the conference here in the foyer, or in the conference room," I said. "Why the chapel?"

Calendula grinned. "We're going to really put on a show. Let the whole county know how we support the trucks, how good they are for our environment, and how this movement should spread across all of Valley County." She paused, frowned.

"Though now, without Sister Marigold, I'm not sure we'll have quite the fanfare. She is such a bold speaker."

That she was.

The large front doors opened and the entire City Council streamed in, along with candidate Ashley Sage. Garth Mendez, wearing an untucked green-striped dress shirt and wrinkled khakis, walked ahead of Matty Buono, who looked like he'd just come from the gym, and they were directed upstairs. The women were left to mill in the foyer. We hadn't yet been invited into the sanctuary.

I approached Cindy Scott, who was standing apart from Ashley Sage and Jessica Alvarez. "What do you think of the monastery getting involved in the truck issue?" I asked.

She bristled, then seemed to remember that I was, at least in some way, connected with the *Quack*. "Citizens have the right and the obligation to be involved in civic affairs," she said sententiously. I blushed, remembering my horribly similar remark to Ernestina Carreras.

Cindy mistook my flush for offense. "Really, though, I'm not sure how they'll tie it in to ecology," she added in a more conversational tone.

"I guess that's why we're here," I said pleasantly.

Ashley came up to us, abandoning Jessica to her lonely fate. She smelled like spa lotion, even as she approached. "So, we're going to find out all about the benefits of the trucks!" she gushed. "The good-for-the-earth sisters are full of surprises."

There was something odd about her phrasing, something unnatural. Then I remembered that she, allegedly, had been sleeping or had slept with Justin March. Did she know he was dead?

"You doing okay?" I asked her gently.

"Sure, couldn't be better. As long as we don't eat from Nate's truck out front, we should be fine."

So she didn't know. Or she was an amazing actress, which was possible.

Before I could pursue the line of thought, Mother Sassafras, in all her four-and-a-half-foot glory, opened the main door to the chapel. "Please, ladies, leave the front two rows empty, but otherwise sit where you'd like. We'll begin the conference shortly."

We filed in, and I noticed that besides the Council members, there was another woman who could be a journalist, with her phone held out to record. Other than the five of us, scattered in the third and fourth rows, there were no other female guests. Up in the balcony there were the four men—two Council, two journalists.

Behind us, I heard a rustling, and turning I saw Carinna enter and sit in the last seat of the back row. I wiggled my fingers at her and she nodded and smiled. I wondered why she was there, and then remembered. Of course. Refreshments.

And as I could see the approaching ranks of green-clad nuns, slipping in the side was Ernestina, Nate's daughter. She slid into the seat next to me. "Practicing to be a reporter," she whispered. I high-fived her.

Then the wave began. As they entered the sanctuary, the nuns, hands folded at their waists and eyes cast down, began to hum. It was the sound of bees, not a tune but a murmur, growing stronger but not really louder, as they made their way to the front. One by one, without altering their tone or looking around, they sorted themselves into the first two rows, remaining standing, still humming.

Then, as if a swarm had turned, some hummed louder, some changed tone, and the sound was nearly visible. It rose, it fell, and now one side was dropping and the other rising, until they met in the harmonic that made the entire air vibrate. It reached a crescendo, then without a visible signal, it stopped. They sat down in unison.

In the silence I could hear my ears still ringing, and my heart beating, my blood flowing in my veins.

I glanced at Ernestina, who stared wide-eyed at the nuns. I let her revel in the weirdness of it all.

At last, Mother Sassafras went up to the dais at the front of the room. There was no altar, no statues, or anything like that, not even the branches of plants that had decorated the front of the room the first time I had visited. This wasn't a service, it was a press conference.

I wondered what fanfare Marigold had been expected to provide.

"Good morning," Mother Sassafras said in her quiet voice. It seemed to travel through the room; the acoustics were excellent. "Thank you for coming to our press conference. I am grateful that we have representatives from the *Quack*," she nodded at me and the men in the balcony craned their necks to see who I was, "the *Valley Dispatch*, the *Marketplace*, and the *Green Times*."

I heard the faintest giggle in the back. That had to be Carinna.

"Sister Pussywillow will make the presentation, we will take questions from you, and our most green and ecological refreshments will be served." She glanced at Ernestina. "Twenty-one and older, of course, for some."

I could barely stand the idea of "Sister Pussywillow," but I was here as press, and I stifled my urge to guffaw as a surprisingly pretty woman, perhaps forty but without seeing her hair it was hard to tell, strode to the dais. I reminded myself that Mother Sassafras had told me, when I first visited the monastery, that they got to choose their own names.

"Hello. I'm Sister Pussywillow." No one laughed. I guess we were all grownups. "You may be wondering how food trucks and the Little Sisters of the Earth tie in together, and how food trucks are good for the environment. After all, we all know that fossil fuels, like gas for trucks and heat sources, are bad, bad, *bad* for the environment. But look at it this way. Imagine you're downtown. You're hungry and it's lunchtime. Let's say you work in the city offices. Name one, just one, restaurant that's worker-affordable. You can't, right? So either you bring your lunch, or you hop in your car, drive the five miles to Valley, and get a bite at a taqueria, a pizzeria, a deli. Then you drive back.

"But it's not just you. Say you work at the downtown hotels. You definitely can't eat at *Schreens*, or at *La Grande*. So you and your co-workers get into one of your cars, good for you for carpooling, yay! And head to the food trucks out by the construction site.

"With the food trucks right here downtown, tourists won't head back down to Valley for their lunch—I mean, they sure aren't going to spend the fortune lunch costs in downtown Simpato when they have dinner reservations at *Petit Canard*. So just in fuel costs alone, putting the trucks downtown saves the world.

"So saving maybe twenty car trips to Valley a day per truck is a savings to the environment."

I wasn't sure her math added up, but I got the point. She went on a bit longer, things we had already heard, and then opened it up to questions.

#

I heard the door open and turned, only to note that Carinna had left the room. When the door opened and closed a second time, I did hear the stairs creak, but I was focused on the other journalists, so I didn't see who entered.

"What's the monastery's role in the food trucks?" a man up in the balcony asked. He was the balding one with glasses and

I noticed a cigarette stuck behind his ear. Waiting, no doubt eagerly, for this to be over.

"I believe we just explained our support comes in light of the benefits to the environment," Pussywillow said crisply.

"Yes, but what is the Order's interest?"

"You mean, Josh, do we have a financial interest in the food trucks?" Her small, triumphant smile told me they'd crossed paths, and maybe swords before. "No. Next question."

"I see that *La Sabrosa* is operating outside your doors," the other female journalist said. "Are you subsidizing their operation in any way?"

Pussywillow shook her head. "I guess, if counting the number of tacos we've enjoyed since Saturday's opening is subsidizing, but it's business. We pay for every single taco, burrito, huarache, tostada, um, what else have we been enjoying? Isn't that right, Ernestina?"

Ernestina jumped. "Um, hi. I'm just here because I wanted to see how a reporter works."

"But your father runs *La Sabrosa*, doesn't she?" Pussywillow insisted. She nodded, eyes wide. "Don't we pay for everything we order?"

"Lay off the kid," I said sharply. All eyes turned to me. "You want to invite her dad in to support your statements? Fine, but she's what, thirteen? Not qualified to testify on financial matters anyway."

I could swear I heard a chuckle from the balcony.

"You know best," Pussywillow said. "Any other questions? Or shall we adjourn for refreshments? As Mother said," she turned back to Ernestina, "over twenty-one for the cookies."

"No answers, no cookies," I heard. I turned. Ashley Page was grinning. She had her hand up.

"Yes, before we break up here," Pussywillow said. "Ms. Page?"

Ashley rose, her lilac slacks and gold and lilac blouse catching the light in the sanctuary. She tossed her long, honey-colored hair, worn loose today. "You know that the City Council is divided on the issue of the food trucks. In fact, we're all here—" a murmur of *you're not on the Council yet* was discernible, "and when the solution of temporarily assigning trucks came up, you were pretty insistent that one be here. And," she added, holding up her hand before Pussywillow could interrupt her, "you made sure that it wasn't Siggy's truck, that's not ready, and it wasn't the Buendías' truck, being assigned to your ..."

Before Sister Pussywillow could answer, Mother Sassafras stood up. "You know, dear, this is a press conference, not a Council meeting. It was I, if you recall, that made this suggestion."

She positioned herself centrally and took a deep, buzzing breath. Now it looked like we'd get some of the fanfare they'd planned. It wasn't enough, and it wasn't interesting, to say, *well, it saves gas.*

Mother Sassafras showed us why she was the Mother Superior. "We support the food trucks downtown because we here at the Little Sisters of the Earth believe in tolerance and equity. Because tolerance and equity are good for the earth, and greed and elitism are not! We want the people of Simpato to have the same benefits as the tourists enjoy: good food, pleasant, honest and family-oriented entertainment, and an opportunity for those who are possibly less fortunate to succeed. In a world overrun with grasping, an elevation of money over the spirit, and a complete denial of the integrity and value of every single human being, regardless of race, color, creed, national origin, we believe in the Earth! And that, ladies and gentlemen," she finished, her voice returning to its normal register, "is why we so adamantly support the food trucks. Now, since there are no more questions—"

She signaled to the nuns to begin their exit humming.

"One moment, Mother Sassafras," came a voice I knew from the balcony. All sound stopped. Devon stepped to the front rail of the balcony, and was now visible to the women below. So that was who came in during the presentation. "I see you've suspended your normal rule limiting male participation in the sanctuary, so I ask that you all remain in your seats while I address you."

The attendees in the sanctuary shuffled to see up to the balcony better. Devon put his hands on the rail, and I mentally shifted back. Heights and I are not friends.

"I'm sorry to be the bearer of bad news," he said. He looked around, and I noticed that his lieutenant, Luke Aureliano, had moved to stand just behind and to Devon's side. Aureliano's gaze went across the group. When he came to me he gave me the smallest acknowledgment, my first ever from him.

For Ernestina, Luke Aureliano had a sharp look and pursed lips. He put a hand on Devon's shoulder, whispered something. Devon nodded and I could see that he mouthed, "It's okay."

I knew what was about to happen.

"Again, what I'm about to share is not what you want to hear. First, there's been a tragedy." The group gasped. "Yes, I'm sorry to say, well, you were mostly there when we heard about Silvestre Sanchez dying." Many crossed themselves. Not all the nuns did, I noticed. "Mr. Sanchez did not die a natural death."

The reporters were scribbling, except for the reporters who were recording with their phones. "Many of you already knew this."

Aureliano's eyes went back and forth, back and forth.

"On Saturday night, another man died. Again, not a natural death."

There was a collective gasp. Before the questions could start, Devon held up his hand again. "And today ..." I tensed. Had someone else died? I looked up at Devon, who avoided my eyes.

"Today, another man is ill and a fourth is missing."

"Who? Who died?" the reporter up on the balcony who had challenged Sister Pussywillow asked.

"Yes, who died?" went across the room.

I looked over at Ashley Page. She was staring, rapt, at Devon. I wanted to see her reaction when Devon made the announcement. Clearly, Aureliano had her in his sights as well.

Ernestina moved close to me, took my hand. I may be childless, but I was a child once, and I knew she was scared, seeking comfort. It was a small community. It would be someone she knew.

"I'm sorry to report that our county health inspector, Justin March, died last night."

Over the collective sigh of relief came a cry, and Ashley Page sank into her chair.

#

Other than Ashley, the rest of the room seemed greatly relieved that someone they deeply disliked had been the newest to die. I looked over at Ashley, her face in her hands.

Aureliano came down from the balcony and moved into the sanctuary, to stand over next to Ashley. This major breach of protocol went unchallenged. "I'm not finished," Devon said. His voice could stop a train. Irrelevantly I thought of his son, who'd abandoned actor training a few weeks ago and was finding his true self while building houses in Honduras. If he had his father's voice, he'd be a success.

Devon held up his hand for a third time. "I said one man died, one was ill, and one was missing. I won't disclose the name of the sick man, because he has the right to medical privacy. But as to the missing man, if anyone knows the whereabouts of Arturo Buendía, if anyone has seen him around in the past few days, please let the police know. There will be no consequences to you, I promise."

Ernestina startled at the mention of the name, then moved even closer to me, her warm young body nearly lined up with mine. Poor child, this was someone else that she knew. I felt an urge to protect her with my life. She looked up at me, scared. "I know," she mouthed.

I frowned. She knew what?

I bent down and she whispered in my ear. "I know where he is."

I breathed, relieved. "Okay. Don't worry. I'll go with you and we'll tell Chief Plata. He'll be grateful."

Aureliano was looking longer at us as his eyes kept sweeping. He didn't want to draw attention to the fact that, well, we had his attention.

"Can we tell Luke instead? My dad is cousins with his aunt's husband, so I trust him more."

"Okay," I whispered. "Let's get out of here."

There was no bee-humming, no crescendo and harmonics. We just piled out of the sanctuary into the large foyer, as the giant campana bell tolled noon. I put my hands over my ears, and looked for Luke Aureliano and Devon. I saw them over by the refreshment table. Given what the cookies likely had in them, thanks to Carinna and her daughter's supply of cannabis, I was sure that they wouldn't indulge. Nor would I.

I watched, therefore, shocked, as Devon took a huge bite of a chocolate chip cookie. We made it up to the table. There was a little sign next to the chocolate chip ones, *Safe for minors and cops.*

"You sure about that?" I asked him.

"I cornered Carinna before I went upstairs. She was laying out the refreshments with one of the young nuns, and I told her to put something non-drugged out, and that she'd rot in jail for months if she lied to me. Of course she laughed, but she promised."

"I'll pass anyway," I said. "Where's Luke? He was just here a minute ago. I need to talk to him."

Ernestina wasn't clinging to me but she wasn't leaving me, either. Devon raised a brow, and his green-gold eyes glinted. I nodded.

"Over by the lemonade," he said.

"I'll skip that, too," I said. "Aren't you due at Edwina's?"

"Wow, word travels faster than light here, doesn't it. I'll be late."

I took Ernestina's shoulder lightly and steered her to Luke. The moment he saw us he cut short whatever banter he was having with one of the younger nuns. Even if most batted for the other team, not everyone was averse to male company.

"Mrs. Keeper," he said to me, addressing me with Simpato formality in front of Ernestina. "What's up?"

I pushed Ernestina a bit forward and, tween that she was, she gave me an irritated look but then took my hand again. "She wants to tell you something."

"*Queobo?*" he said to her, switching to colloquial Spanish for *what's up*. Then he added, gesturing to me with his head, "She understands."

"I know where Mr. Arturo is," she said softly, using the title to refer to her elder. I thought of Amparo, calling Mikey Mr., and Mr. Jack.

"Good girl," Luke said gently. "Want to tell me?"

"I won't get in trouble, right?"

"Well, girl, unless you killed him you won't." It was meant as a joke but she stepped back.

"He's not dead," she said. I felt my insides relax. "He's, well, Señora Amparo took him there. To the place. You know, where the drunk men go. I think it's called the Dry Duck. *El Pato Seco.* On the way to Cragstown, but not quite."

"When?" I felt Devon behind me before I heard him.

"Tuesday night? No, I think Wednesday night, kinda late. We all saw it. Their house is the back one, two lots down from ours. It was the day after the big meeting about the trucks. So, yeah, I think it was Wednesday night. Because when I came home from school on Wednesday afternoon she was scream- ing at him because he'd been too drunk, or something, to go to work. They had a gigantic fight, she pulled out her *bruja* knife."

I thought back to what Mikey said. Never missed a day, but wasn't always sober. Maybe it finally caught up to him.

"He was yelling back at her, saying that Mr. Jack didn't pay him what he should have, or something. My mom and my lit- tle brothers were all watching, because sometimes Mr. Arturo would get nasty and try to hit Amparo, and my mom would throw water on him with a big pot, like two dogs fighting. But not if she had her knife."

This was getting more and more convoluted. Devon gently stepped in. "So, try now to remember when you saw him last. We'll talk about all the other things later. Think, now."

Ernestina closed her eyes, then opened them. "After their fight, Amparo went off with her truck to do the afternoon meals, and when she came back Arturo was asleep in the yard. She woke him up by pouring a whole pot of salsa on him. He was so mad, all covered in tomatoes and chiles." She giggled, then stopped.

"So then she took out her knife and said if he didn't go in the car with her to the Dry Duck place, she was going to ... I can't say those words—but she said she'd put a part of him in his throat. He started crying, he said he loved her, he'd never drink again. They had *that* fight a lot, so we all started to go inside our houses again because *same old same old*, but then she said that another part would be going in his throat after the first one if he didn't get in. So that's what happened."

"She put his—"

"No! He got in the car. And she came back around four in the morning, so that was already Thursday, my dad was up getting his meat ready for the tacos, that was the day before there was going to be the big drawing. She was, well, she's crazy anyway, but she was screaming at everyone, and on the phone, and crazy. So that's where he is. At *El Pato Seco*."

Devon shook his head. "Well, truck a duck.

CHAPTER THIRTEEN

I left Ernestina eating a chocolate chip cookie at her dad's truck. Nate glared at me but didn't say a word. As soon as I was out of earshot I punched in "call" to Marigold's number. Sure enough it went straight to voicemail, the automated kind that gave you the number as well as the unavailability of your target. I left what I hoped was an enticing message.

It's Sal DeVine. I know something you don't. Call me.

Perhaps since I wasn't in her contacts my call had been suppressed. I quickly called again to explain a bit more of why I was calling. It was answered this time and knowing that there hadn't been enough time for her to listen to my message, I said, "Hey, Margo, it's Sal DeVine." But it wasn't Margo Schwartz, a.k.a. Sister Marigold on the line.

"Now this is a pleasant surprise," a man's voice came through.

I couldn't place it. "Sorry, who's this?"

"Hmmm, not good with voices, then?" He spoke quickly, his voice was vaguely familiar, but no, I couldn't guess.

"Nope. So if it's a pleasant surprise, who do I have the pleasure of surprising?"

He laughed out loud. "Good one, Sal. It's Jack. Jack Partridge. We met the other night at my place, remember? You and Mikey were enjoying some of my wine, after eating some of my food. Remember?"

I stopped. I was less than a half a block from home, and I could see the house. There was a white van parked on the street outside my house, on the front door side, and from what I could see, there was a police car in my driveway. And I had Jack Partridge on Marigold's phone.

"You there?" he asked.

I took a breath. "Uh, yes. How come you're answering Margo's phone?"

"I thought it might be her, you know, calling to find her phone. She left it here yesterday, after the tasting. I didn't know whose it was, and it had been ringing and binging and buzzing and bonging—" he stopped and laughed at his own joke, "—and I figured I'd better pick it up this time. I was too late to grab it the first time."

Too much of this didn't make sense, but at least this told me two things: that she'd been there, maybe at a tasting but that was pretty pricey for a local, and that she wasn't there now.

I didn't like Jack, he made me nervous both now and the first time we'd met, but I had what looked like a bigger problem on my hands here at the house.

"Hey Jack, thanks for letting me know, but I've got to go right now. If Margo stops by to get her phone, tell her the whole monastery is looking for her—"

"What? She didn't go home last night?" He sounded truly alarmed.

"No, I guess not. Anyway, when she gets her phone she'll see that they've been trying to reach her. Thanks, I've got to go."

"Wait! Now I'm worried about her," he said. "Can you come by, get her phone? Take it to the nuns or something?"

I remembered that I was meeting Mikey later.

At that moment, two police came around the side of my house, both carrying black contractor bags. "Sure," I said quickly. "I'll be by a little later, so yeah, I'll get her phone. Bye." I hung up. A much more pressing problem was presenting itself.

#

"What are you guys doing?"

"Hi Sal," Tilly Green said. "We're taking a bunch of evidence from your house!" She grinned, delighted to be part of something higher than desk duty.

"What!?"

"Yeah! Want to talk to Sergio?"

As I stood next to my front door, young officer Sergio Gallego, son of the coffee purveyor and currently the most junior officer on the force, until Tilly becomes a full officer, approached with a contractor bag.

"What the hell, Sergio!" I said.

"Um, yeah, um, not *in* your house. Just, you know, *around* your house—"

"On my property. So, warrant?"

Sergio looked at Tilly, who shrugged. "You're the senior officer on this one, Sergio."

Now there was a scary thought.

"What's in the bag?" I said. Tilly looked at Sergio for direction. This was absurd. "What's going on?"

"We aren't going to arrest you or anything," Sergio said.

I was still holding my phone in my hand, so I scrolled to Devon's number. It went to voicemail.

"Devon," I said into the recording, "why are Tilly and Sergio in my yard, with contractor bags, gathering what they're calling 'evidence'?" I paused. Should I pretend he was on the line? Sergio looked aghast. His mouth was open and he kept glancing around from Tilly to the cop truck and back.

"Okay," I said, which could go either way after that short delay. I pressed end and turned to the young officer and officer-to-be. "Spill it. Now."

Tilly put her bag down. "We got a call. It was anonymous, it was," she paused, awkward, "a white guy, but not one I knew. I'm good with voices." She was observant, quick, and good with lots of things, so I listened. "He said that it looked pretty bad with the cops not even arresting Amparo Buendía for poisoning Silvestre Sanchez, and that if people kept dying from food truck poisoning then it was going to be really bad for Simpato."

"Well, he has a point," I allowed. "But my yard?"

"I was doing some research on arsenic," Tilly went on, "because that's what the Chief said it was, and it says that arsenic is found all over the place, and here in Valley it's in the dirt, in the wine, and it's in rice, and anyone who works here has a certain level of arsenic already in their blood. So I told Sergio about it, and we decided that we'd go and get some dirt and send it for testing."

"Yeah," Sergio chimed in, "so we figured we'd get some dirt from your yard, because it's so big you'd never miss it, and it's so close to everything, and besides, you're friends with the Chief, so you'd be cool with it."

I stared at him for a few seconds. "Why the contractor bags?"

"Oh, that!" Tilly laughed. "I told Sergio we didn't need too much, because the labs only want a small amount, so we decided to clean up your yard while we were at it. Do a good deed."

I shook my head. Either they were lying or they were so, so young. "Whose van is that?" I asked instead of pursuing the issue.

"Dunno," Sergio said. "It's been parked there all morning. It's a public street," he added pedantically. "I thought it was those developer guys who came by earlier."

Tilly shook her head. "Nah. They drive a Tesla." Tilly had been on parking enforcement for a year, and she knew who drove what around here.

"Wait. The developers were back?"

"Yeah," Sergio said. "I hope we didn't screw up any sales plans you have. I mean, having cops hanging around can hurt values. But then, having trash around could, too."

"I don't have plans—I don't have trash around."

"Not anymore," Sergio grinned.

I sighed. "Tilly? You were on parking duty. Recognize the van?"

She shook her head. "I don't, and I don't like those kinds of vans, you can't see into them." She walked off to the curb. Then she paced to the corner. "Eighteen feet. Needs to be twenty." She pulled out her ticket book and wrote out a citation.

"Now we'll be able to find out whose van it is," she said. "I'll run the plates when I get back to the shop."

"Meanwhile, what are you going to do with those bags?"

Tilly glanced at Sergio again. "Um, we'll just take them. I'll put whatever we don't need for the arsenic lab into the green can at the station."

They were lying. I didn't like that. I was going to find out why, but whatever it was, it was going to have to take a back seat to all the other problems I was trying to solve.

#

I went into my house and changed into sneakers. My pretty shoes were getting ruined with all the walking on the uneven sidewalks. Now in black stretchy capri pants, a long melon-hued silk T-shirt, and my flat pink dance shoes, I felt like I could move a bit more.

I made a cheese sandwich, supplies still quite meager in the pantry department. I figured I should eat something, though, as it was unclear whether I had an afternoon date with Mikey.

If Mikey and I were going to eat out, I didn't want to spoil my appetite, but on the other hand I didn't want to arrive starving.

The men of Simpato were extremely unreliable.

It was too early for wine, I'd had enough coffee, if such a situation were possible, and the water in Simpato tasted like a duck pond. I poured some orange juice in a glass and topped it with Perrier. Some prosecco would have been better.

I texted Mikey, telling him would swing by Perdiz in a bit. I didn't mention any ulterior motives, just that I was looking forward to hearing how Amparo did at the tasting on Saturday and how he pulled off the cooking on Sunday. After a moment, I added that I was also going to pick up Margo's phone. And that if he still wanted to go out, somewhere out of county, it was a lovely day for a drive.

I waited for an answer. In my mind, questions kept swirling. What the heck were Tilly and Sergio doing in my yard? What was in the bags?

Jack Partridge said Margo'd been at the tasting yesterday. That was odd in itself. I would get as much information as I could on that from Mikey as well, and avoid Jack if possible.

I wondered how Devon was getting on in his interview of Alicia. His phone had been off when I called him about Tilly and Sergio. I texted him, too, with equally silent results.

Alicia.

There was something off here, and I had felt it yesterday but hadn't been able to pinpoint it. I went out on my back deck from my kitchen and sat in one of my lounge chairs. I closed my eyes.

I startled awake at the sound of the first four bars of "Never on Sunday." I must have dozed off, I realized, as August's truck roared by, August waving jovially from the cab. At least he didn't pull in, jump out, and bound up the decks. He just drove by.

I got up, and something caught my eye on the edge of the deck. It was like a piece of green fabric snagged on a splintering board, and a bunched up white cloth napkin on the ground below.

I approached it carefully. I reached to unsnag it, but the smell of feces, or dead animal, or something gross stopped me. It was the smell that I'd smelled in Alicia's house.

My next thought was that when Tilly and Sergio had been cleaning up my yard they'd unearthed some old garbage and some of it had gotten away from them. Then I remembered that they were lying, and I didn't have garbage around the house.

I went inside and got a pair of pliers from my little tool box. They were a cute number, with red vinyl handles, but they did the job. I pinched the cloth napkin with the pliers and gingerly put it into a plastic bag. I used a separate bag for the green fabric, and then put both in a third bag. Not the most scientific thing I'd ever done, but I wanted to preserve and not contaminate them.

Though they sure smelled contaminated. I scrubbed my hands. What had Tilly and Sergio found?

I was about to call Devon again, when I remembered the rest of my conversation with August. Alicia was a longtime member of the community here. Her father was a taco truck guy. Everyone knew her mother had died. Everyone knew she'd made it to college, and not just to college but to UC. Why wasn't the community, at least the Latino community if not everyone, rallying around her? Where were her relatives? Why weren't there ten aunties cosseting her, cooking her food, making a funeral?

For that matter, where was Father Jim?

How did it have to do with Silvestre's being from New Mexico? I thought of my speculation regarding the Crypto-Jews, and went to my computer.

In no time I learned a lot. There were many descendants of secret Jews in New Mexico, and in fact there was an entire society devoted to the study of them. Many, or most Crypto-Jews, depending on which website I looked at, were practicing Catholics, though. So where's the church when Alicia needs them?

Ask Alicia! I texted a summary of this to Devon.

He'd suspended notifications at this time. Did I want to send it anyway?

Hell yes.

#

The Prius at first refused to start. For a car that never broke, it was mighty temperamental, but I'd learned to listen to its moods.

"What's the matter?" I said to it.

It remained mum, our conversations usually being verbally one-sided, as it preferred to manifest its views through actions. Finally it gave in to the starter motor and allowed me to back out of the driveway.

As I pulled out of the driveway I noticed that the white van was gone. Good riddance, if it was the developers. I headed out to Perdiz.

I passed *Happy Tacky*, and business was booming. How lucky Angelo had been, I thought, to pull the bridge site. Siggy still wasn't up and running, despite a prime spot, but I realized it had only been three days since the drawing. Nate's spot at the monastery had proved lucky for him that Saturday, when they let him use the kitchen. Now that Justin March was gone, rest his soul or whatever, I wondered how the health department would handle the trucks.

Justin had evidently been holding everyone up for whatever he took as bribes: money from Silvestre Sanchez, sex from Amparo Buendía, and no wonder Arturo hated him, and was he squeezing Angelo either way? Certainly, though, *Happy Tacky* remained happy, at least externally. And it seemed that Nate just wouldn't play ball. So *La Sabrosa* kept getting tagged.

Any one of those guys would have been happy to see him dead, not just Amparo. Arturo had been conveniently bundled off to dry out at the Dry Duck, right before March was poisoned. But if Amparo was truly having relations with Silvestre, as everyone implied, it was one of the oldest motives for murder around.

All those people intertwined. And no one was helping Alicia.

I pulled up to the Perdiz lock-pad and punched in the code. The gate swung open. It looked different at two in the afternoon on a sunny Monday than it had on Friday at sunset. The vines were giving off a vibrant green glow, row after row, their arms around each other's shoulders like a twining arboreal kick line. The air smelled of earth, of fecundity and growth.

As I came around the turn, the wrought-iron-decorated stone archway rose over the road, and I passed under it to the cobble-paved parking area. The glass double doors reflected the vines behind me, the golden-cream stones flanking it were warming in the afternoon sun.

I stepped out of the Prius, and once again it sighed before turning off. "You don't like it here, do you?" I said to it quietly. "Don't worry. If Mikey's not here, it will be a quick visit with Jack, so keep your cool. And keep an eye on me, okay?"

Now who was crazy?

I entered the open double doors into the foyer, its yellow-cream tiles softened by the warmth of the red and gold carpet on the floor. "Mikey?" I called out.

There was no answer, so I tried the French doors leading to the courtyard, with its inviting little fountain burbling away directly onto the stone floor. I stepped into the courtyard, following the path around the blossoming lantana, Europs daisies, and a circle of lavender. This time, being daylight, I was able to see a thin drain line that allowed the water that didn't seep through the stones to keep from flooding the courtyard, on, say, a rainy day. The water had a slightly sulfuric smell that indicated the natural spring source.

"Beautiful, isn't it?" I turned to see Jack emerge from the opposite side, from a carved wood door with no window. His white-blond hair rose and fell a bit with the little breeze that had picked up, despite the sheltering courtyard. He looked very much the gentleman farmer-winery owner, in a striped blue and yellow T-shirt, not skin-tight but well-fitting, and perfectly worn jeans. He wore flip-flops on his feet, though the temperature was now closer to seventy than eighty.

He squinted at me. "Bright out," he added. He fished out from his jeans pocket a pair of aviator sunglasses in a style that was no longer popular, and slipped them on. "Much better, Sal," he said. It occurred to me that he was also nearsighted.

He crossed the courtyard and held out his hand. "I'm Jack Partridge. I know we met once, but I was not at my best. Sal DeVine, right?"

Maybe he deserved the benefit of the doubt. After all, it had been his body language, all coked-up and bristling at the word 'Shabbat,' that had set me off, not anything he'd said. If he wasn't drugging, maybe he'd be normal.

"Right," I said, and shook his hand briefly. It was cold, almost morgue cold. "I came by to get Margo's phone," I added. "I'll take it back to the monastery, so when she gets back it'll be there."

"Oh yes, Margo's phone. Sister Marigold." His face crinkled as he winked behind his shades. Well, it was funny. "I think it's in the kitchen. I found it in the tasting room."

I followed him into the building through the doors I'd entered, remembering that the kitchen and the tasting rooms were to the left of the entry, or the right as we came in now.

"Mikey around?" I asked.

Jack whirled. "Mikey? Uh, no. Day off."

I frowned. It was Monday, and Mikey had suggested a drive today because he was free, but we hadn't set a time. Maybe he'd gone on an errand somewhere.

Mondays were not a popular day for wine tasting. Now that I thought of it, the gate had been closed, no sign out, no "open, walk-ins welcome" that usually graced the entry of a winery on weekends, and a deserted parking lot. "So, you closed today?"

Jack was walking ahead of me into the kitchen. "Yeah, we do allow visitors in the morning, but this afternoon we closed at one. Mikey's not here at all today, said he needed some personal time for something in the morning, so I did the gracious host thing for one or two folks stretching out their weekend, and then closed at one." He grinned. "I can only be gracious so long."

I believed him on the last part, though the first was more detailed than a casual visitor was entitled to.

The kitchen was in some disarray. There were dishes piled in the sink, there were pots and pans on the stove, food crusting and dry, but the floor shone like a mirror, and the big table where Mikey and I had eaten was clean and smelled of lemons.

"Damn, I told that girl to clean up before she left," he said.

"Girl?"

"Yeah, Amparo came and cooked in her good-for-nothing drunk husband's place yesterday, again. She's almost as good a cook as he is, when he's sober, but she left this place a goddam mess."

It rang hollow. Mikey had told me *he'd* cooked on Sunday.

Jack had said he had Margo's phone, so he'd been in here earlier in the day. Now he was acting like he was just finding out that the place was a mess.

"So, Amparo was cooking for you yesterday?"

He nodded, as if distracted. I wasn't distracted. "Any idea when she left?"

"Huh? Why?"

"Just making conversation," I said. "Margo's phone?"

He looked around. "Damn. Where'd it go?"

"Any idea when Margo left last night?"

"Last night? Who said anything about last night?"

"Oh, I meant the tasting. What time was that? And before you ask, it's so I can help figure out where she might have gone. Same deal with when Amparo left, since she would have seen Margo, maybe noticed her phone first, right? So if you happened to notice either one ..."

Jack smiled a little lips-but-not-eyes smile. "Nope. Tasting went to about four. Mikey, dear boy, was a little under the weather, and went home right afterwards. Amparo was supposed to clean up, but obviously she just took off. No better than her husband. And Margo, Sister Marigold, must have left with all the other guests. Happy now?"

I shrugged. I just wanted her phone. Though Mikey had said that Arturo was *neat as a pin.*

Jack continued to look around the kitchen. "Maybe I brought it back into the tasting area," he said, moving into the private room. I followed, and once again was struck by the beauty of the tapestries on the wall.

Before I thought, I said, "They're gorgeous. Really stunning, the way the colors and the fabrics pick up the textures of the vineyards."

Jack turned and glared at me. "Yeah. Thousands of dollars' worth of string goes into those." I'd forgotten that they were done by his now-estranged or possibly divorced wife, Victoria. "Not here," he added, after a quick look around for the phone.

He walked away, into the public tasting room, looking under tables and over the bar.

Victoria had also been Justin March's lover, or so Tiffany said. And whether she tired of him, or refused him, Justin March had, in a rare turn of events, called the cops to report that Victoria was abusing Jack. Looking at his muscular arms and tight physique, I had trouble imagining the rail-thin woman I'd seen on Facebook scaring him. I suppose she could if she was armed, and abuse could go either way. Without facts I'd suspend speculation.

Or Justin was just jerking both of them around. Another nice reason to be rid of him.

Jack went behind the bar, looking to see if somehow, in his distraction, he'd put the phone there. It made sense, to put it away from where others could mistakenly pick it up.

But he'd picked it up when I called.

"Wait!" I said. "Let me call it!"

"Of course!" he said. "Thought it was buzzing, not ringing, when you called earlier. But if we're quiet …"

"Where were you when I called? Think back."

"That's just it. In my memory, and it's only been what, two hours, I was in the—no, not the kitchen, I was in the private tasting room. I hadn't gone into the kitchen. Was I there?"

I called. Nothing.

"No, wait. I took it with me, and ... Okay, come, follow me."

We went back through the private tasting room and into the foyer. I looked across to the other door, with its large metal hasp. Wasn't that where Mikey lived? So if he was "out," was he just here in the other part of the building?

Something was really not right here.

Jack took a large key from his pocket, something out a medieval chatelaine's ring, and slipped it into the big lock. When the lock clicked, he pushed the heavy door open.

"Come on in, this is the office side."

"I thought Mikey lived on this side," I said.

Jack shook his head without turning around. "Is that what he told you? No, it's the way to the wine cave, where we store the barrels."

Why would Mikey lie to me about the fact that he lived on-site?

I stopped. A mental tile just clicked into place. "No, I'll wait here. You get the phone."

"Don't be silly," Jack said. "Don't you want to see the wine caves? It's the most beautiful part of the tour. It's magical, trust me."

He motioned me forward, ahead of him. My brain was trying to tell me something, and I needed quiet to figure out what it was.

The hallway was dark, and there were two doors, one behind me, just past the door we'd entered, and one that, if I wasn't completely turned around, faced the structure that enclosed the right side of the courtyard. That was the door that Jack opened.

"The offices are this way, before the cave, and now I remember, after I talked to you I went into the office. No, wait, I'd gone in to look over the ordering, when the phone buzzed. It was in my pocket. I must have left it on my desk."

He came to another door, and took out another key. "A lot of security," I said.

"Definitely," he nodded, unlocking the door. He stood aside, gentlemanly, and bade me proceed. The door swung open. The air was unexpectedly cold. He pushed me through. It was dark, and I stumbled forward as the door slammed behind me, cutting off the rest of the light.

CHAPTER FOURTEEN

I put my hand against a stone wall to steady myself and breathed slowly. There was the aroma of wine, of course, but it was superseded by another, stronger smell. It was the same smell as at the hospital, and at Alicia's, but without the added stench of death.

It was like a gas station bathroom after someone had failed to flush, underlaid with fermentation of grapes. I gagged against the smell, and reminded myself that I was not unwell. It was whoever had made this stench. I closed my eyes to help them adjust to the darkness, then opened them. Turning, I reached until I felt the door. There was no handle inside. I felt some more, until I sensed an indentation, a place to pull it shut or push it open, but nowhere to lock or unlock it. I pushed. No surprise: nothing happened.

As my eyes adjusted to the darkness I noticed that there were tiny windows at the top of the room on two sides where the walls met the ceiling. They seemed no more than a foot above my head, which meant that this room had very low ceilings or there were steps and I was at the top of them. I would have to move very carefully if it was the latter.

I ran my hands along the wall, feeling for a light switch. It was likely that if there were one inside the door it would be nearby. The little light from the ceiling windows was helping me adjust, and I saw that I was in what looked like a small ante-room. At the end it was darker. I kept my hands on the wall and slid my feet forward to avoid any unseen stairs, obstacles or walls.

I put my left hand out, swinging it slowly in front and to the side of me, until I reached a wall facing me. It was solid for what felt like a foot, then it opened directly before me, and using my right hand now, I felt until I reached the other side of the opening. I shuffled a foot forward, and tottered as it reached empty space.

I inhaled sharply, regretting it instantly, as I took a step back. Stairs. Stairs I could have catapulted down. But there was something on the wall, something rectangular. I palpitated it. Yes. I pushed, and was blinded by a white light that blasted overhead.

I took another step back, covering my eyes. Then slowly I released them, allowing my vision to permit the entry of the glare. I looked around. I was indeed in a small anteroom, and what had seemed like an endless trek was merely a five-foot walk from the door. The walls were smooth and the same warm cream as the stones that adorned the outside walls of the building. The little windows, now visible as slits, gun-turret style, were at the top of the walls on both sides, so one must be towards the courtyard, one to the vineyards.

But it still stank.

At the head of the stairs I saw that while they were rather narrow, they were constructed of shiny wood, and there was, thoughtfully, a railing on both sides. Once again I went back to the door and pushed, seeing the indentation that made for an inner handle, but again I found the door immovable.

Given the undertone of wine along with the bodily excretions—and I was getting used to the smell enough that it was still bad but not unbearable—this had to be what Jack said it was: the wine barrel cellar.

I had no real choice. I looked down the stairs. It was dark below, but not completely. Now that I saw that the anteroom was set up in a civilized way, I felt sure that there would be a light switch at the bottom.

I pulled out my phone, and took a quick video. I had to tell Devon where I was, and that I was trapped here by Jack, before I tried to find another way out. I activated the phone. That there was no reception came as no surprise.

I recalled reading that even when calls didn't go through, texts sometimes did. They could transmit if there was a sudden bit of reception, as a satellite went by or something. I wished I knew more science, but at this moment all that mattered was letting Devon know.

I typed out a text and hit send. It looked possible, it could go out, it didn't say it didn't. I knew that sometimes a failure notice took a while. I sent a second one, and sent the video as a third. With the extra weight of the video it was less likely to transmit, but worth the possibility.

And I sent one to Edwina for good measure.

I stepped down onto the first step and said a quick prayer. And took a second step.

#

There were twelve steps first, then a small landing, and eight more. No turns, so I was still paralleling the courtyard. At the bottom of the stairs I found another light switch. I pressed, and the light from the foyer went out. Damn. I turned it back on.

Although the space I was entering was only lit from the stairs, I could see barrels of wine, labelled, row after row. They were wood, and the smell was of red wine.

The barrels receded into darkness, with a single-barrel-width space between them. I looked around, not wanting to leave the bottom of the stairs and the only light in the room. There had to be another switch on the cave wall.

And then I heard it. A retch and a moan. Someone was down here, and they were sick. "Mikey?" I called out.

The moan that answered was too high-pitched to be Mikey.

I felt around for the switch, and not finding one, patted my way using the light from the stairs, and staying close to the wall when I could. I went around the barrels when I had to. "Who's down here?" I called out.

Though I got an answer, it was indecipherable, and followed quickly by another retching sound. "It's okay," I said. It wasn't, but whoever it was was worse off than I was.

Something brushed my face. I squealed and jumped back, banging my arm hard on the barrel behind me. In the dim light, I looked up, and saw it was a dangling string. I reached and pulled on it.

The room was suddenly flooded with light. I was between two rows of barrels, stacked two high and thus above my sight-line, with a passage of about three feet between rows. At the end of the aisle I was in, barrels ran crosswise, but I could see that there was a space to walk left, as the row on my right continued along the wall.

It was cool down there, and I shivered in my short-sleeved T-shirt. Where was that person? "Where are you?" I said loudly.

"By the toilet," it was a woman's voice weak but clear.

"I'm coming," I said. Jeez, good thing she was by the toilet, whoever she was. I kept following the path, realizing that it was really the only option. Not a maze then, a labyrinth. At least in a labyrinth I couldn't get lost.

A few more turns and I came to a cleared area. I gasped and stepped back.

In the open area without barrels were a small table with two carved wooden chairs, an ornate brass single bed with a mattress, blankets, pillows and bolsters, made up and unmussed, and a long piece of furniture that could be a credenza or a kitchen isle, depending on where it was.

This had to be where Mikey lived. In a wine cave.

On the wall behind the bed, inserted into the wall, was a shelf with wine glasses, and below it was another shelf, with implements whose use I could only guess. A shelf of towels stood next to a small door in the wall.

The door was ajar, and I could see a bare leg extended out into the room. A woman's leg. "Oh my god," I said aloud.

I approached the little door, though that was where the bad smell was coming from. I pulled it open.

There, in a tank top and panties, on her knees facing the toilet, was Margo Schwartz.

Her hair, now that I saw it for the first time, was matted in front, but neatly tied into a bun in the back. She wasn't wearing her glasses. The toilet was flushed, but spattered all around with what had clearly been a nightmare of excretion.

I grabbed some towels from the stack and ran water in the small sink. I handed them to her and she mopped her face. She was greenish pale, her eyes were dilated, and I knew exactly what was wrong.

I raised her to near-standing, as best I could. "How long have you been getting sick?" I asked her, helping her onto the bed. Clearly she'd been too weak to do it herself.

I propped her up with pillows. "How long?" I repeated.

"I don't know," she said. "What time is it?"

"About three in the afternoon. On Monday," I added.

"Jeez. Twenty four hours, I guess. I'm actually feeling a bit better now. Just really, really tired. And thirsty. I couldn't reach the water in the sink. Can you get me some?"

She looked exhausted and pale. I reached for her neck. I was a lawyer, not a doctor, that was for sure, but I found her pulse and counted. "Um, about ninety beats a minute. I think that's good." If seventy or so was average, ninety couldn't be that bad.

I didn't know if water was good for her or not, and I remembered my reading that there was arsenic in our water, but I didn't want her to die of thirst on my watch. I didn't see any cups in the bathroom, but on the credenza there was a silver tasting cup. I took that.

"No! Don't touch that!" Margo said.

"For the water," I soothed.

"No! Find something else!"

I looked in the silver tasting cup. Sure enough there was a residue of powder in it.

"He made me drink from it."

I shook my head. I dragged over a chair and carefully got up on it. That was what I had to do to reach that shelf, so this was set up for someone much taller than I was. I took down one of the wine glasses, filled it from the sink, and Margo slurped a bit from it. Her hands shook and she rest spilled down her front.

"Even that helps," she said. She leaned back against the pillows. I looked around. This was not an ordinary wine cave. "I think I'll sleep."

"Oh no you won't," I said, pulling Margo up. "We need to get you to a hospital. We need to get out of here."

"Right," she said, her eyes closed, "and I need to write my story."

I let that pass. "I'll look for another exit. The one at the top of the stairs is locked. You tell me how you ended up here."

"And let you scoop me in that silly little *Quack*? No way, sister."

I sat back down on the bed. "Look, Margo. Whatever story you're chasing, it's not of any interest to the *Quack* or to me. We're a weekly local, not a national rag like you write for. But there's something more here than the gossip we print. There's a murderer out there. And unless we want to be victims four and five—"

"There's been more than one?"

I grinned. "Not telling. Now, you want to die or you want to live to write your story? Because if you don't tell me what you're doing here, I'm leaving you here. And you're sure as dead then, when Jack comes back and finds you resting on the down pillows and bolsters. And heaven knows what people do with the rest of this stuff." I looked around and shuddered.

"I don't think it's heaven that knows," she muttered. "Come on, let's get on that exit. This is bigger than both of us."

"Tell me how you ended up here," I repeated as she struggled to swing her legs over the edge of the bed.

"Hold on," she said, and facing away she retched briefly. "I think the worst is over." She wiped her mouth.

"Let's hope. You'll need to be rehydrated, though. If this is what I think it is, you've been poisoned with arsenic."

"Arsenic? What do you think this is, the twenties?"

"Actually, it is."

"You know what I mean. Jeez, no one can get arsenic anymore," Margo said, leaning on my shoulder to stand.

She was at least four inches taller than I was, so that made me a convenient crutch. Convenient for her, that is.

"Trust me, they can. Some grape-growers still have it, though they're not supposed to. Apparently it's a terrific antifungal, and keeps the rats away too. And that's what you got. So spill it."

Margo was now fully upright, but without shoes or proper clothing. Nevertheless she was covered.

"Why don't you wash your face and hands, and, um, whatever else needs washing, while I find the door. There has to be one, since they don't roll those barrels up and down the stairs, or do the bottling here."

At least she complied with the washing without arguing. For a woman on the brink of death by poisoning she was pretty difficult. From what I'd read, though, it looked like she'd survive this round.

If we got out.

She emerged looking more lively.

"Where's your habit?" I asked. "I'm not used to seeing you without the jumper, cape, and veil."

"Part of the story. Let's find the door."

Still leaning heavily on my shoulder, Margo and I made our way away from the bed-and-poison nook. I knew it had to open to the outside, not the courtyard, but at this point it didn't matter since there was only one path through the barrels. "Of course, it could be locked from the outside," I said, meaning the door to our escape.

"I'm sure it will be," Margo said.

"Talk."

She sighed. "There's a story here, and I'm going to write it. But this is what happened. I've been tracking Jack Partridge for about six months. He's a winemaker, sure, but he's also one of the principal sources of cocaine in the entire winery industry. Among the landed gentry, that is. And it's not just Valley county, but the other tourist meccas—so, not Cragstown, we can leave the meth to them—and he runs a distribution center out of his 'private tastings.'" She made air-quotes around *private tastings*.

She stumbled against a barrel. We stopped to let her get her breath.

"About once every six months, he and his, well, ex-to-be-wife Victoria, would host the elite of the industry for a wine dinner. Among them are the purveyors of fine blow to the wine stars. Arturo Buendía, his cook, was kept on a string of addiction and withholding, and was working for free most weekends for his fix."

"So it wasn't just alcohol, then," I said.

"Duck, no. That's what tipped me off a few months ago, when the health inspector was called out for some violation or other, and tagged the tasting room. A fancy place like this doesn't get a health tag. So I started looking into it, and sure enough, that inspector, Justin March, he's on the take. Only the take isn't always money. It's coke from Jack, and sex from Victoria. Or at least he was trying to get it on with Victoria. No one seems to know if he's been successful."

Well, that filled in a few blanks for me. It also told me that she, nosey reporter and all, didn't know that Justin March was dead. The word *scoop* floated briefly through my mind before I wrenched my thoughts back to our current calamity.

"So you came here to confront Jack? In your little nun outfit?" I smirked.

"What's so funny? That nun outfit, as you call it, gives me more cover, literally and figuratively, than anything you wear."

I looked down at my capris and T-shirt. "Maybe. So where's the habit now?"

She smiled a little acknowledgment of the pun. "I really don't know, but I do know that I puked and, well, everything else all over it. I guess Jack took it off me, but—" she was quiet. "I think I don't remember."

I thought she did. How horrible. I turned my attention back to the story. "So that's it? A drug ring?"

"What more do you want?"

Was it possible that she didn't know about the rest?

We made one last turn and there on the wall ahead was a huge door. As I'd thought, the door was definitely large enough to accommodate a truck or the barrels. It had an old-fashioned barn door lock, the type with a heavy iron bar that came down into a holder across where the double-doors met. The bar was about three feet long, at least as wide as my arm, and would be impenetrable from the outside. It would take both of us to lift it, but unless there was a lock on the other side, it was do-able.

I turned to Margo. "We'll have to lift it together."

She nodded. "Too bad you're such a shrimp," she said.

"Hey. I'm rescuing you, remember?"

We positioned ourselves so that I was the fulcrum, she was the lever. It didn't budge. Margo swore. I had to laugh. I'd never thought I'd hear a nun swear. But sweat was running down her face and arms. I had to remember that she was poisoned.

We tried again, this time with me putting the strength of my legs into lifting as well as Margo's arms. It made a noise, but didn't move. We both took deep breaths, and in the silence of our breathing we heard something else.

We heard the clap of flip-flops coming down the stairs. The confident steps belonged to someone who knew the layout and didn't need to find his way. I felt myself go cold. Then the steps were coming across the cave. "Quick, we need to try again!" I said.

Margo shook her head. "We can't do it."

She backed to the door, leaning against them for support as her knees weakened. Her eyes were wide with fear. And she didn't even know about the murders.

"Let's at least hide behind the barrels," I whispered. But it was too late, as Jack emerged around the path between the barrels, carrying a long-handled ladle.

"Maybe a man can help you ladies," he said. "You'll never open it otherwise."

We cowered against the barrels, and I saw from the corner of my eye that Margo was shaking.

"What's that?" I asked him, to distract him if nothing else. His eyes were glittering, like when I had met him that first time, and his hand with the ladle moved back and forth almost like he was swinging a golf club one-handed.

"This? We use this to take a little taste from a barrel, see how the wine is progressing. I was just about to start doing it, knowing I had a couple of lovely gals down here to help me—though I didn't count on you being able to drink quite yet," he added to Margo. "Maybe another dose?"

Margo shrunk as much as she could into the doorway.

"How about you, Sal? Care to taste the wine with me?"

"Well, I do like wine," I said, thinking furiously. It was pretty obvious, once I added in Margo's facts, what had happened. Well, at least most of it. "Let's go back upstairs," I said. "I don't know why you pushed me in here, or left me here, but I just came because of her phone."

"My phone?" Margo said, patting her underwear.

"Sure," I said. "I was trying to call you, no one was answering, then Jack answered, and told me he had it."

"I don't remember," she whispered.

Jack grinned. "I'll bet the whole night's a blank, huh, *Sister Marigold*."

I stifled the urge to swing at him. I had to play along, nauseating though that was. "So here I am, mixed up in whatever little fun and games you two are enjoying. Not my cup of tea, I'll tell you."

I screamed when the ladle hit my arm.

I put my hand over the place where he'd hit me. "What are you doing? What the he—"

Jack was winding up for another crack at me. "Stop!" I yelled. "Don't! What's going on?"

"You really expect me to believe you?" Jack laughed, more like a snarl. "I saw that photo and your story in the *Quack*! I know what you're up to! You and your fake nun friend." He swung around faster than I could follow and hit the side of Margo's face with his ladle.

"Leave her alone!" I yelled over her scream. She put her hand to her face, and I saw blood well up under it. "You've done enough to Margo!"

Another laugh. "Yeah, Margo Schwartz, our favorite nun. Another one of your tribe. You all stick together, don't you? Thick as thieves. Which is what Mikey is, you know. A thief. Not a Jew. At least not that I know of. He's French, which is probably worse."

He was talking faster and faster, making less and less sense.

"So, Margo left her phone here by mistake, and you were just calling to get it back? Right. You couldn't think I was that stupid. And I didn't think I'd get this lucky."

He swung the ladle again, this time catching me under my jaw. I felt my teeth vibrate, then tasted blood. My ears started ringing.

"Let her go," Margo said. "It turns out she really doesn't know anything."

"Don't be a hero, girl," he said. "She's a lawyer, on top of being one of you. I think she'd enjoy a nice lunch, a fine bit of wine."

My head was spinning. Lunch? What?

Suddenly Margo groaned, and doubled over, clutching her belly. "It's starting again. I need to get to the bathroom."

He took a step back, disgust on his face. Using the momentary distraction I threw myself against Jack, while Margo dashed past him towards the little bathroom where she'd been sick before. It was my last chance.

"Sorry," I said, pushing away from him. "She'll need help."

He grabbed at me but his momentum was in the other direction, and he dove against a barrel. I was a step ahead, and ran back along the path between the barrels. It wasn't a maze, I reminded myself as I turned the first corner. It was a labyrinth, with only one way in and out. I'm no runner, but in this case the adrenaline was coursing. I followed the path of the barrels, grateful that I couldn't get lost, and quickly came to the stairs.

I grabbed the string that controlled the light, and pulled. The cave plunged into darkness. *Sorry, Margo*, I thought. But the stair landing was lit where Jack had come in, and the door was open.

I went up those stairs like an Olympic athlete. I could hear Jack pounding behind me, his flip-flops a hinderance on the smooth floor, giving me the tiniest of advantages. I knew that the door locked from the outside. As soon as I was through the door I pushed it hard. Just as Jack reached the top of the landing I swung it shut, and he slammed against the hard wood. One more step and his greater size and strength would have stopped it. I made sure I heard the lock click shut.

I grabbed my phone from my pocket, and as I opened it I heard the swoosh of my texts going through. There was no time for texts though. I pushed *call* on Devon's number. If he didn't pick up right away I'd go to 911.

But he did. "Where the hell are you? I've been calling and calling, and instead of calling back I get no answer, and then, just now, a text with a photo—"

"Hold on, Devon. We need help. It's an emergency. I'm at Perdiz, Jack poisoned Margo—" I spat out blood and something hard, a bit of tooth.

"Who?"

"Sister Marigold! Send some officers and an ambulance and hurry!" I didn't even address his indignation at my failure to answer his calls. That particular score was about ten to one.

"I'm on my way," he said.

I could only hope for Margo's sake that he was fast.

#

Valley Hospital had gotten good at arsenic poisoning in the past four days. Other than a chipped tooth and a seriously ugly bruise on my arm where the ladle had caught me, along with sore muscles from running, I was unhurt. My jaw hadn't broken, thank goodness. There was only one dentist in Simpato, and she'd try to work me in on Friday.

Margo had given nearly as good as she'd gotten, and Jack almost needed the ambulance more than she did. She was going to be fine, and her system had processed the arsenic to the point where the hospital only needed to rehydrate her and keep her overnight until her blood pressure and her kidney numbers stabilized.

She did need two stitches over her eyebrow where the ladle had smacked her, but Jack's nose was broken and he certainly was not going to be tomcatting around for a while.

#

I was sitting at Mikey's hospital bedside. His arms were black and blue from the chelation shots, and the room smelled like rotten eggs from the medication, but he was definitely on the mend.

"It was the photo that sent him over the edge," Mikey said. "The photo of me at the Buendía taco truck, that you took for the *Quack.*"

"But you got sick on Sunday night."

"Yeah. The problem was that your pal, Ed Sharp, sent it over to me and Jack on Sunday, to get permission to print. Me, because I'm in it, and Jack because of the Perdiz sign. I sent back an okay for both, not realizing that Jack would see it."

"I don't know why that would send him off the deep," I said.

Mikey sighed. "He was really against the trucks being downtown, and he was furious that I was having a taco at Amparo's, but it was all about Justin March."

Of course it was. I didn't think that having food trucks downtown was reason enough to poison one's manager.

Mikey was talking.

"He suggested I sit down with him, and he poured me some wine. Said it was a new bottling, wanted my opinion. I took a couple of sips—I don't actually swallow wine if I'm doing a real tasting, but we were sitting in the tasting room, just before the big party we had was due, and he handed me a tasting glass. I had a couple of sips, said it was odd. *Try it again, it grows on you*, he said. But I knew it was off. I told him not to serve it, and he said, *try it after it's been open a while*, and left it behind the tasting counter.

"And then, I saw that the reporter-nun, Sister Marigold, had come in. She wasn't there for the pairing, she didn't have a reservation, she said she was just there to see Jack. She was pretty insistent. And he poured her some of that wine, and I thought, *that's gonna make a lousy impression*. Then he took her down to see the caves, I got busy with the pairing, and I didn't see her leave."

"Had you started to feel bad?"

He nodded. "Yeah, but stupid me, I tried that wine three or four times over the course of the afternoon, and when I texted you I was just not feeling all that great. Nothing compared to an hour later."

"Did you know about the blow?"

"I knew he did coke. I knew he gave Arturo coke when he'd show up too drunk to work. But I can't imagine now how I was so blind. His winemaker dinners, his insistence that only Arturo cook—"

"And Justin March?"

Mikey tried to laugh, and gave a little hiccup. "It explained everything, when I ended up here with arsenic poisoning. Remember when you came over on Friday night? And Jack came back all furious? And was going on about how Arturo was a thief?"

I nodded. "You know he jumped about three feet back from me when I told him I had to go home for Shabbat."

Mikey grinned. "I didn't know that. I figure he hates everyone equally. Well, anyway, Saturday morning, just after you took your photos, Justin paid us a little visit. In fact, he was pulled up on the side of the road, and Amparo probably saw him in her mirror as she was leaving. He went up to see Jack, said he had an appointment. I think he was putting the squeeze on Jack because of Sanchez—I think everyone knows that Amparo poisoned Silvestre Sanchez, but where did she get the bad meat? From Arturo. And where did he get it? Here. I mean at Perdiz."

"Wait—"

"Yeah. So there he was, Justin March, charging around the kitchen, laughing, and saying that Jack was, well, a bad word for cuckolded, and that now he was going to go down for murder, and Jack said, *Justin, let's just talk this over, man to man, like we planned. I've got lunch all prepared.* And they went into the caves, and that was the last I saw of Justin March. Just like Margo Schwartz."

"Wait. So Jack had poisoned meat in his own kitchen?"

"I couldn't find things when I started cooking the meal we were going to have, remember? Beef was missing, and Arturo usually took pork home. Jack had been fooling around in the kitchen earlier, and I think he was going to have Arturo make up some kind of special lunch for himself and Justin, to *talk things over*, but Arturo didn't show up, and the doctored meat was gone. Thank god, because I would have made our empanadas out of them."

I shivered at the close call.

"And then Jack himself went out and got some pork, and he never, ever does the shopping himself. I order all the meat delivered. Amparo used that for the tasting dinner. But Jack had his own plans, I guess."

The last penny dropped. "I need to go. I'll be back tomorrow."

He raised his hand—whether to stop me or in exhausted farewell, I don't know—but I was walking as fast as I could out of the hospital. I tore down the stairs and out into the parking lot, but Devon was gone.

I'll be at the police station in 15 minutes, I texted, *make sure Sergio or Tilly is there. Get Amparo if you can.*

I knew it was ludicrous for me to tell the Chief of Police what to do. I could only hope he'd do what I asked.

I was on my way, but I needed to make one more stop.

CHAPTER FIFTEEN

Edwina Sharp lived alone, it turned out, with two grey cats, in an old converted church just past the biggest of the geysers that dotted Valley county. It was nearly six o'clock when I got there. This had to be the longest Monday in history.

Edwina let me in. Alicia was curled up in a chair in Edwina's den. She was scrolling on her phone but I could see that she wasn't looking at anything specific.

I pulled Edwina into the kitchen. I hadn't ever been to her house, and it was full of rich rugs, beautiful furniture, real art. This would bear exploring another day.

"I need to take Alicia to the station. But I don't want to scare her."

"She's already scared, and starting to grieve. Devon was here for two hours today, more or less grilling her, poor thing. Her dad was killed, and she's carrying the whole load."

"Where's her boyfriend?"

"I have a feeling that even though they live together—or at least sort of do—he's not the most mature of guys. Tech bro in his twenties, from the sound of it."

"Okay, but I need her to go with me …"

"I'll go too," Edwina said. I shook my head.

"You guys are whispering about me." Alicia strode into the kitchen. She was in sweats and a green No-Duck T-shirt, barefoot, and her beautiful hair was limp.

"Yeah, sorry," I said. "I just need to get you to come with me to the police station for a minute, so I was letting Edwina know—"

"Right. Instead of just asking me."

She was right. "You're right. I'm sorry," I said again. "Can you put some shoes on and come with me, please?"

"Why? I talked to the Chief for, like, a hundred hours already today, and I don't have anything else to tell him."

"I know. But I do. And you need to hear it. Edwina, I promise you the scoop, but for now I just want Alicia. Alicia, will you come? I can't make you, of course, but I need you."

She shrugged, but I heard her go up the stairs, and a minute later she was back, in jeans and a black top, her hair brushed and glossy. Oh to be young ...

In the car I asked as carefully as I could, "Alicia, you know I'm not Catholic, right?" She shrugged, but I felt her tense up. "And your dad was from Santa Fe, in New Mexico, wasn't he?"

This was coming out stupid. Evidently Alicia thought so, too. "Okay, so yeah. He was not Catholic, either. Not inside. But I was baptized, and Amparo was my godmother, and my mother, God rest her soul," Alicia crossed herself, the first time I'd ever seen her do that, "was buried here in the church. And now that my father is gone, that whole thing is over."

"But is that why the community isn't rallying around you? No one is helping you?"

She laughed, a bitter little laugh. "Right. No *tías* cooking for me, taking me in, helping me clean, like they did when my mom died. Because he was from the line of *conversos*, and even six-hundred years later they weren't considered real Catholics. Mostly because they weren't. Do you know my dad still lit candles on Friday night? He didn't eat pork? Can you imagine a taco truck without pork? No wonder he never made any money."

We were at the police station. She went on. "You think that's why someone poisoned him? You think Amparo, even though she's my godmother, killed him because he's not a real Catholic? If that's what you think, well, you're—that's just nuts."

She was furious, sitting there not unlocking her seatbelt, not moving to get out of the car.

"No, she didn't," I said. "I mean, she did, but not on purpose. Come on, we need to see the Chief."

#

Devon's eyebrows went up when he saw Alicia. She gave him a look that nearly rivaled Amparo's glares, and then kept her focus on her shoes.

"Can you set us up in two rooms?" I asked.

"Awfully demanding, aren't you?" he said, but passed us both through the locked doors and into the break/witness/conference room. "We have an additional room, for, um, sensitive questioning. Would you like to go in there?"

"Actually, I think it might be best for Alicia to wait there, if that's okay?"

"You drag me all the way down here and then put me in a room by myself?" She started to swear, a non-duck-sanitized word, and stopped herself. "Coming back here makes me into a child again. I apologize. If you need me to wait, show me where."

"You're entitled to be mad," Devon said, surprising me. "I'd be pissed too. And I don't know what Ms. DeVine has in mind, frankly, but she's been right before, so you and I are both going to see how it plays out, okay?"

Only in Simpato.

He came back alone. "Okay, what's going on?"

I sat down at the all-purpose table. I yearned for some of that good coffee, but I didn't dare ask for any. I'd pushed my luck as far as I could.

"Is Amparo here?"

Devon nodded. "We have a couple of holding cells. She's in one of them. She came willingly. I asked if she wanted a lawyer, and she snarled but said no."

"You won't be arresting her, at least I don't think so." My entire web could come unraveled so easily. "I do need to ask Tilly or Sergio something before I go on."

"Sergio's off duty. Tilly's here." He got up, and came back with her, and mercifully, coffee. "Here," he handed me a cup. To Tilly he said, "Take notes, please."

She looked relieved, since that was more along the lines of her regular duties, rather than getting in the trouble she suspected she was in.

"Sal?"

I took a deep breath. "Tilly, this morning—" Tilly took a breath, and Devon looked sharply at her. "This morning, when I got back from the monastery, you and Sergio were taking bags of something from my yard."

"What??" Devon said.

He must never have even heard my message, what with all the later texts.

Tilly looked terrified. Everything she had worked for, her burgeoning career must have flashed before her eyes.

"Who called you, and what were you taking, and why?" I said.

Tilly looked at Devon. He waited. She didn't answer, and finally he said, "Sal, if this is a citizen's complaint, I would prefer that you make it privately to me. But if it's connected to everything else that's been going on, Tilly, please answer."

"It's connected," I said. Tilly nodded. "Please tell the chief, Tilly."

She shut her eyes a moment. "We got a call. Later, I recognized Jack Partridge's voice. I'm good with voices," she added.

So, she'd lied to me before, when she said she didn't know who had called. "If you'd told me," I said, "the rest of the day would have gone very different."

Devon nodded. "Go on," he said tersely.

"He said that there was something in the Keeper's yard we should have. And that it looked like the Keeper might be involved in the poisoning of Mr. March. I asked his name, but he hung up. So I told Sergio, and he said ..." She stopped.

"At that point the fact that March had been poisoned, or was dead, wasn't out in public," Devon said.

"I know! So I was kind of shocked. And that's when I— okay, this is how I do it—I scrolled through my mind for the voice, and then I got it, it was Jack Partridge. So I told Sergio, we should go to Sal's house and see what he meant, and we did. And Sergio thought we should bring some evidence bags, but when we got there, we saw all this green and white cloth, and I knew it was a nun's habit from the monastery, and it was covered in puke and poop. Our evidence bags were way too small, but Sergio had some contractor bags in the police car because one of the foremen from the hotel that's being built had called in a theft of a bunch of cement ..."

I knew about that one.

"We picked up the clothes and took them here, but they stank, so I put them out by the trash. But they're not there anymore."

"Oh my god, Tilly," Devon said. "You know the trash pickup was this afternoon."

Tilly covered her face.

"I have some," I said. "They missed a few scraps. That completes the puzzle, by the way. It must have been Margo Schwartz's habit."

Devon nodded. She'd been in her panties and tank top when he'd gotten to Perdiz. "He was trying to shift the blame to you," Devon said. "Did you think to call me, Tilly? Get a warrant? Call Luke?"

Tilly looked at the table. She wasn't going to throw Sergio under the bus, either.

"I wonder how the clothes got there," I said. "Ever figure out whose van was in front of my house?"

"Yeah, it's Siggy's." Tilly looked relieved to be back to facts.

"Mark Segismundo?" She nodded. "I wonder what he was doing parked in front of my house."

"Yeah, we thought it was the developers who came by first."

"You're thinking of developing your property?" Devon asked, frowning.

"Nah, it's my ex-husband's scheme to solve his tax problems. I keep telling them no, but that's a story for another day. I wonder if Siggy was watching my house for Jack, to let him know when I was out so he could get Margo's clothes dumped there."

"Easy enough to find out," Devon said.

"He's the one with a downtown spot, right here at the fountain, and no truck. It would be easy enough to fall under Jack's spell, if you thought he'd help fund your taco truck," I said.

"Thank you, Tilly," Devon said, dismissing her. "I'll speak with you and Sergio later."

"Yes, Chief," Tilly said.

I hoped he would be kind.

"Now," Devon said, once Tilly had left, "we've addressed your citizen's complaint. What's—"

"Hey, this is more than that. It's falsely planted evidence! Now we need to speak to Amparo. And Alicia needs to be there."

"I'm not going to put a victim in with the perp."

"It was a mistake."

"It sure was."

"No," I said. "Amparo made the mistake. Because of Arturo, and Jack. Silvestre Sanchez didn't eat pork."

Devon shook his head like he was clearing the cobwebs.

"Because he was a crypto-Jew, a *converso*. From New Mexico. Get Alicia."

Devon glared.

"Please."

#

Alicia folded her hands on the table like a well brought-up girl. Tilly returned, this time with the tape recorder and her notepad. Devon asked the questions.

"Alicia, tell us about your father. Where he came from, what set him apart."

She took a sip from her coffee cup. "This is good," she said. Devon nodded. "As Sal, um, Mrs. Keeper, Ms. DeVine—"

"Sal's fine."

"As she said, my dad is, was a descendant of a line of *conversos*. Somehow, over six hundred years, since 1492, they kept their Jewish faith in secret. But outwardly they were Catholic, and most were only vaguely aware of their heritage, and why they did certain things. My dad knew, though. He was born in Santa Fe, in New Mexico, where there are a lot of them. And he was a good student, and even went to a year of community college, and even studied poetry with the great Miriam Sagan there. And he learned about the reasons for his customs: he lit the candles on Friday night, he didn't eat pork or shrimp, and he always washed and changed his clothes on Friday before dinner.

"He was poor, and he had that math learning problem so he couldn't do any arithmetic in his head, but he was a good cook. He ran out of money so after a year he quit college and made his way out to California. He met my mom. She was just a regular Catholic, you know, my grandparents were from Mexico, and my mom was born in Salinas, here in California. They were migrant workers, and she ended up here in Simpato working in one of the wineries. Then she married my dad.

"Amparo and Arturo, and all the truck people, were all part of my mom's community, so that helped my dad start his truck. He called it *Tacos Santa Fé*. But even though he was smart, he never made a lot of money, especially when he couldn't add and he wouldn't cook pork or carnitas or anything like that.

"My mom always did the money part of the truck. And sometimes she would cook carnitas over at Amparo's, and then my dad would sell it, but not very often. You know my little brother died? Hit by a bus when he was eight?"

I nodded.

"We were already different, but people started saying we were cursed. When my mom got sick, I was in middle school by then, she didn't work much, and she stopped doing any cooking, just the accounts. When she died, everyone was still really kind, and helped me a lot, but we were called a *bad luck family*. Folks started to avoid us. Except Amparo. She didn't turn her back on us. Not then."

Alicia was clearly relieved to be able to tell her story.

"Even though my dad was smart and had gone to college, it was really surprising to everyone, including me, that I got into UC. Everyone was super-proud, especially Amparo. She came over a lot, because Arturo is such a jerk. Where is he, by the way?"

"Amparo forced him to go to *El Pato Seco* to dry out," I said.

Alicia laughed. "Seriously? He's finally at the Dry Duck? She's been trying to get him there for years."

"We checked on it," Devon said, "he's really there. And it's not just alcohol. I probably shouldn't tell you ..."

"No, don't. It's alcohol and cocaine, right?" I said.

"Coke? How does he get the money for coke?" Alicia exclaimed.

"Jack Partridge. He kept Arturo on a string, making him work the fancy tastings, giving him just enough to come back for more."

Alicia shook her head. "No wonder he's such an SOB. But long story short, now that my dad died, no one knows what to do. How to bury him. I mean, I don't think Father Jim will bury him in the Catholic church for the funeral, and we don't know how to do a Jewish one, which is what I was going to ask you about as the Keeper that night, but then all that stuff happened. Besides, I'm not even sure if he'd want that."

Tears shone in her eyes, and she blinked them away. Devon looked at me. "I know the Jewish customs," I said, "but maybe we can make a combination. Is the body ready to be released?" I asked Devon.

He nodded. "Yes, but we still have major unresolved questions."

"Maybe the next part will help. Alicia, we can figure out a beautiful way to celebrate your dad. I'll help you. But right now, we need Amparo."

Alicia started. "I'm not ready to see her." She put her finger up to the cut on her face, already healing. The butterfly bandages were off, and it probably wouldn't scar. But Alicia was still talking, "Even if she's my godmother, she cursed me that night."

"You don't have to," I said. "Can she wait in the other witness room, then?"

Devon was nodding, but Alicia changed her mind. "No, on second thought. I need to see this through."

"If you're sure. I'll have Luke come in, too. Extra security."

"Luke's not here now," Tilly said.

"Right, I forgot. Who do we have? Anyone other than you, me, and Lori answering the phones?"

"Greg from the Sheriff's office should be here any minute."

"Okay, as soon as he's here, we'll get Amparo. Tilly, I want to talk to you outside."

#

The room was very small with Amparo in it. Her energy took up all the oxygen. Her hair was in its usual bun, and she was wearing black sweats and a grey T-shirt that covered her hips. She had chewed a lot of her red lipstick off, but her eyeliner extended nearly to her temples, and her eye shadow was a dark, forest green on the lid and a lighter green below the brow. She had darkened her black eyebrows into slashes.

She sat, declined coffee, and stared at me.

Devon cleared his throat, then looked at me. I guess I was leading. I could feel my heart in my ears. Alicia looked like a startled child, her feet tucked under her legs. It was Tilly who spoke.

"Señora Buendía, I'm Tilda Green. You know me as Tilly, the parking officer, and you can call me Tilly as usual. You're here voluntarily, right?"

Devon had a little smile on his lips, but said nothing. Amparo matched him.

"You can leave whenever you want, okay?"

Amparo didn't react, didn't look at Tilly or Alicia, just at me.

"So, we know that you took Mr. Buendía to *El Pato Seco*, and we're all grateful for that."

Amparo finally turned to her. "That's none of your business."

"But it is," I said.

"I wasn't talking to you."

"I know, but I have to tell you something. You made a mistake." Amparo started in her seat. I held my gaze. "You knew that Silvestre Sanchez, your goddaughter's father, didn't eat pork. You were his," I paused, "good friend. And you brought him beef empanadas that you made from the beef that Arturo brought home from work, right?"

She didn't move, but I could see the pulse in her throat.

"You didn't know the meat was bad, did you? That Jack had put something in that meat, not a lot, just enough to make you sick, make Arturo sick, so that he could keep Arturo weak and not come to work for a few days. And to prove that he'd been stealing meat for years."

"He was a devil!" Amparo said.

"Arturo was a sick man," Devon said.

"Not Arturo, you idiot," Amparo said. Devon was too experienced to react. Besides, I realized he did it on purpose.

"It's that Jack. *Mister Jack*," she sneered. "He gave Arturo the drugs to make him crazy. He would drink to try to calm down. Then Jack would give him more. And yes, Arturo took meat for our trucks, because Jack was taking his manhood. Making him work like that, for the drugs. And you know Jack was selling the drugs to all the fancy white men who run the wineries, right?"

"I believe we do," Devon said gently.

"And I'm sorry, Alicia, you shouldn't hear these things, but Silvestre was kind to me, when Arturo was crazy from the drugs. And I was kind to him when he was lonely."

Amparo seemed softer for a moment, but she picked up speed again. "Jack was stealing Arturo's manhood, but it was Mr. March making us all pay, one way or another. Even Jack, is what I heard. He went after Jack's wife, Mrs. Victoria, but she didn't play. I wish I had her balls. Do you know what he made me do?"

"You can tell me," Devon said.

"I'll tell your lady policewoman, this is women's business. But Mr. March, he took something from everyone. I'm glad Mr. March is dead, he was a very bad man, but it was Jack who killed him, not me. I wish I had."

"We've arrested him, Mrs. Buendía. For poisoning Margo Schwartz—»

"*Quien?*" Amparo switched to Spanish.

"He poisoned the nun?" Alicia exclaimed.

If I had tried, I could not have imagined Amparo looking as surprised and human as she did.

"—but we'll get evidence to charge him with Mr. March's murder, for causing Mr. Sanchez's murder, for poisoning and Mikey Charolais—"

"He poisoned the nun?" Amparo echoed. "And Mikey?"

"I hope the DA can make it all stick," I said. "It's up to him what gets charged."

Amparo's scowl returned. "Of course. And Jack has money. He's got the money, and we're the ones who pay. Always."

#

Devon and I were sitting at the picnic table outside the station, near the fountain, eating tacos. Siggy still didn't have a truck.

He'd hoped that Jack Partridge would fund him, in exchange for his keeping tabs on Mikey, me, and Margo, and anyone else who offended Jack, but it hadn't worked out that way.

Amparo's truck was parked at the curb, and the special today was *tacos de pato*. Rich and delicious, the juices ran down to my wrists. I mopped them with the ample napkins I'd grabbed. "One to a customer," Amaparo had snarled.

"Is this a date?" I asked Devon.

He coughed on his duck. "Date? In broad daylight?"

I guessed not.

"When is Silvestre's memorial?" he asked, changing the subject.

"Next Tuesday, instead of a Keeper session. He's been cremated, and we're going to do some traditional things from both faiths, since he was a combination, and that's what Alicia wants. I wonder if Margo's going to write her story, now that Jack's been arrested." It was my turn to jump subjects.

"Well, he's still in the county jail. Murderers don't get bail easily in this county, and he's definitely a flight risk and a danger to society," Devon said. "She'll know where to find him to interview him."

"That's why we have the fifth amendment," I replied.

"I'm sorry," Devon said.

"About?"

"My dumb answer. It's such an instinct. So let me try again. Maybe this isn't a date, but a nice dinner out, maybe even go hear some music, would be a date."

I thought of Mikey, offering the same thing, but without the baggage. Perhaps I could have a little of both. "I would like that, especially somewhere outside of Simpato," I said. Because it was true. I didn't have to make choices, and I wasn't promising anything either. "Maybe even out of state."

"Right," Devon said, "because there's no privacy in Sin-Pato."

* * *

TACOS DE PATO

(Duck Tacos)

Makes four tacos

#

1 *cup cooked duck meat*
1 *cup orange juice, fresh, divided*
2 *limes - one juiced, one quartered*
1/2 *head red cabbage*
2 *scallions or green onions*
3-4 *TBS mayonnaise*
1 *fresh jalapeño 1/2 sliced thin, 1/2 minced or 1/2 tsp red pepper flakes*
Cilantro
Salt and pepper
4 *fresh corn tortillas (use 8 if they're "street taco size" and use 2 per taco)*

#

Shred the cooked duck and put it in a bowl. Add 1/2 cup orange juice and the juice of 1 of the limes. Let it sit while you make the slaw.

Shred the red cabbage into a bowl, slice the green onions not too thin, add the other 1/2 cup of orange juice. Let that sit for 10 minutes.

To the slaw, add **3** TBS mayo and stir. If it's too soupy, drain off some liquid. If it's too dry, add some more mayo. Add some minced jalapeño or red pepper flakes to taste. It will get hotter as it sits so don't overdo it. Add some cilantro, reserving some for topping, and salt and pepper to taste.

Drain the duck meat. Heat a skillet dry, and add the duck. Toss just to heat. On another burner, char up the tortillas.

Scoop some duck into each tortilla (or tortilla pair), top with slaw, top with sliced jalapeño, top with cilantro, and serve with a quarter of lime.

Notes on duck meat:

For home use: 1 confit duck leg, available at the Duck Shop for about twenty bucks, but it will make four tacos.

For a dinner: buy a duck breast, cook as directed, cool and shred. Set aside a cup of meat per four tacos. Figure on 2 tacos per person, at least.

For the taco truck: first, shoot a duck.

Author's Note

Simpato is, of course, my own invention.

Sure, Calistoga, California, where I live, is a small, grape-growing, wine-producing town, with gourmet restaurants and chic boutiques. Sure, its founder meant to name it Saratoga, California, and in a haze named it Calistoga. Naturally, we have food trucks, a city council, and a monastery with (regular) cookie-selling nuns.

But nothing that happens in *Truck a Duck* is real. No person, living or dead, is portrayed in this book. Any resemblance is purely coincidental.

The truth is, I made it all up. Come to Calistoga, see for yourself!

ABOUT THE AUTHOR

CLAUDIA HAGADUS LONG is the author of 8 novels, including the *Simpato Mystery Series* and the *Zara and Lilly series*, one of which has been optioned for a major feature film. When she's not writing stories, she's a lawyer in Northern California, where she lives amid wineries and geysers, with her husband and too many animals. She's a passionate weaver and spinner, a dedicated cook, and the doting grandmother of three perfect grandsons. She relies heavily on coffee.
www.claudiahlong.com

ACKNOWLEDGMENTS

While the city of Simpato is a creation of my imagination, the city of Calistoga has graciously accepted me as a newcomer of merely three years. My special thanks go to Copperfields Books of Calistoga, and Julia, the manager, for welcoming me several times for events, book sales, and signings.

There are indeed food trucks in Calistoga, serving delicious tacos, burritos, and many, many other delicacies. Daisy of Mi Cocina kindly explained the rules they operate under, and let me look "under the hood" if you will, to see how a truck operates. Any mistakes are mine, and the evil goings-on are purely invention.

Our former Chief of Police, Mitch Celaya, was incredibly generous with his time, giving me a complete tour of the Calistoga police station and explaining how things work here. Simpato's police station works a little differently in the interest of the story, and I can assure you that in this case, any mistakes or lack of protocol are completely, and unquestionably mine!

Last, I am always grateful to my agent, April Eberhardt (through thick and thin!), my publisher, Sibylline Press and Vicki DeArmon, the cover designers, and the editors.

Clyde, without you, none of this would be possible.

STUDY GUIDE QUESTIONS

1. Do the residents of Simpato like the fact that everyone knows their business, or do you think they crave more privacy? Have you ever felt like there were no secrets in your town?

2. The role of Keeper of Secrets that Sal's mother created and Sal inherited, is like a steam valve for the town. It keeps them from exploding. What are some other ways society lets us blow off steam, or release tensions, safely?

3. Language is important in Simpato, and nearly everyone is bilingual. Do you think knowing a second language helps the residents get along better? Or does it cause problems for them? Are there any reasons for speaking more than just one language in your city?